D0786419

Unearthly Things

Also by Michelle Gagnon

Strangelets

Don't Turn Around

Don't Look Now

Don't Let Go

Unearthly Things

Michelle Gagnon

This is a work of fiction. Names, characters, places, and incidents either are the product of the author's imagination or are used fictitiously, and any resemblance to actual persons, living or dead, businesses, companies, events or locales is entirely coincidental.

Published in the United States by Soho Teen
an imprint of
Soho Press, Inc.
853 Broadway
New York, NY 10003

Library of Congress Cataloging-in-Publication Data

Gagnon, Michelle
Unearthly things / Michelle Gagnon.

ISBN 978-1-61695-696-7
eISBN 978-1-61695-697-4

1. Guardian and ward—Fiction. 2. Social classes—Fiction.
3. Orphans—Fiction. 4. Secrets—Fiction. 5. Ghosts—Fiction. I. Title
PZ7.G1247 Une 2017 DDC [Fic—dc23 2016025805

Interior design by Janine Agro, Soho Press, Inc.

Printed in the United States of America

10 9 8 7 6 5 4 3 2 1

For Mom and Dad

Who instilled a love of the classics and taught me that girls can do anything

"No sight so sad as that of a naughty child," he began, "especially a naughty little girl. Do you know where the wicked go after death?"

"They go to hell," was my ready and orthodox answer.

"And what is hell? Can you tell me that?"

"A pit full of fire."

"And should you like to fall into that pit, and to be burning there for ever?"

"No, sir."

"What must you do to avoid it?"

I deliberated a moment: my answer, when it did come, was objectionable: "I must keep in good health and not die."

—Charlotte Brontë, *Jane Eyre*

Chapter I

Rain, wind, and darkness filled the air; nevertheless, I dimly discerned a wall before me and a door open in it; through this door I passed with my new guide: she shut and locked it behind her.

"This is the place," the driver said. "Home, right?"

"Not really," I muttered. The ride from the airport had passed in a blink. But then, my whole life felt like that lately. Every time I closed my eyes, the world seemed to jump forward to a new and terrible place.

Less than three weeks ago, I'd been sitting on our back porch watching the tide come in. When a car pulled into the driveway, I figured my parents were back early from their "day date." Then the doorbell rang, which was weird; weirder still, when I answered it, there were two serious-looking cops standing there. The older one asked, "Are you Janie Mason?"

The next time I blinked, two caskets were being lowered into matching dark holes, while a priest talked about lives cut tragically short. Blink: I was in a lawyer's office, my bare legs sticking to a leather chair as he droned on. *Your parents appointed the Rochesters to serve as your legal guardians. They live in San Francisco . . .* Blink: I was on a plane, watching Kona International Airport recede in the distance. Blink: at the bottom of the airport escalator, a chauffeur was holding a sign with my name on it.

And now I'd arrived at the home of total strangers, like so much driftwood cast ashore.

I fought the urge to cry as I tucked stray hairs into the hood of my anorak. The rain was coming down in sheets, making it difficult to see more than a few feet past the car. The driver hurried around to retrieve my suitcases from the trunk. Girding myself against the downpour, I climbed out of the backseat.

The wind drove the rain into me, quickly soaking my clothing. It rained all the time in Hawaii, but those drops were warm, more like a caress. These icy pellets were a different beast entirely. Shivering, I tilted my head back and stared up at the house.

"Whoa," I muttered. It was a mansion: huge, imposing, and starkly different from our cozy beach cottage. The kind of place you could actually get lost in; especially since it was completely dark aside from the light above the door.

The driver carefully set my battered suitcases on the front porch before pressing the doorbell. I joined him beneath an awning that blocked the worst of the storm.

"You're sure this is it?" I asked after a minute, trying to keep the tremor from my voice.

"It's the right address." The driver frowned at the door, then pushed the buzzer again. We both listened as doleful chords bounced off the walls inside. "Sure they're expecting you?"

"Yeah. I mean, I think so," I said.

He smiled at me, and I felt badly about forgetting his name. "If you'd like, miss, you can wait in the car."

"No, thanks. I'll be fine."

"I'll wait with you until they answer," he said, laying a comforting hand on my shoulder.

He was only trying to be kind, but I flinched at the contact. For the past few weeks I'd felt like a rag doll being passed from person to person, hugged and patted and consoled. Even my parents' lawyer, Mr. Briggs, had offered an embrace. I was seriously done with being touched by virtual strangers who claimed that everything was going to be okay, when obviously it wasn't. Nothing was ever going to be okay again.

The door slowly creaked open. I sucked in a deep breath and plastered a smile on my face.

An elderly Asian woman squinted up at us. She was tiny, barely five feet tall. A ratty gray bathrobe brushed the top of her slippers. Enormous round eyeglasses made her look like a wizened owl; the dark wig perched crookedly on her head only heightened the effect. Her scowl deepened, and she barked, "No."

Then she slammed the door shut.

My jaw dropped. Was this some sort of joke?

The driver grumbled something and rapped hard on the door. It didn't open. I pictured the elderly woman standing on the other side, willing us to go away.

For a second, I felt a flash of hope. Maybe this had all been some sort of huge mistake. I'd call Mr. Briggs and explain that the Rochesters didn't seem to want me after all, and he'd get me on the next flight home. I could live with my friend Kaila instead. By this time tomorrow I'd be back on my surfboard, waiting for a set of waves to come in . . .

The door opened. The owl lady peered at us again, frowning.

"I-I'm Janie," I squeaked. "Janie Mason. The Rochesters should be expecting me?"

Wordlessly, she stepped back and opened the door wider.

The driver cast me a quick, questioning look. When I reluctantly nodded, he picked up my bags and shifted them inside.

"Good luck," he said, sounding relieved. Then he raced back to the car, head ducked against the rain.

Owl lady closed the door and bolted it while I surveyed my

surroundings: *my new home*, I told myself, but the thought was so absurd I almost laughed. In the dim lighting, it was hard to make out much aside from the thick Oriental rug I was dripping on and some huge, dark pieces of furniture.

"So," I tried again, "are the Rochesters here?"

"Not home," she muttered in a thick accent. Looking me up and down appraisingly, she added something that sounded like, *"Kung backit mo deeto?"*

"I'm sorry, I don't speak Filipino," I apologized, recognizing the language. Tourists from the Philippines tended to make the same mistake, since I'd inherited my mom's hair and skin tone.

You speak it. Why didn't you ever teach me? I'd demanded in fourth grade, jealous of Yuko Osumi's ability to rattle off Japanese phrases at recess.

It brings up too many bad memories, Mom had replied, looking sadder than I'd ever seen her.

What memories?

She shook her head. *You're too young. I'll tell you someday.*

NOW THERE WOULD NEVER be a someday, I thought. My lip quivered again, and I bit it to stop the tears.

Owl lady's frown deepened, either because I didn't speak the same language, or because I was clearly a mess. She motioned for me to pick up my bags. As she turned and shuffled down the hall, I followed, thinking that if I spoke Filipino, maybe she'd explain where the Rochesters were.

Mr. Briggs had assured me that they'd been in constant contact over the past few weeks. He'd also said they sounded great on the phone, and were looking forward to meeting me.

Wait, what? That can't be right.

I'd spent the past half hour fixated on Mr. Briggs's quivering mustache as he read my parents' will, so I'd missed most of what he'd said. I frowned. *Did you just say that I'm supposed to go live with some random family in San Francisco?*

Yes, the . . . He glanced down. *Rochesters, James and Marion.*

But I don't know them.

Mr. Briggs squirmed uncomfortably. *No?*

No. I shook my head hard to underscore the point. *I want to stay here.*

I'm afraid the will is quite clear. If your grandparents are no longer alive . . . and they're not?

No, I muttered, thinking that I'd never met them, either.

Well, in that case, you're supposed to go live with this family.

But that's nuts. My parents wouldn't do that to me.

Mr. Briggs gave a small shrug. *Apparently, they did. You'd be surprised how many people forget to update their will . . .*

THE ROCHESTERS HADN'T EVEN made it to the funeral, although they'd sent a huge bouquet. They'd agreed to raise me from here on out, so it seemed a little strange that they hadn't made the effort to say goodbye to my parents. Based on their huge house, it looked like they could've afforded the plane tickets.

But apparently they couldn't even be bothered to stay home to greet me, I thought, disgruntled.

I dragged my bags along until we reached a door at the end of the hall. Owl lady opened it and gestured inside. My insides clamped when I realized it was a tiny elevator. I hated small spaces, and this would barely hold the two of us.

Owl lady waved her arm again, looking exasperated, and I grumbled, "Fine, I'm going."

I dragged the bags inside and pressed myself against the back wall. As the doors slid closed, I shut my eyes and tried to steady my breathing. Unfortunately, my companion was wearing a pungent mix of scents: jasmine perfume mingled with cold cream and Tiger Balm. It was strong enough to make me gag. I swallowed hard and waited for the nausea to pass.

When we reached the third floor, the door slid open and owl lady stepped out. I hurried to keep up as she marched down another dark corridor. Near the end, she threw open a door and stepped aside to let me pass.

This room was dark, too. I was about to ask where the light switch was when she flicked it on.

I froze, gawking.

The bedroom was several times the size of my old one; heck, it was roughly the size of my former house. A chandelier dangled from the ceiling. The poster bed in the corner was draped with velvet and silk, brocade drapes covered the windows, and two small chairs sat in front of a fireplace. Someone clearly had a thing for red, because everything in the room ranged from maroon to crimson. It was probably supposed to look rich, like the inside of a jewelry box; instead, it reminded me of those posters detailing the inside of the human body, where everything was coated in a thick layer of blood.

I turned to ask if she was sure this was the right room, just in time to see the door shut.

"Great meeting you, too," I muttered. "A real pleasure."

I peeled off the soaked anorak and spent a few minutes debating where I could hang it without ruining some insanely expensive piece of furniture. I finally draped it over the door handle and set my shoes on the hearth. For a second, I toyed with the idea of starting a fire; the room was chilly, and sitting in front of roaring flames might cheer me up. But I decided against it. I'd never used a real fireplace before, and burning the place down on my first night would probably make a bad impression.

The only other door led to a bathroom, complete with a modern walk-in shower and more marble than I'd ever seen in one place. No adjoining door, so apparently I'd have it all to myself, which made me feel unexpectedly lonely. Back home, we'd all shared a bathroom. Most days started with the three of us accidentally elbowing each other as we brushed our teeth. I looked around for a note, something to indicate that the Rochesters were sorry they hadn't been here to greet me, but there was nothing.

I collapsed on the bed, tears pricking my eyes again. I'd spent the past few weeks numbly getting through it all: the funeral, the packing, the goodbyes. Nothing felt real, nothing penetrated.

But being here drove the reality home. My parents were gone. My dad's helicopter had crashed into the jungle on the way back from Mauna Kea, killing them instantly. The house I'd grown up in had a FOR SALE sign hanging out front. And now, the only thing left was me, alone, in a strange house.

I gave in to the grief and lay there sobbing. I was crying so hard, minutes passed before I realized someone was knocking quietly on the door.

I swiped my hands across my cheeks. Maybe the owl lady had brought up a snack; at the thought, my stomach growled. I hadn't eaten anything since breakfast.

"Coming!" I said in a strained voice.

When I yanked open the door, a little boy in navy pajamas was standing there. His light brown hair was tousled from sleep, and he was clutching a stuffed rabbit. Seeing me, his whole face split in a wide grin.

"You're here!" he chirped.

"Hi," I said dumbly.

"I'm Nicholas," he said, brushing past me to enter the room. "And this is Bertha."

He held up the rabbit, paw extended. Gravely, I shook hands with the bedraggled stuffed animal and said, "Pleased to meet you, Bertha. I'm Janie."

"Are you really from Hawaii?" Nicholas peered around the room expectantly, as if hoping I'd managed to magically transport some of the Big Island with me.

"Yup," I said.

Nicholas sighed. "I love Hawaii. We went to Maui once. Were you crying?"

"A little," I admitted, conscious of the tightness of dried tears on my cheeks.

"That's all right," he said cheerfully. "I'd cry, too, if my parents were dead."

"Um, thanks," I said. "Isn't it past your bedtime?"

"Yes, it is." Nicholas lowered his voice to a stage whisper. "Don't tell Alma, or I'll be in big trouble."

"Alma?"

"Our maid. She probably let you in."

"I won't tell," I promised. So far, Alma wasn't high on the list of people I planned on confiding in anyway.

He beamed again. "Great."

"Is anyone else here?"

"Oh, they all went out," Nicholas said. "To an *important* society event."

He pronounced it reverentially, as if attending society events was roughly akin to curing cancer. *Seriously?* I thought bitterly. *Going to a party was more important than greeting me?* But I forced a smile and said, "Guess I'll meet them tomorrow."

"Oh yes, definitely." He bobbed his head. "Breakfast is at seven-fifteen sharp. You won't see me, though. I eat in the kitchen with Alma."

I furrowed my brow. "Really? Where does everyone else eat?"

"In the formal dining room," he said.

"Is there an informal dining room?" I joked.

Nicholas's eyes went wide, and then he started laughing so hard he almost fell over. When he caught his breath, he said, "Informal dining room! Like a place where you'd eat in your pajamas!"

"Yeah, like that," I said, making a mental note to not wear pajamas to breakfast.

"You're funny, Janie."

"Thanks." Even though Nicholas was charming, these tidbits of information were worrisome. Why did he have to eat separately from the rest of the family? And who went to a party on a Monday night, anyway? I was getting the sense that the Rochesters might not be as "great" as Mr. Briggs had promised. "Well, I hope I get to see you before you leave for school, at least."

"I hope so, too!" His exuberance was infectious; it was impossible not to smile back. "Eliza can't wait to meet you. She's sorry she couldn't come tonight, but she's busy."

"Eliza?" I asked, wishing I'd paid more attention when Mr. Briggs had rattled off the names of the people I'd be living with for the next couple of years.

"My twin sister," he said. "Anyway, I have to get back to bed. Alma will be so mad if she catches me."

I walked him to the door. "Good night, Nicholas. And Bertha."

"Good night, Janie," he said solemnly, suddenly sounding much older.

I waved, and Nicholas trotted off down the hall, then took a left. A few seconds later, I heard the muffled sound of a door closing.

I shut my own door. If Nicholas was any indication, the rest of the Rochesters were also probably a wonderful, loving family that just happened to live in a big scary house. Maybe tonight's party had been super-important. And there was nothing wrong with formal dining, I just wasn't used to it. In our house we sometimes even wore pajamas to dinner.

Blueeeeeeberry pancakes for my girls! Dad sang as he danced around the kitchen, brandishing the spatula like it was a mic.

Mom laughed as he bent low to croon to her. They were both wearing matching threadbare Brown T-shirts and navy cotton shorts. Dad held the spatula out, and she obligingly added, *Put choooocolate chips in mine, pleeeeasse!*

I rolled my eyes. *You guys are so lame. And you're dressed alike again.*

That's because weeee've got style, Dad responded, and Mom clapped as he took a bow.

THE MEMORY MADE THE lead ball in my gut sink another inch. Suddenly exhausted, I dragged myself across the room and collapsed into bed. It was past midnight, and breakfast was apparently in precisely seven hours. I set the alarm on my phone for six forty-five and plunged into sleep.

I WOKE UP FEELING shaky and disoriented. Ever since the helicopter crash, I'd been plagued by bad dreams. There were minor variations, but in all of them I was trapped, surrounded by fire. I could hear voices through the smoke, the sound of someone crying; but no matter how loudly I screamed, no one ever came to rescue me.

It took a minute to remember where I was. The overhead light was still on; I'd been too tired to turn it off. According to my phone it was 3 A.M.

I ran a hand through my hair as I shuffled across the room. My mouth tasted terrible, and I debated digging through luggage for my toothbrush.

As I flicked off the chandelier, there was a bloodcurdling shriek. I froze, then fumbled for the switch. The room flooded with light again, illuminating the goosebumps along my arms. I couldn't pinpoint where the scream had come from, although it had sounded like it was directly above me. I strained my ears, but it was dead silent.

I wasn't even completely certain it had come from inside the house; maybe someone was being attacked in the street? San Francisco was a big city, after all. I didn't have a clue whether or not Pacific Heights was considered safe, although mansions weren't usually in the bad part of town.

I hurried to the window and drew back a curtain. Nothing but impenetrable darkness—the backyard, probably.

I sat there barely breathing for five full minutes, but the house remained still. I chewed my lip—maybe it had just been my imagination? After all, I'd just had a nightmare in an unfamiliar place. And I'd gotten so little sleep over the past few weeks, it could be affecting my mind. But what if it had been something? Shouldn't I tell someone?

Of course, the only person I'd met so far was a kid, and I wasn't even sure I could find his room. Conflicted, I toyed with the drawstring on my pajama bottoms and kept listening.

After a few more minutes I gave up and went back to bed, leaving the lights on again. But even with them blazing, I kept catching moving shadows in my peripheral vision. Each time, I jerked up in bed and snapped my head around; but of course there was nothing there, and I was left feeling ridiculous.

Hours passed. I finally drifted off to sleep as daylight seeped beneath the curtains.

Chapter II

There is no happiness like that of being loved by your fellow-creatures, and feeling that your presence is an addition to their comfort.

Waking up felt like dragging myself to the surface of the sea with clumsy strokes. My head ached, and my whole body seemed to have been recast in lead.

I sat up and groaned. Hopefully the Rochesters wouldn't have any big plans for my first day. I lifted my phone and squinted at it: 7:45 A.M.

"Crap!" I dropped the phone on the bed and scrambled to my feet. Nicholas had given the distinct impression that being late to breakfast was frowned upon. I was kind of surprised no one had knocked to wake me. Maybe they were letting me sleep in.

I was tempted to grab a few more minutes of shut-eye, but my stomach protested. It had been nearly twenty-four hours since I'd eaten anything, and that was only a half bagel. *Maybe I can take a nap later,* I thought, throwing on a pair of sweatpants and my dad's old sweatshirt.

On the threshold I paused. I had no idea where the "formal dining room" was. The hallway was only slightly brighter than it had been last night. My feet sank into a plush rug. Dark oil paintings lined the corridor like grim soldiers, flanking marble statues. I let out a low whistle, thinking there were probably museums that weren't this nice.

There was a flight of stairs on my left; at least I could avoid the elevator. As I started down, I heard the faint sound of conversation, and something inside me quailed. I was half tempted to go back to bed and hide under the pillows.

"C'mon, Janie," I muttered out loud. "Don't be such a baby." Steeling myself, I continued descending.

Two flights down, I emerged in the front hall. It was much larger than I'd realized, probably fifty feet wide. Prettier, too, now that it was filled with sunlight. An archway led into what appeared to be a ballroom.

The voices were coming from that direction. I couldn't make out what they were saying, but it sounded a lot like arguing. I hesitated. Should I just go back to my room and wait? I had very little experience with this sort of thing—my parents rarely fought. And when they did, it always ended with Dad cracking a dumb joke and banging out a song on our piano about strong-minded women and the men who fell for them. Mom would start laughing, and then they'd—

I gritted my teeth, forcing back the memory. *Enough, already.* Time to meet the Rochesters.

I followed the voices through three more rooms, each more intimidating than the last. Chandeliers swooped down from the ceilings, spotlighting furniture that didn't look like it was meant to be touched. I kept my arms crossed in front of my chest, terrified that I'd accidentally send a priceless heirloom crashing to the ground.

The fourth room turned out to be the formal dining room. *Informal dining room,* I thought, and had to repress a laugh. The mammoth table could probably comfortably seat twenty. Three people sat at the far end: an older man and woman, around my parents' age, and a teenage girl. They immediately fell silent, which made me wonder if they'd been talking about me.

"Um, hi," I said, feeling painfully self-conscious in my sweats. *Nicholas was right, no pajamas here.* Mr. Rochester was wearing a suit, and his wife had on a navy dress and pearls. Even the girl looked perfectly turned out in her prep school uniform. She smirked as her eyes ran over my outfit. I forced myself to take another step forward. "I'm Janie."

Mr. Rochester was already rising out of his seat. He was imposing: easily six-five, with broad shoulders and a slight gut. He crossed the room in long strides, then reached out and clasped my elbows. "Jane! We're all *so* glad you're finally here. Welcome!"

It was hard to miss the strain in his voice, or the fact that Mrs. Rochester hadn't joined him. She scrutinized me as if I was something she'd ordered that had arrived damaged, and she was considering returning it for a refund. "Thanks," I managed.

"Please, have a seat." He guided me around the table and held out the chair next to the girl, pushing it in once I'd sat down. "This is my daughter, Georgina; she's just a year older than you. And my wife, Marion. No need to be formal, you can call me Richard."

I almost said that "Richard" sounded pretty formal to me, but managed to catch myself in time. This didn't seem like a crowd that appreciated humor. Marion Rochester inclined her head but didn't say anything. Despite the hour, her hair was coiffed, makeup perfectly applied. Her skin was flawless, too, not a wrinkle in sight. I suspected that a talented plastic surgeon deserved credit for that.

"Hi everyone," I muttered.

"Hello," Georgina responded coolly, not meeting my eyes as she took a sip of orange juice. She would have been intimidating under any circumstances—model-tall and thin, with her mother's sharp cheekbones, silky blonde hair, and enormous gray eyes. She even managed to make a hideous school uniform look like something every teenage girl in the country should rush out and buy.

"So." Mr. Rochester cleared his throat. "What can the cook get you for breakfast, Jane?"

"It's, uh, Janie," I said, feeling my cheeks flush. *The cook?* I thought. *Seriously?* "Anything is fine, really. Maybe some cereal?"

"You should really try an omelet—Grace makes the most amazing omelets. Doesn't she, Georgie?"

"I told you not to call me that anymore, Dad," Georgina said, rolling her eyes.

"Right, I keep forgetting how grown up you are now." He winked at me. I tried to smile. Despite his efforts to lighten the mood, the atmosphere in the room had passed oppressive and was rocketing toward funereal.

"Jane, I realize it's your first day here," Marion said crisply, "but in the future, I trust that you'll be on time for breakfast."

"Of course," I said weakly. "Sorry."

"How could she have known?" Richard scoffed. "We weren't even here to meet her last night." He turned to me and said earnestly, "I really am sorry about that, but we had to go to this awful—"

"It was a very important benefit," Marion interrupted in a voice that could chip ice.

"Still, I feel terrible about it," he went on. "I know that your dad would have wanted us to greet you properly." At the mention of my father, his eyes looked pained.

"It's okay, really," I said. "And an omelet sounds great." I reached for the bread basket in the center of the table, narrowly avoiding knocking over a glass of juice. I grabbed a blueberry muffin and started picking at it, although I'd lost my appetite again.

For the next few minutes, the only sound was the clink of silverware against plates. I sat there, desperately uncomfortable. In spite of myself, I flashed back to breakfast at our house.

Can you turn the radio down, hon? Mom said. As always, Dad had NPR blaring to be heard over the grind of our orange juicer. *Janie, aren't you showering before school?*

Why bother?

Because you just went surfing, Mom said reasonably.

Yeah but mid-tide is at three, so I'm going back out then, I said. *The waves are supposed to be epic today.*

Cool. Can I come with? Dad asked.

Sure, I smirked. *If you think you can keep up.*

Big talk, Dad said. *Remember who taught you, little grasshopper.*

The pupil becomes the teacher, I retorted.

I don't know why I even bother sweeping, Mom said, frowning at the pile of sand around my chair. *I swear, we might as well live in a tent on the beach.*

Sounds good to me, Dad said, holding out his fist for me to bump.

THE MEMORY WAS ALMOST too painful to bear, especially since this breakfast felt like something out of a stiff British period drama. To break the silence, I blurted out, "I met Nicholas last night. He seems like a really sweet kid."

Mr. Rochester lit up. "Oh, good! He was so excited to meet you. Watch out, he'll talk your ear off if you give him half a chance."

"That's okay. I like kids." I took another bite of muffin, feeling better. I swallowed, then continued, "Does Eliza eat breakfast in the kitchen, too?"

Dead silence.

I looked up from my plate to discover them all staring at me. Marion's fork had actually frozen halfway to her mouth. Georgina was slack-jawed. Even Richard looked like I'd just called him a terrible name.

"If you'll excuse me," Marion said, setting down her fork and abruptly pushing back her chair. "I really must get on with my day."

She swept from the room without a backward glance.

I stared after her, perplexed. "Sorry, did I say something wrong? I just—"

"Who told you about Eliza?" Georgina spat, glaring at me.

Puzzled, I stammered, "Nicholas. He said she was his twin, and that she wanted to meet me . . ."

Richard's whole face sagged and he slumped in his chair, his napkin gripped in his right fist. In a heavy voice, he said, "We lost Eliza last year. I'm afraid we're all still in shock over it, Nicholas especially. He's developed some . . . unique coping mechanisms."

"Oh, God. I'm so sorry." I pushed my plate away, remembering how Nicholas's face had lit up when he talked about his sister. So this family knew about loss, too. And I'd managed to drive a knife into the wound in less than five minutes. No wonder they'd avoided my parents' funeral, and didn't seem completely delighted about taking me in—I was carting even more tragedy to their doorstep.

"You couldn't have known," Mr. Rochester said gently. "Your father and I hadn't been in contact in some time, so . . . well, let's just forget about it, okay?"

I managed a nod, although I didn't dare look up again. I could still feel Georgina's eyes drilling into my skull.

"Anyway," he continued, "you girls had better hurry if you're going to make it to school on time."

"School?" I said, startled. "What, today?"

"Marion wants you to get into a routine as quickly as possible," Richard said, although judging by his tone he didn't necessarily agree. "We were extremely fortunate—the Hamill School, where Georgina goes, has agreed to accept you midyear."

"Guess how much that cost them," Georgina muttered, just loud enough for me to hear.

"But . . . today?" My mind spun. Even on a full night's sleep, the thought of walking into a strange school was terrifying, and I hadn't even unpacked yet. "I'm not sure—"

"Your uniform arrived last night. I'll have Alma bring it to your room." Richard glanced at his watch, then said, "You better hurry, the car leaves at eight-fifteen. Have a wonderful day, girls."

And with that, he left the room.

I gaped after him. He couldn't be serious, right?

Apparently he was, because Georgina pushed back from the table next. As she passed my chair, she snapped, "I'm meeting someone before class. Don't make me late."

Then she was gone, too. I stared down at the muffin on my plate, which looked like a squadron of mice had been tearing at it. My stomach roiled, and for a second I was pretty sure I was going to throw up.

You don't have time for that, I reminded myself. I had less than ten minutes to get dressed and find my toothbrush. I stumbled out of the chair and ran back to my room.

"YOU CAN'T WEAR THOSE."

Startled, I jerked my head up. Georgina was leaning against my bedroom door, her gaze fixed on an iPhone.

"Why not?" I demanded, struggling to tie the laces on my Vans with shaking fingers. I'd thrown on the uniform, brushed my teeth with my index finger, and knotted my hair in a sloppy ponytail. All things considered, I was feeling pretty pleased with my progress.

Without looking up she said, "There's a dress code. No sneakers."

I swallowed hard. Aside from flip flops, the only other shoes I owned were plain black pumps I'd bought for the funeral, and

I'd ruined those by walking in the surf afterward. Georgina was wearing a pair of brown leather loafers that probably cost a few hundred dollars. "I don't have anything else."

"Seriously?" She cocked an eyebrow.

"Yeah." I cleared my throat, trying to hide my embarrassment. I'd never needed fancy shoes before, certainly not for school. What kind of high school banned sneakers, anyway?

"What size are you?"

"Why?"

"Maybe I can loan you something."

I hesitated. "I'm an eight."

"Me, too." Georgina smirked at her phone, then tapped on the screen as she said, "I'll bring them down. The car's already waiting."

"Okay." She still hadn't made eye contact. I had a bad feeling that whoever Georgina was texting was hearing all about this. "Thanks."

"Whatever." She vanished down the hall.

I padded downstairs in stocking feet. The cold seeped through my thin white socks as I waited. I'd pulled my anorak on over my uniform; hopefully the Hamill School's dress code didn't apply to jackets.

I'd never worn a uniform before, and it was even more ugly and uncomfortable than I'd expected: a green and white tartan kilt, a plain white shirt, and a green neckerchief. I examined myself in the mirror by the door: my dark hair looked lank, and strands of it had already escaped the ponytail. There were deep circles under my eyes, and my skin was paler than normal. I looked like a beleaguered, overgrown Girl Scout.

Georgina swept into the hall, still gripping her phone in one hand. She dropped a pair of identical loafers at my feet. "Here. I was going to send these back anyway."

I slid on the loafers, wincing as they pinched my feet. "Thanks," I muttered. "These are great."

"Sure," she said breezily. "We can work on the rest later. Now move, we're going to be late."

The rest? I thought, following her to the black Lincoln Town Car that was parked in the driveway. A man in a dark suit stood beside it, holding open the rear door.

"This is Bob, he's been our driver for ages," Georgina said, waving a hand in his direction before sliding inside. "They hired a car to get you last night."

"Nice to meet you, Bob," I croaked.

Without making eye contact, Bob nodded and carefully closed the door behind me. The leather seats were stiff and uncomfortable. Georgina pulled a mirror down to check her makeup, then started reapplying lipstick. I wasn't wearing any, because I never did. I wondered if that was just one more thing that would make me stick out like a sore thumb.

The school was close by; probably near enough to walk, I couldn't help thinking. It seemed silly to drive a few blocks, then edge forward in a long line of luxury cars that disgorged girls once they reached the entrance. But I kept my mouth shut and climbed out after Georgina, who trotted up the front steps without a backward glance.

I paused, staring up at the building.

My old high school had been a series of prefab trailers hunched on cinder blocks above a reclaimed lava field.

The Hamill School was something else entirely. With enormous gilded windows and marble columns, the building would have been right at home on a college campus. There was even ivy snaking up the sides.

I joined the stream of girls who chattered away as they bounded up the stairs. I'd never been the new kid before: from preschool on, I'd shared classes with the same fifty kids from our section of the island. I didn't have a clue how to act or what to say. I couldn't remember ever making a friend; they'd always just kind of been there. Kaila and I had learned to do everything together: walk, talk, surf. She was practically a sister. I felt a fresh pang of grief. *What had my parents been thinking, choosing total strangers to be my new legal guardians? How could they have done this to me?* That spurred a fresh wave of anger, followed immediately by guilt.

I actually preferred the grief, all things considered. It was less messy.

TEN MINUTES LATER I was squinting at a map. The day was kicking off with chemistry, my least favorite subject—not a good sign.

"Lost?"

I turned to find a small, pixie-faced girl smiling at me; in the uniform, she looked even more like a Girl Scout than I did. Her reddish hair was cut in a bob, and she was wearing glasses with thick black frames that looked like they belonged on someone much older. "Yeah. I'm new here."

"Sure, you're the one from Hawaii. I'm Helen Leaven."

"Hi. Janie."

"Where are you supposed to go?" Helen peered at the map in my hands, which was already crinkled and slightly moist from my sweaty palms.

"Chemistry 101, with Miss Scatcherd."

"Oh, she's the worst," Helen groaned. "Sorry. This way."

She walked me down the hall and up a flight of stairs, depositing me in front of a lab. Girls were already seated on high stools in front of long desks filled with lab equipment. "Thanks."

"Good luck," she said with a grin. "See you around."

Helen scurried down the hall. *Well, she seemed nice enough,* I thought. I probably should've asked if we shared any of the same classes, or better yet, a lunch period. *Too late now.* Sighing, I shuffled into the room.

A tall woman with gray hair wound into a tight bun stood in front of a Smart Board. As I entered, she threw me a disapproving look. "And you are?"

"Janie Mason," I muttered.

"You're late, Miss Mason. Please take a seat."

There was a single empty chair in the back. The class was dead silent as I made my way to it. A whisper to my left, then someone giggled in response.

I could barely concentrate as Miss Scatcherd rattled off a series of formulas. My eyelids kept drooping, my head bobbed from lack of sleep. Halfway through, I nearly lit my hair on fire with the Bunsen burner.

So all in all, a good start.

The rest of the morning passed in a blur. Between bells I wandered the halls in a near panic, trying to locate my next class. Three times I was reprimanded for lateness. Apparently the Hamill School faculty, like the Rochesters, didn't believe in cutting people slack on their first day.

Lunch period finally arrived. My stomach growled as I waited in line. When I reached the front, I stared up at the menu—seriously, a menu, as if it was a restaurant—trying to figure out what to order.

"Um, I guess I'll have the tuna melt?" I offered, digging my wallet out.

The woman behind the counter squinted at me. "Tuition includes lunch, honey. Put your money away."

"Guess I should've ordered the lobster," I said, taking the tray from her.

She laughed and shook her head. "Just you wait for canapé day. That's the one everyone loves."

I couldn't tell if she was kidding or not, so I offered a weak smile. Turning around, I drew a deep breath. The lunchroom was a long, narrow hall lined with family style tables and benches. Nearly every seat was taken. The sound of high-pitched chatter reverberated off the ceiling. Streams of light shone through windows that overlooked the city.

Less than a month ago, I was sitting under a palm tree with Kaila and Taka, eating a bag lunch my mom had made.

Spam sandwiches again, Kaila complained, curling her lip in disgust as she peeled up the bread. *Seriously disgusting, Mom.*

Taka was eating a peanut butter and jelly sandwich. Seeing Kaila eye it, she sighed and handed half to her.

Love you, mean it! Kaila said.

You better, Taka snorted. *That's, like, the third time this week. You're slowly starving me to death.*

Hey, what about me? I complained, holding up my turkey sandwich.

Is it spam? Kaila asked.

No, but it's nasty anyway.

Eating an animal is disgusting, Taka sniffed. *In any form.*

Except burgers, Kaila joked. We'd teased Taka about being a vegetarian since she swore off animals in second grade, after we caught our class hamster eating its babies.

Mmm, nice, juicy, burgers, I said, closing my eyes with fake relish.

You guys are the worst, Taka said, reaching over and snatching the sandwich back. *You seriously wouldn't last a day without me.*

We could, but we wouldn't like it, I acknowledged.

C'mon, Taka. I'll trade you my totally humane lemon cake, Kaila wheedled.

Deal, Taka said, tossing the sandwich back. *So are we going to the bonfire later?*

ONCE AGAIN I FELT the pressure of unshed tears against my eyelids, but I was determined not to cry here.

I searched the room for Helen, but there was no sign of her. I finally found a seat in the middle of the room, surrounded by much younger girls. They jabbered away as if I wasn't there. I ate slowly, methodically chewing each bite without tasting it. After finishing my milk, I stood to clear my plate. A ping on my cell: opening it, I saw a text from Kaila; maybe she'd somehow sensed how much I'd been missing her.

Hey girl. How was the trip? Love you, mean it!

That nearly broke me. I managed to collect myself enough to return my tray to a window where a woman in a hairnet and rubber gloves took it from me. Then I rushed to the bathroom.

I closed myself in a stall and sat down on the toilet seat, tugging at my hair until my scalp ached. *Don't cry,* I admonished myself. *Not here, not now. Wait until you get home.*

The door creaked open, and I stiffened. Two girls entered, chattering about a dance.

"Oh, you should totally wear that," one said.

"I don't know," the other replied. "I'm seriously over DVF. You up for a trip to Saks after practice?"

"Can't, I'm meeting Jake at Tacolicious."

"Classy," the other girl teased.

"Shut up." The sound of a faucet running.

"Hey, did you see the new girl?"

"God, yeah. What a hot mess."

I went rigid. Part of me wanted to block my ears, dreading whatever came next, but I couldn't help myself. I leaned forward to listen.

"I heard Georgie's folks spent some serious cash getting her in."

A snort, then, "Please. Like they'd ever turn a minority away. Especially an Asian chick."

"I know, right? I swear, they don't even have to be smart anymore."

Whatever else they said was cut off by the door slamming shut behind them.

My chest tightened, making it hard to breathe. I remained

bent forward, trying to get control of myself. It was so tempting to bolt out and call them a couple of ignorant racists. To scream that I was actually biracial, since my dad was white. But the truth was I had very little experience with this sort of thing. Where I grew up, pretty much everyone was a mix of something: Japanese, Hawaiian, Chinese, Korean, Filipino, white, black. Very few of my classmates could check off a single box under "race," and no one had ever really seemed to care.

Thinking back on my classes that morning, I realized that they'd all been a sea of white faces. It was jarring, like I'd stumbled across a clone army comprised of girls with hair highlighted identical shades of blonde. Well, with the exception of Helen, of course.

Did they really think I'd only gotten in because I was half-Asian?

Worse yet, were they right?

I wasn't sure if the payoff Georgina alluded to made it better or worse. One of the things that had been drilled into me from an early age was to never, ever accept charity. Whenever tourism declined and my dad's helicopter business took a hit, we'd just eat a lot more rice and beans. My dad never asked his parents for help, even though judging by overheard scraps of conversation, they could have afforded it. And I'd been fine with that, since based on what little he had said, they sounded like jerks.

So I really didn't want to end up indebted to the Rochesters for the dubious privilege of attending this miserable school.

I left the stall and splashed some water on my face, then bent forward to examine myself in the mirror. I had my mother's coloring and hair, so yeah, I could pass for full Filipina. But I had my dad's blue eyes and chin, too.

They don't even have to be smart anymore echoed in my ears. I stormed out of the bathroom like I was heading off to war.

MY NEXT CLASS WAS English class: finally, something I could at least be competent in. I was developing a rough sense of the layout of the school, so I managed to find the room right as the bell rang. I grabbed a seat in front and ignored the whispers, fixing a glare on the chalkboard.

A young woman came in, probably not much older than we were: Ms. Temple, according to my schedule. That was weird, too; at my old school, we just called our teachers by their first names. Dressed in khaki pants and a button-down shirt, with auburn hair piled messily on top of her head, she almost looked like a normal human being—at least compared to the battle-axes I'd been dealing with all morning. She dumped a stack of ratty paperbacks on her desk, then straightened. Seeing me in the front row, she blinked and said, "Oh, hello. Are you new?"

"Yeah, hi. I'm Janie Mason."

Pursing her lips, Ms. Temple shuffled through a stack of papers on her desk while I tensed, inwardly braced for more of the cold welcome that seemed to be a Hamill School specialty. Pulling out a ragged form, Ms. Temple squinted at it for a minute, then her eyes widened. "Is your middle name really Eyre?"

I cringed, inwardly cursing my parents for the gazillionth time. Their little joke was both the bane of my existence and the delight of every English teacher I'd ever had. "My mom and dad were big readers. That was their favorite book."

"Jane Eyre!" Ms. Temple actually clapped her hands together, like a little kid. "I've waited my whole life to meet you!"

The class tittered. I winced; apparently my day wasn't improving after all.

"It's Janie," I muttered. "And I've never read it." Silently, I added, *And now I never will.* It would only remind me of my parents.

"No? That's such a shame. It's one of my favorites. Brontë's views on social hierarchies and the limited options for women in that era were really quite groundbreaking." Apparently noticing my discomfort, Ms. Temple added more kindly, "It's a lovely coincidence regardless. We're currently reading *Wuthering Heights*, by her sister, Emily. Do you know it?"

I shrugged. "Sure. We studied it last year."

"Wonderful. Then you'll be all caught up in no time."

ENGLISH CLASS TURNED OUT to be the high point of my day. Ms. Temple was, at least based on initial impressions, a great teacher. She led an animated discussion on whom Heathcliff's modern day counterpart might be, and whether or not the relationship would've been easier or harder. I didn't participate, but managed to stay awake, so that was something.

By the final bell, my feet were covered in blisters from Georgina's shoes, my eyeballs felt like they'd been dipped in sand, and my head was throbbing. I collapsed in the car, inordinately grateful to be driven the five blocks home.

"Where's Georgina?" I asked as Bob pulled away from the curb.

"Miss Rochester has riding lessons after school most days," he said, meeting my eyes in the rearview mirror.

"Thank God," I muttered. Bob flashed me a small smile but didn't say anything. I slid down the seat and closed my eyes.

THE HOUSE WAS QUIET when I entered. "Hello?" I called out, letting my new Hamill School backpack slide off my shoulders and drop to the floor.

No answer. Not that I was really in the mood to talk to anyone, but still. I was seized again by loneliness.

Go upstairs and call Kaila, I told myself. *That'll help.*

I dragged myself upstairs and dialed: it went straight to voicemail, and I remembered belatedly that Kaila was two time zones behind me. Right now she was sitting in American history, probably staring longingly at the back of Tommy Oliver's head. After that, she'd be surfing until dinner.

Closing my eyes, I could practically feel my longboard beneath me, rising and falling on the swell. Another lump rose in my throat; when would I get a chance to do that again? My board should arrive in the next few days, but I had no idea how close a surf-able beach was, or how hard it would be to get there.

One thing at a time, I reminded myself, echoing the advice Kaila's mom had given before I left. *Just get through today.*

Thanks to Hamill's "stringent academic standards" (their words, not mine), I had hours' worth of homework ahead of me anyway.

I flipped open my chemistry book, determined to get the worst of it out of the way. But my attention kept wandering. The crimson bedroom looked better by daylight, but not by much; even with the curtains open, light barely penetrated the gloom. Would it be too pushy to ask if I could paint the walls a different color?

I pictured Marion's expression at breakfast that morning; she didn't seem like the type to welcome constructive criticism of her decorating skills.

Sighing, I shoved aside the textbook and flopped down on the pillows, staring up at the red ceiling. I'd left my door ajar, and the sound of muffled conversation drifted in from down the hall. I debated whether or not I was up for human interaction; but with every passing moment, my bedroom felt more like a cell. I pushed off the bed and wandered out, following the sound.

Around the corner, I spotted Nicholas. He was sitting in front of a closed door, staring at it as if it were a portal to another dimension. His bunny Bertha was propped up beside him, facing the same way. Nicholas was speaking in a low, urgent voice. As I approached, he said, "No, you'll like her, really. You don't have to be so angry about it."

Seeing me he fell still, a grave expression on his small face.

"Hi, Nicholas," I said.

"Hello." His eyes flicked to the door, then back. "How are you?"

I laughed at the formality in his voice. "I'm cool. You?"

"I'm cool, too." He said the word *cool* as if he were tasting a new dessert, one that felt strange but sweet on his tongue.

Something about his quirkiness reminded me of Kaila, oddly enough. The Eliza thing was weird, but then I'd been acting pretty strangely since my parents died, too. I wasn't exactly in any position to judge.

I settled on the floor beside him and crossed my legs. "So. No playdates today?"

His brow furrowed and the corners of his mouth turned down. He drew Bertha onto his lap and said sorrowfully, "I never have playdates."

"Why not?" I asked. "You go to school, right?"

He nodded solemnly.

"So do you have friends there?"

His eyes shifted back to the door, then he slowly shook his head. In a whisper, he said, "She doesn't like it when I make friends."

Something in his tone made my skin crawl. The lights in the hall were dim, and shadows crept along the walls toward us. I inched closer to him. "Who doesn't? Your mom?"

He just sat there, mutely staring at me. Finally, I said, "Well, then I guess we should have a playdate."

Nicholas's face lit up. "Really?"

"Really. What should we play?"

He glanced around as if checking for spies, then said in a low voice, "Eliza and me always play the same game."

Referring to his dead twin as if she was sitting there with us was creepy as hell, but I tried not to let it show on my face. "All right," I said. "How do we play?"

Nicholas took me by the hand and led me to his room. Along the way, he eagerly explained what sounded like an extraordinarily complex game set in an imaginary world. I tried to focus, but most of what he was saying blew past me. I eventually gathered that my primary role was to move figurines of knights on horseback around the castle in the middle of his bedroom. Apparently my knights were trying to rescue a princess from an evil sorceress.

Nicholas had come up with elaborate requirements for every character: each knight had specific powers and could only move at certain times in certain ways. And the sorceress kept changing her appearance, sometimes even appearing as a knight.

Honestly, I'd played less complicated games of chess with my dad.

Sure you want to do that? Dad asked, cocking an eyebrow.

I hesitated, them moved my rook back and squinted at the board. He'd already taken all my pawns, and had my queen cornered. If I didn't do something . . .

I sucked in a breath as I saw the perfect move. Quickly moving my queen, I sat back and said, *And that's check! Boom!*

Dad held up his hand for a high five. *Yes! I was wondering if you were going to pick up on that . . .*

"JANIE, SILLY, SHE CAN'T go there!" Nicholas exclaimed.

I started, abruptly pulled back to the present. "Oh, sorry." I moved the sorceress out of the moat and back onto the parapet. "Better?"

He scrutinized the castle. "Not really. If she stays there, the red knight won't be able to fight her."

"Okay," I said. We were an hour into the game, and I still

didn't understand it. I grabbed the red knight, set him back on his horse, and let out a loud neigh.

Nicholas collapsed in giggles. Despite my other weaknesses, he was a big fan of my ability to make horse noises.

"You're getting better," he said. "I bet next time we play you'll win."

There's a way to win? I thought, but just said, "Thanks. You know, I'm actually a real princess."

Nicholas's eyes widened. "Really?"

I hesitated; this kid obviously lived in a dream world, and it probably wasn't a good idea to fuel that. Still, I nodded sagely and said, "You may call me Princess Janie."

"Wow," he said. "A real live princess. I can't wait to tell Eliza!"

Without warning, the knight in his hand went flying. I jerked sideways as it flashed past, missing me by inches. I turned back to face Nicholas. He'd gone pale.

"Nicholas," I snapped. "Did you throw that at me?"

"No," he said in a small voice.

I hesitated. He looked scared. The knight was small, but made of cast iron. It could have gouged out my eye. "You're not supposed to throw things, Nicholas."

"I know," he said miserably. "I'm sorry. Eliza gets angry sometimes, no matter how hard I try to keep her happy." His shoulders started to shake, and tears poured down his cheeks.

I hesitated, then pulled him onto my lap. Nicholas buried his head against my shoulder as he sobbed; I stroked his back lightly, trying to calm him down. I played the incident over in my mind: had his hand drawn back? I was pretty sure it hadn't, but the knight had flown halfway across the room. I shivered; the room was freezing. I could practically see my breath.

Wasn't it supposed to get cold when a ghost was around? I repressed a shudder.

You're being ridiculous, I told myself firmly. Nicholas was just acting out. Pretending that Eliza was still talking to him was a coping mechanism, like Richard said.

Still, as Nicholas cried into my shoulder, it was hard to shake the sense that we were being watched. When I finally led him sniffling down to dinner, I was relieved to find Alma ensconced at the kitchen table. I deduced from her grunted responses that the other Rochesters had gone out again.

Nicholas and I sat side by side at the table, eating silently. I wondered how often we'd be left alone like this. I couldn't decide if it was good or bad. As I watched Nicholas chew his steak with the same seriousness he applied to everything else, I flashed again on the soldier flying at me. *What was going on?*

Chapter III

There were but eight; yet somehow, as they flocked in, they gave the impression of a much larger number. Some of them were very tall; many were dressed in white; and all had a sweeping amplitude of array that seemed to magnify their persons as a mist magnifies the moon. I rose and curtseyed to them: one or two bent their heads in return, the others only stared at me.

Despite the hideous uniforms, it quickly became apparent that at least in terms of academics, Hamill was light-years ahead of my little island school. I'd always been near the top of my class, but here I felt like the village idiot. I was determined to catch up; I might not be able to change my social pariah status, but I could do something about passing chem.

Not that I was completely alone. I'd found Helen again on Wednesday, and she'd shared something that was key to maintaining my sanity: it was okay to eat lunch in the library. So every day at noon, we hung out for twenty minutes. Not a lot of time to get to know each other, but so far I'd discovered that Helen was a fourth generation San Franciscan whose mother and grandmother had both attended Hamill. She had an older sister and a younger brother, spent most weekends at a house they owned in Napa, and she was a huge gamer. She had a tendency to go on and on about Skyrim, some video game that apparently involved giants, cheese wheels, and a Dragonborn, whatever that was.

I'd never even owned a console; the thought of sitting in

front of a screen made me twitchy. But I was short on friends, so I made approving noises as she prattled on about it. Frankly, I was mystified that she managed to find the time to do anything extracurricular. I was barely getting through my homework every night as it was.

"You could come over sometime and play," she offered. "I bet you'd really love it."

"Um, maybe," I said, picking at the remains of my sandwich. The tuna melt was pretty much the best thing about Hamill, as far as I was concerned. "I'm not very good at games."

"Oh, you'll like this one. Even though I should warn you, it's got a tough learning curve." Helen grew increasingly animated as she continued, "It's so worth it, though. Your avatar can be any gender, any race, and the women are just as strong as the men. Building a great avatar is really the key."

"I'll bet." I nodded mechanically. "So how do you win?"

Helen laughed. "Oh, it's not really about winning. I mean, the cool thing about it is that there's this whole world to explore, you know? Maybe I could show you this weekend!"

"Maybe. My surfboard arrived yesterday, though, and I was actually thinking—"

"There you are!" Someone cried from the doorway behind me.

Helen was staring past me in disbelief, as if a unicorn had suddenly strolled into the library. I turned to see Georgina approaching. As always, she held her phone in one hand, and her eyes flicked back and forth from it to me. She casually perched on the edge of our table, hardly seeming to notice Helen.

"Um, hi," I said. My interactions with Georgina had been limited to breakfast and the drive to school. We'd still barely spoken. According to Nicholas, she'd been deemed old enough to attend society functions with her parents. And those seemed to occur every single night; Mr. Rochester must have an entire closet full of tuxedos. In this case, I was grateful to be excluded. I'd rather give up surfing forever than be forced to put on a dress and make small talk with a bunch of stuck-up strangers.

Taking in my half-eaten sandwich, Georgina wrinkled her nose. "You're eating in here? Really?"

"Sure," I said, fighting to sound casual. "It's nice and quiet."

Georgina's eyebrows shot up. I could practically see the snarky reply forming in her head.

Helen stood. "I've got to get to class. See you later, Janie."

"Bye," I said.

Georgina's eyes narrowed as she watched Helen leave. "Is that Blanche Leaven's little sister?"

"Her name's Helen," I muttered.

"Hm. Well, Blanche got all the looks." She smirked. "Not that there were many to start with."

"Yeah, well, looks aren't everything," I snapped, hearing an echo of my mom's voice in mine. I realized belatedly that this wasn't exactly supportive of Helen, either, and added, "Besides, she's cute. And super smart, and nice . . ."

Georgina was tapping furiously on her phone again. She glanced up and said, "Sorry, what?"

Fuming, I asked, "What do you want, Georgina?"

"Well, you of course." She tossed her hair. "We're going shopping after school. You know, for the dance."

"The what?" I asked, mystified.

"The dance, silly," Georgina said with exaggerated patience. "There's a mixer with Country Day tonight, and I need something to wear. You do, too."

I wanted to protest that I had plenty of things to wear. But she was right, my dresses were mainly suited for a day at the beach. "Wait, tonight? Like, in six hours?"

She sniffed. "Well, no one actually gets there on time."

"Um, okay." My mind was still spinning. "Is the dance mandatory?"

At that, she laughed. Georgina had a surprisingly nice laugh, louder and rougher than expected. "Oh my God, Janie, you are too much! Of course it's not mandatory. But it kind of is, too. You know?"

"No," I muttered.

She brushed away my confusion with one hand. "Bob will pick us up at three-thirty."

And with that, she was gone.

I sat there for a few more minutes, trying to decide what was more shocking: the fact that Georgina wanted to take me shopping, or that I was expected to go to some sort of fancy dance with her. I suspected that Richard was behind Georgina's sudden invitation; she certainly didn't seem to want to spend any more time with me than was absolutely necessary.

Still, I could use a shopping trip. I needed warmer clothing. I'd also love to replace what I'd privately nicknamed "the blistering loafers of death" with a more comfortable option.

The bell rang, and I scrambled to gather up my books.

AS PROMISED, GEORGINA DRAGGED me along on a shopping "mission," as she called it. To Saks Fifth Avenue, no less. And when they say Fifth Avenue, they're not kidding; the first price tag I checked almost made me choke. I'd never spent more than fifty dollars on a single item of clothing in my life. Our high school dances were basically beach parties; shorts and a T-shirt were the standard attire, maybe a sundress if you were trying to impress someone.

But I realized quickly that this mixer was going to be something else entirely. In the changing room Georgina scrutinized me, then sighed and said, "Well, at least you're skinny."

Then she proceeded to order around a slew of beleaguered sales girls.

By the end of the first hour, the level of excess had me feeling drained and slightly nauseated. I tried to feign interest as Georgina executed a twirl in a stunning silver lamé dress. I could practically hear my mom commenting, "Good luck sitting down in that."

"So?" she asked.

I shrugged. "It's great." *Just like the other twenty,* I added silently. Georgina made the world's most heinous school uniform look chic; what she did to designer clothing shouldn't be legal.

"I know," she said, frowning over her shoulder at her reflection. "But still not quite right."

I groaned inwardly. I was still half-heartedly trying on dresses, but I couldn't even afford the straps for one of these, never mind the whole thing.

"We might have to go to Barney's after all," she complained. "I swear, the buyer here should be *shot.*"

"That seems fair," I mumbled sardonically, checking my watch. It was almost six o'clock; the dance was supposed to start soon. Maybe Georgina wouldn't find anything and we could both skip it. I tried to picture us sharing a pint of ice cream in front of a cheesy movie, the way Kaila and I spent most Friday nights. Somehow, that seemed like a stretch.

"Now *this* is more like it."

Looking up, I had to admit she was right. The deep red halter dress swooped low in the back, with a hem that hovered a few inches above her knees. It showed just enough skin to be sexy without pushing it.

"Definitely," I said, relieved. "That's the one." *Now can we get out here?*

"So you're getting the periwinkle Marchesa, right?" Georgina was giving me her best innocent, wide-eyed stare.

I scoffed. "Yeah, right."

"Why not?" Her brow furrowed with genuine puzzlement.

Was she for real? "It's eight hundred dollars," I said, enunciating each word. "As in, money I don't have."

Georgina stared at me for a minute, then burst into laughter.

"What?" I demanded. If she'd only brought me here to mock how poor I was, it was time to storm out.

"Um, hello?" Georgina pulled a black credit card out of her purse and waggled it in front of me. "This is on Daddy Dearest."

"Oh, I can't—" I protested.

"Please. It's not like he ever even sees the bill. We've got people who handle all that."

"I really can't. It wouldn't be right."

Georgina's eyes narrowed, making the resemblance to Marion even more striking. "Of course you can." Her voice hardened as she continued, "You're family now, right?"

"I guess," I murmured reluctantly.

"Good. This is how our family does things, so get used to it." Her face brightened as she added, "Now let's go check out the shoes!"

"I'M GLAD TO SEE you and Georgina getting along so well."

Startled, I nearly dropped the dress I was holding up in front of the full-length mirror.

Richard Rochester was standing in my bedroom doorway. He smiled wanly at me. "Sorry. Didn't mean to make you jump. Okay if I come in?"

"Sure," I said, suddenly self-conscious about my unmade bed. I spread the dress across the foot of it, then surreptitiously straightened the covers. I turned to find him scanning the room with a slight frown.

"A little grim, isn't it?"

I laughed, surprised. "A little, yeah. Red's not really my favorite color."

"Well, you'll have to let us know what you'd prefer. I'll call the painters as soon as you decide."

"That's okay," I said, uncomfortable again. I didn't want to seem ungrateful, complaining about this huge space they'd given me. "I don't mind it so much."

"Nonsense," Richard said with forced cheer. "This is your home now. It should be arranged the way you like it."

"Um, okay." I gestured toward one of the chairs beside the fireplace. "Do you want to have a seat?"

His face lit up. For a brief moment, he looked like an older version of Nicholas. "I would, thanks." He settled down in the chair and crossed his legs. It was ridiculously small, making him look like a giant at a tea party. "So how do you like Hamill?"

"It's fine, I guess." I leaned against the bed. It felt weird, talking to him like this. We'd managed a few strained conversations over breakfast, but that was the entirety of our interaction. This wasn't the sort of family that pulled out a board game after dinner or piled on the couch to watch TV. I still couldn't wrap my mind around how weirdly formal and stilted they were with each other. They acted more like the victims of a shipwreck, unexpectedly stranded on an island together, than blood relatives.

"I know it must be hard for you," he said sympathetically. "I can only imagine how different this all is."

I shrugged. "I'll get used to it."

"I hope so. And really, Janie. Anything you need, don't hesitate to ask."

He got up, straightening his jacket. He was nearly at the door when I screwed up my courage enough to say, "Excuse me, Mr. Rochester?"

"Richard, please," he replied in a pained voice, turning back around to face me.

"Okay, Richard." I drew in a deep breath, then said, "I was just wondering if you knew . . . I mean, the lawyer said my parents chose you to be my backup guardian. Did they ever tell you why?"

His features softened. "Honestly? The phone call from Mr. Briggs came out of the blue. I was more than a little astonished, myself."

"Huh. That's . . . interesting." I sank onto the bed, feeling another flare of frustration. I was old enough to have been asked where I wanted to live. Why hadn't my parents trusted me?

"Janie," he said gently.

I looked back up. "Yeah?"

Richard rocked slightly back and forth on his heels as he spoke, again reminding me of Nicholas. "Your father was my best friend, all the way through college. We were roommates at boarding school; did he ever tell you about that?"

I shook my head. I hadn't even known he went to boarding school.

Richard continued, "Your dad was something else. People always liked him."

"My mom used to joke that he was the unofficial mayor of our town," I said, remembering. It seemed like the entire island had turned out for their funeral. At the service, so many people got up to tell funny stories about my dad, the priest finally had to cut them off with a request to share anecdotes on the memorial website instead.

"Mayor, huh?" He flashed a sad smile. "I'm not surprised. To be honest, it used to make me jealous. They even asked him to organize our senior prank. Somehow your dad dyed the local lake bright orange, our school color. It stayed that way for weeks."

I smiled, too. "Last year on April Fools', we convinced my mom that my temporary tattoo was real. Dad said he'd gone with me to give permission. Mom was so angry." I could still remember her raging at us while Dad rocked silently, barely able to contain his mirth. We both finally burst out laughing. He'd had to take her out to dinner that night to make up for it.

Richard laughed. "I'll bet! Oh, your dad loved April Fools'. One year we dumped itching powder into Alma's lotion. I honestly thought she was going to kill us."

"So Alma has been with you that long?" I asked, surprised.

"Since I was about Nicholas's age." Seeing my expression, he held up a hand. "I know how she comes across, but Alma was like a mother to me and your dad."

I tried to picture Alma nurturing another human being, and failed. She'd still barely spoken to me—in fact, whenever she saw me, she headed in the opposite direction.

I suddenly noticed that Richard was examining me closely. He was frowning again. "Your parents never talked about any of this?"

I shook my head. "Honestly, they didn't talk much about how they grew up." Which was weird, I now realized. When I was younger, I'd pestered them with questions about what their lives had been like when they were my age, but they always gave what in retrospect were overly evasive answers. After awhile, I stopped asking.

"Well, we were quite close, the three of us. Inseparable, really." His voice grew strained, he'd choked up again. I felt a flood of warmth for him. This was nice, sharing memories of my parents. Maybe he'd fill me in on more of their past; in a sense, that would keep them alive for both of us.

"So what happened?" I asked, trying to imagine my mom and dad hanging around with a younger version of Richard Rochester.

He shrugged, looking uncomfortable. "We had a falling out. At the time, it seemed like a big deal. So we didn't talk for a few years. And then, as time went on, we just never reconnected. I'll always regret that."

There was a fine sheen of tears in his eyes. We sat in silence for a minute.

"I'm sorry they dumped me on you like this," I said awkwardly. "Mr. Briggs thinks they just forgot to update their will when I got older. But I know it's bad timing."

Richard took a deep breath and blinked several times, then

dug his hands back in his pockets. "The one thing I've learned, Janie, is that life has a way of surprising you. I think that in the end, your coming here will turn out to be a great thing for our family. I think you're just what we needed."

There was an odd fervor in his voice. I wasn't sure how to respond. Aside from Nicholas, none of them had exactly seemed delighted by my presence. "Um, thanks."

"You're welcome. Let me leave you with this. San Francisco was your parents' hometown. They probably thought that if anything unexpected ever happened, you'd end up here, living with your grandparents. And you'd get a chance to experience some of what their childhoods had been like."

"I guess," I muttered. "It's still weird to me that they didn't change their will."

"Believe me, this was a wake-up call," Richard said. "I realized that we hadn't updated our estate planning since Georgina was born. It's just one of those things that slips your mind, even though it shouldn't. After all, you never expect—"

He stopped speaking abruptly. My eyes were glassy again, the urge to cry had forced its way back up my throat. "I'm sorry, Janie," he said with concern. "I didn't mean to upset you."

"That's all right. I just can't help it. I miss them so much." A sob escaped, despite my efforts to choke it back.

"I miss them, too," he said quietly. "And believe me, I'm going to do everything I can to make sure you're happy here."

"Thanks," I said weakly. He was trying to be nice, but I couldn't imagine any scenario in which I'd be happy. It was hard to imagine this house, this city, ever feeling like home.

And yet everything in Hawaii would just remind me of them. It didn't feel like I really belonged anywhere anymore.

"Might as well start with tonight, right?" he said with forced cheer. "I should probably let you get ready for the big mixer."

"Right," I said, glancing back toward the dress on my bed. A ball of dread was already forming in my stomach; *how had I let*

Georgina talk me into this? But sitting around my room sulking wasn't exactly helping matters. Maybe the mixer would turn out to be cool, if I gave it a chance. "Thanks, Mr. Rochester."

He held up his hands in mock exasperation. "What will it take to get you to call me Richard?"

I laughed. "Thanks, Richard."

"Of course." He paused in the doorway and threw me a stern look. "And no matter what Georgie tells you, there is a twelve o'clock curfew in this house."

"Midnight. Got it," I said.

"Good night, Janie."

Once he was gone, I turned back to the bed with a sigh. There was still a little time; maybe I should try to call Kaila again . . .

"Open the door!" Georgina cried out.

The intensity in her voice took me aback; I hurried over and threw open the door. She was standing there with a small suitcase. "Are you going somewhere?" I asked, perplexed.

"Makeup caddy," Georgina explained, huffing slightly as she rolled it into the room. She dropped the handle and straightened. "You already showered, right?"

"Uh, no," I said, as she unzipped the bag with a flourish. Inside, dozens of compartments were stacked with what appeared to be the entire contents of a Sephora store.

"Well, hurry up. This is going to take some time."

"What's going to take some time?" I asked as she pushed me toward the bathroom.

"Your makeover, silly. Don't wash your hair, it'll be easier to curl if it's a little dirty."

MY NEW LIFE IS *dominated by a series of increasingly painful shoes,* I thought, shifting from foot to foot in the corner of Country Day's gymnasium. The silver pumps with four-inch heels that Georgina had talked me into (for five hundred bucks, no less) seemed determined to zero in on my only remaining blister-free zones. My arches already ached, and I was terrified to move more than a few feet in either direction; I'd rarely worn heels before, and never ones this high. Outside the ocean, I wasn't exactly graceful. I'd been forced to lean heavily on Georgina's arm just to get here from the car; and as soon as we were inside, she issued an excited squeal and abandoned me, rushing off to her group of friends.

At least I'd managed to make my way to the long table arrayed with food. Apparently this wasn't a chips and salsa kind of crowd; there were actual trays of sushi. Tiny finger sandwiches stacked on tiered silver platters. A watermelon carved into a cornucopia, with smaller pieces of fruit tumbling out. Delicate puff pastries and mini-quiches and tarts. A catering crew bustled back and forth, refilling platters every time the slightest dent was made in them.

No DJ, either, but an honest-to-God band. One that I'd actually heard of, with a hit song a couple years ago.

Not that anyone was dancing. Clumps of teenagers huddled together, laughing and chattering as if this was all completely normal. The boys wore suits and ties, the girls expensive semiformal gowns. Judging by the price tags I'd seen today, there was probably a million dollars worth of clothing squeezed into a high school gymnasium that reeked of sweat and floor polish. I felt an unexpected swell of gratitude toward Georgina; she'd been right, if I'd shown up in something from my closet, I would have looked like an alien.

All in all, pretty darn intimidating, I thought to myself. It was like a scene culled directly from of those teen flicks my friends and I always scoffed at. I could practically hear Kaila protesting, *Yeah, right, like a high school dance would ever look like that.*

Apparently they did, sometimes.

I held a tiny plate stacked with food in one hand and let my eyes rove across the room, taking it all in. Despite the fact that my feet killed, and the dress was cutting off my circulation, I was still glad I came. This was definitely worth seeing once, although I doubted I'd ever go to another one.

"Would you like another mushroom quiche, miss?" A caterer asked, leaning over the table to be heard.

I shook my head, since my mouth was already stuffed with two of them. I washed them down with lemonade. Unfortunately, I tried to breathe at the same time, and ended up having a coughing fit.

I tottered away from the table in my heels, bent double. Sounding concerned, the caterer asked, "Are you all right, miss?"

I waved to indicate that I was okay, even though it felt like I was choking up a lung.

"Here." A cup was forced into my free hand: Water.

Gratefully, I gulped it down, instantly easing the tickle in the back of my throat. After wiping my mouth with my hand, I turned to hand the cup back.

The "thanks" died in my throat. Instead of the caterer, pretty much the hottest guy I'd ever seen in my life was looking down at me. He was easily six-two or six-three. Built like an athlete, with broad shoulders. His hair was dark and wavy, and he had big brown eyes with long lashes and a cleft in his chin.

He grinned. "Can't let a Hamill girl die in the middle of a mixer. The alumni would freak out."

I realized that I was still gaping at him like an idiot. "Thanks."

"You are okay, right?" His brow furrowed.

"I'm great," I said, collecting myself. "Wrong pipe, that's all."

Internally, I winced. *Wrong pipe? Seriously, Janie?*

"Hate it when that happens," he said sympathetically, tucking his hands in his pockets. Instead of a suit—which most of the other boys were wearing—he was in a navy jacket and khaki pants. "So, are you new?"

"Yup," I said. "I just moved here this week."

"Really?" He raised an eyebrow. "Pretty brave to show up at a shindig like this your first week."

"Tell me about it," I muttered.

"So where are you from?"

"Hawaii. The Big Island."

"Yeah?" His face lit up. "I love the Big Island! Hey, have you been to the Four Seasons in Kona?"

I shifted uncomfortably; the Four Seasons was by far the fanciest resort on the island, and that was saying something. I'd only been once, to visit a friend who was working in their beach shack. And they'd actually escorted me off the premises for not having "official permission" to be there. "Yeah, I've seen it."

"I love that place," he said reverently. "We used to go for the holidays every year."

I sighed: yet another rich kid I could never relate to. "Great," I said without enthusiasm.

We stood in an awkward silence for what felt like an eternity. My eyes wandered to his tie, which had a weird and oddly familiar pattern of faces in black and white. I did a double take, suddenly recognizing it. "Hey, that's the Sergeant Pepper tie!"

His eyebrows shot up, and his grin widened. He held the tie out for me to examine. "The one and only. You like the Beatles?"

"My dad had that tie," I blurted out.

"Oh." His smile faded.

I scanned the room for a hole to crawl into. God, you'd think I'd never talked to a boy before. *Get a grip, Janie,* I chastised myself. "That came out kind of creepy-sounding, huh?"

"What, that I remind you of your dad?" His head tilted to the side. "I thought I had a good response to that, but then I said it in my head and it sounded even worse."

I laughed. "Oh, now you *have* to tell me."

"Nope. Not happening. Your dad has good taste, though."

"Yeah." I flashed back to the last time he wore that tie: on my birthday a few months ago, when he flew us to Oahu for dinner. Suddenly I was blinking back tears.

The boy looked alarmed. "Hey, are you . . . crap, what did I say?"

"Nothing," I mumbled. "I'm fine. Thanks again for the water."

I stumbled away from him, tottering even more unevenly on the heels.

Outside, I sucked in deep breaths of air. Tears rolled freely down my face. It felt like I was going to throw up everything I'd just crammed in my mouth.

"You're ruining your makeup."

I raised my head to find Georgina looking down at me critically. "What?"

"I wouldn't care, except I did a fantastic job with that smoky eye look." She held out a flask. "Here."

I shook my head. "I don't drink."

"Suit yourself." She took a swig, then said, "I'm heading over to the after party. Coming?"

"After party?" I managed to stammer. "But we just got here."

Georgina threw me a look of disdain. "Really, Janie. No one stays for the dance. You make an appearance, then you leave."

"I don't feel very good," I mumbled. "I just want to go home." Another flash: of my old bedroom and the way it looked after the movers had left—barren and sad, with chipped paint and a dusty rectangle where my bed had sat. More tears came, too many to wipe away.

Georgina crinkled her nose. "God, you're a mess. Bob can take you back. I'll catch a ride."

And with that, she turned on her heel and walked away.

I sank into a crouch and wrapped my arms around my legs. It was almost a relief to have Georgina acting normal toward me again; I didn't know how to handle her being nice. A breeze swept over my bare arms, and I shivered. It was always so cold here. "I hate it," I said out loud. "I want to go home."

But there was no home to go back to. I sat there wallowing in self-pity for a few more minutes. Then I dragged myself back to the car and asked Bob to take me home.

Chapter IV

To this crib I always took my doll; human beings must love something, and, in the dearth of worthier objects of affection, I contrived to find a pleasure in loving and cherishing a faded graven image, shabby as a miniature scarecrow.

When I woke up the next morning, sun was streaming past the curtains I'd forgotten to close. I climbed out of bed and went to the window. Sunlight glinted off the rooftops, casting them in mauve and violet. In the distance, the graceful red arches of the Golden Gate Bridge swooped toward Marin. Alcatraz Island hunched in the middle of the bay like it was trying not to be seen.

Gazing at the water lifted my spirits. Remembering my total meltdown at the dance the night before, I cringed.

Enough whining, I chided myself. *You need to get a grip.*

The rest of my things had arrived yesterday, including my surfboard. I'd stacked everything in a corner of the room until I could figure out where to put them. My board stretched nearly to the ceiling. I unzipped the case and ran a hand lovingly over it, the bumps and ridges of surf wax familiar against my palm.

"All right," I said with determination. "Let's go see how they do it on the mainland."

The house was still silent, and I didn't encounter anyone as I clumsily carried the board downstairs. I came close to knocking a few vases off their perches, and heaved a sigh of relief when

I made it to the front door without shattering something irreplaceable. I left my board propped against the wall and zipped to the kitchen to grab an apple.

I had to take three different buses to reach my destination: Ocean Beach. Fortunately, there weren't a lot of passengers at 6 A.M. on a Saturday. I sat in the back row each time, keeping my board propped at an angle so it was out of the way.

During the ride I skimmed surf sites on my phone, checking conditions. According to them, Ocean Beach had one of the best surf breaks in the world, but it was also notoriously dangerous. Between the undertow, riptides, and freezing water temperature, there were lots of warnings about leaving this beach to the pros.

I wasn't a pro, but I'd been surfing from the moment I could stand on a board. My dad came to the sport later in life, but he was a natural, and he'd taught me everything he knew.

Paddle! Paddle! Dad cried. I struggled, digging my hands into the water frantically. The wave was already passing beneath me. I wanted to scream with frustration—I was missing it again!

I can't do it!

You can, Janie! Now, two more big paddles, then stand!

Dad was twenty feet behind me. My board was rushing toward the break. I drew a deep breath, dug in my right hand, then my left, then pushed quickly to my feet the way we'd practiced on the beach.

And suddenly, I was flying, the board hurtling along the wave. I screamed and threw my arms up . . .

. . . which sent me flying off the board. I broke the surface, gasping and choking. Dad was already there, an expression of glee on his face. He picked me up out of the water and swung me around, yelling, *You did it! I knew you could!*

I SNIFFLED AND INHALED deeply: *No more crying,* I told myself. At least, not today.

After an hour and a half, the final bus deposited me at the corner of Sloat Boulevard and the Great Highway, where three sites claimed you could find the best waves. A breeze whipped off the dunes across the street, sending tufts of sand flying upward. *Offshore wind,* I noted. *Perfect.*

At the first break in traffic, I trotted across the street and scrambled up the dunes. At the top, my heart caught in my throat.

Spread below me was a glorious panorama. Dusky sand stretched in both directions, the tide lines marked by clumps of dark seaweed. Overhead, pelicans glided past in tight formation. The water was darker than I was accustomed to, more violent and wild looking in shades of green and black. But it was still the Pacific—*my* Pacific. The wind teased my ponytail. For the first time since arriving, I finally felt like I was home.

I struggled into the wetsuit, muttering curses as I fought the unforgiving neoprene. But as soon as my bare fingers touched the water, I was happy to have it. The water was almost unbearably cold. I dove in and came up sputtering; it felt like my head had been encased in ice, and my teeth were already chattering.

How on earth do people stand this? I wondered as I hopped on my board and started paddling out.

I sat shivering for ten minutes before a rideable set finally came in. I paddled hard to catch the first wave, pushing up to standing as soon as the board caught and lifted below me.

I let out a whoop as the wave swept me along, bringing me racing toward shore. I'd timed it perfectly: my board tore along just below the crest. I cut out before it broke, chasing foam over the top before settling my board onto the wave's back.

I was grinning like a crazy person as I paddled back out to wait for another wave. Sure, the water was icy, it took forever to get here, and the neoprene was chafing the hell out of me.

But in spite of all that, I was happy—truly happy—for the first time since I'd left home.

I caught another dozen waves, each better than the last. I understood immediately why surfers discussed Ocean Beach with reverence and more than a little fear in their voices. My breath caught each time a wave picked me up, it was like being lifted by a giant hand that was debating whether to carry or crush me. I'd surfed some unruly breaks before, but this was a whole different beast.

A couple hours in, I decided the next wave would be my last. The tips of my fingers were wrinkled and blue, my toes numb despite the neoprene booties. Surfing an unfamiliar break when I was tired and cold would be a mistake; that's when people got in trouble.

I caught the next wave, a perfect left. As I was coasting down the front of it, knees slightly bent, arms out to the side, I saw movement in my peripheral vision. Frowning, I tilted my head: another surfer was approaching at warp speed.

He yelped and tried to pull out, but it was too late. A lurch as our boards collided, and I was sent flying.

I somersaulted through water churning with sand and foam, immediately losing all sense of which way was up. My lungs strained as my body finally stilled. This was exactly how most surfers drowned: they ended up swimming for what they thought was the surface, and ended up on the ocean floor instead. And then their air ran out.

The important thing was not to panic: my dad had drilled that into me from day one. So I waited, the roar of water abnormally loud in my ears. After a few long beats, my hands floated up. I kicked in that direction, following them.

I surfaced just in time to see another huge wave bearing down on me.

Sucking in a deep breath, I dove back down, letting myself get spun around again. After kicking to the surface a second time, I found myself caught in a trough, the gap between waves. I gulped in another breath and swirled back into the spin cycle.

I could feel myself weakening; fighting the waves consumed too much energy. My head throbbed from the cold, and my ears burned. *Please let this be the last one,* I prayed. Waves usually came in sets of three, but that wasn't a hard and fast rule. I couldn't do this for much longer.

Of course, I could stop fighting, I suddenly realized. Just let go. There were worse ways to die. Drowning would be relatively quick and painless.

For a moment, I saw my parents as clearly as if they were standing right in front of me. Their arms on each other's shoulders, the sun setting behind them. They smiled and reached for me . . .

No, I thought. *They'd never forgive me.*

Weakly, I kicked back to the surface.

The incoming wave was much smaller, and gentle enough to ride in. Enormously relieved, I floated on my back, letting it carry me toward shore.

Abruptly, someone grabbed me by the armpits and started dragging me through the breakers.

"Hey! What—" I struggled against my attacker. "Let go of me!"

"I got you," he gasped. "Just hang on."

He dumped me unceremoniously on the edge of the beach. I lunged to my feet and whirled around. "What are you doing?"

"Saving you." The guy's hands were on his knees, his back heaving as he tried to catch his breath. "Man, that was close."

"Saving me? You nearly killed me! What the hell were you thinking, dropping in on my wave?"

"Dropping in?"

"Yes, you moron." I resisted the urge to throttle him. Dropping in on a wave was pretty much the worst offense a surfer could commit. Once you caught a wave, it was yours and yours alone. Sharing waves was too dangerous, because you could crash into each other—the way that we had. "Don't you know anything?"

He straightened, and the tirade caught in my throat.

It was the guy from the dance, the one with the Sergeant Pepper tie.

He stared back at me, looking equally perplexed. "You."

"Yeah, it's me," I grumbled, still miffed.

"So you're a surfer girl?" A slow smile broke across his face. "Cool."

I tried not to notice how the wetsuit stretched across his broad shoulders, and nipped tightly around his waist. With water dripping from his curls, he looked even better than he had in the jacket and tie. *Snap out of it,* I reminded myself. He was cute, but he'd almost gotten us both killed. "And you're what, a gremmy?"

"What's a gremmy?" he asked. A smile still danced across his lips, like he found me wildly entertaining. Which only annoyed me more.

"A rookie," I snapped. "Someone who doesn't know better."

At least he had the good grace to look embarrassed as he shrugged. "I've only had a few weeks of surf camp, so I guess I am a gremmy." He ran a hand through his wet curls. "Sorry I ran into you."

"Well, you should be." As I squeezed the excess water out of my hair, my hands encountered knots gritted with sand. I probably looked like a drowned kitten. "Aren't there easier breaks to learn on?" I turned to scan for my board, spotting it being tossed by the breakers twenty feet away.

"I usually go to Linda Mar, down the coast," he confessed, surveying the waves ruefully. "But I thought I was ready for this."

"You're lucky we didn't both drown," I scoffed.

"I know. Let me make it up to you," he offered. "With breakfast. My treat."

I weighed the offer; it wasn't like I had anywhere else to be, and I was starving. Plus the thought of climbing back on a series of buses for the long ride back to the Rochesters was too depressing for words.

"Fine," I said. "Breakfast."

TWENTY MINUTES LATER, WE were ensconced at a table in a Denny's a few blocks away. I'd changed back into my clothes, and was uncomfortably aware of the fine layer of sand covering me. There were no showers at Ocean Beach, or palm trees to hang out under while the sun baked you dry. Still, I reminded myself, it had been a pretty good morning. As I perused the sticky menu, my stomach growled.

"I'm Daniel, by the way."

"Janie."

He reached a hand across the table, and I shook it awkwardly. Did kids really shake hands here? It seemed so weird.

"So you just started at Hamill?" he asked.

"Yup. I'm five days into my sentence," I said.

He laughed. "That bad?"

"Worse," I muttered. The waitress finally came over, and I ordered a grand slam with a side of extra bacon. His eyebrows arched up. "What?" I asked.

"Nothing. It's just nice to meet a girl who actually eats. Most Hamill girls count lattes as food." He crossed his arms on the table and leaned forward. "So I'm guessing you grew up surfing?"

"Pretty much. I was doing it every day, up until a few weeks ago."

"I'm jealous," he said. "How do you like it here so far?"

"I hate it," I admitted. "It's cold, and school sucks, and I have to wear a uniform that makes me look like a ten-year-old."

He laughed again. "Don't hold back. Tell me how you really feel."

I felt a flush spread across my cheeks. "Sorry. I just miss home."

"I get that," he said sympathetically. "So why'd you move?"

The lump climbed back into my throat. *Don't you dare cry,* I admonished myself. "My parents died."

His face fell. "Oh, crap. God, I'm really sorry, Janie."

The pity in his eyes was almost too much to bear. "Don't look at me like that."

"Like what?"

"Like you feel sorry for me. People have been giving me that look since the accident, and I hate it."

"Okay," he said gravely. "Do you prefer this look?" As he drew back from the table, his eyebrows shot up, and his mouth gaped open in mock horror. "Better?"

He looked so ridiculous, I couldn't help but laugh. "Not really."

"How about this, then?" He cupped his chin in one hand and wrinkled his forehead.

"Worse. Much worse."

"Well, I give up." He threw his hands up in mock surrender. "I could go Blue Steel on you, but it would render you completely powerless."

"Really." I rolled my eyes. "And that works on all the girls?"

"Some," he said, flashing a cocky grin.

"I'll bet," I mumbled. Daniel seemed nice enough, but it was hard to trust a guy who was so attractive. He was probably a player, like Tommy Oliver.

Our food arrived, and we both dug in. I was mopping up the last of the eggs with my toast when I caught him watching me. "What?"

"Nothing. It's just . . . do you think you could teach me?"

"To surf?"

"Yeah."

"What about surf camp?" I teased.

"I'm guessing you know more than they do."

"What do I get for it?" I asked, emboldened.

Daniel looked amused. "What do you want?"

A real date, I thought before catching myself. "A ride home. I had to take three buses to get here."

"Done," he said solemnly, reaching across the table with his hand again.

I stared at it, then shook my head. "Lesson one. Surfers don't shake hands."

"They don't?"

"Never," I said gravely. "Makes you look like a true gremmy."

"Man." He sat back in his seat. "Clearly I have so much to learn."

"Stick with me, little grasshopper. I'll make a surfer of you yet."

DANIEL PULLED UP TO the Rochesters' front door. We both sat for a minute, staring up at the house.

"Georgina lives here, right?" he finally said.

"You know her?" I asked, startled.

"Oh, yeah," he said with an odd laugh. "Everyone knows Georgie."

"Knows her how?" I asked, not liking his tone.

"Never mind." Avoiding my eyes, he added, "See you tomorrow, right? Bright and early?"

"Yeah, tomorrow," I mumbled, already getting out of the car. I retrieved my surfboard from the hatch and carried it to the foreboding entrance, then propped it against the side of the house. There had to be a better place to keep it than my bedroom, especially now that it was covered in sand. The garage, maybe?

I was debating what to do with it when the front door flew open. Marion glared at me, her face livid with rage.

"Where were you?" she demanded, drawing out each syllable.

"Surfing," I said, taken aback. "What's wrong—"

"Janie!" Richard appeared at her shoulder. "Oh, thank God. We were so worried."

"Worried?" I said, confused. "Why?"

"Get inside," Marion hissed. "I will not discuss this in public."

I glanced back over my shoulder, thinking, *Public? There's no one in sight.* But I shuffled into the house. Marion slammed the door and then spat, "You snuck out of the house like a criminal." She eyed the board. "Were you at the *beach*?"

She pronounced it the way you'd say, "crack house" or "brothel."

"I didn't think it was a big deal," I muttered. "I thought I'd be back before everyone woke up."

"You thought wrong," she said coldly.

"Yeah, sure. Sorry," I repeated, trying to quell a sudden surge of anger. I'd barely even *seen* Marion this week, aside from passing her in the halls. She'd been taking breakfast in her room, and every night the Rochesters were at some society function. Before today she hadn't shown any interest in how I spent my time, so what was the big deal with going surfing? Still, to appease her I said, "I guess I should give you my cell number for next time, huh?"

"Next time?" Marion repeated, her nostrils flaring.

"It's okay, Janie." Richard stepped forward, as if trying to physically shield me from Marion's wrath. "I know you're still adjusting to how we do things around here."

I bit back a retort; *no one had even told me what the rules were, so how was I supposed to avoid breaking them?* Instead, I said, "I'm a little tired. Is it okay if I go to my room?"

"*Your* room?" Marion glared at me, then turned to her husband. "I am done, Richard. Do you hear me? Done. You deal with her." She spun and stormed off down the hall.

I stared after her, flabbergasted. My parents had been considered strict, in that I actually had a curfew. But even the few times I'd gotten in trouble, Mom and Dad had never reacted like this. I felt sick. Marion clearly hated me, and I had no clue why. The lump in my throat returned. *Why was everyone so awful here?*

Richard offered me a faint smile. "We were supposed to head

up to Napa this morning," he said. "Marion is a little put out because we had to wait for you to get back."

"Napa?" I said dumbly.

Richard nodded. "There's a fundraiser tonight, and the whole family is expected to attend. You included," he added pointedly.

My heart sank; I was supposed to go surfing with Daniel tomorrow. "I can just stay here. I have a lot of homework to catch up on anyway—"

Richard was already shaking his head. "We leave in a half hour. Be sure to pack something semi-formal. The dress from last night will be fine, if it's still clean. If not, I'll have Georgie lend you one."

He strode off, apparently concluding that the conversation was over.

I stood there, stunned. Why on earth did they want me to go with them? Marion couldn't stand being in the same room with me. And now we were supposed to spend the rest of the weekend together?

I dragged myself upstairs to my room. Seeing the door ajar, I frowned; I distinctly remembered closing it when I left.

Entering, my jaw dropped.

Everything had been dragged into the center of the bedroom. Boxes had been opened; clothing and personal items spilled out the tops. My jaw clenched at the thought of someone going through my things. Had Marion done this? Or Georgina? But why? I couldn't imagine that my third grade swimming medal would interest them.

Something propped up on my bed caught my attention. Bessie, the doll I'd slept with when I was little, lay on top of the pillows. Her skirts were pulled up over her head.

What the hell?

I picked her up and smoothed her clothing. Turning her over, I gasped.

There were two gaping holes where Bessie's blue eyes used

to be, surrounded by jagged red marker lines. It looked like she was weeping blood.

A noise behind me.

I whipped around: Nicholas was hovering on the threshold, a guilty expression on his face.

"I'm sorry," he said with a hitch in his voice. "Eliza made me do it."

"I SAID I WAS sorry," Nicholas pleaded. "I'll have Daddy get you another doll. I promise."

We were sitting in the back of the Town Car, with Bob at the wheel. He kept casting concerned glances back at Nicholas's tear-streaked face. Alma sat on his other side, her jaw set in a tight line. I wondered if she understood what we were talking about; she didn't seem to speak much English. Georgina had opted to go to Napa with one of her friends, and Richard and Marion were driving separately in their Tesla. Which made this the car equivalent of the kids' table.

It also made me wonder why they'd bothered waiting for me in the first place.

But Marion's unwarranted fit about me going surfing had fallen to a distant second place; right now, I was determined to find out why Nicholas had disfigured Bessie. Remembering her face, I shuddered. I didn't have a lot of experience with grieving kids (other than myself, of course). Still, ripping out a doll's eyes didn't seem like normal behavior.

"I don't want another doll," I told him gently. "I just want to know what happened."

"Eliza made me do it," Nicholas insisted again, his lower lip quivering. "I told her I didn't want to, but she said if I didn't, she'd do something worse. Much worse."

It was hard to argue with a kid who was convinced that his dead twin sister was still ordering him around. I had to try, though. "Nicholas, I know it was probably pretty upsetting, finding out that I was coming to live with you. If you're worried about getting less attention from your parents—"

"No!" he interrupted. "I was so excited. And you actually play with me, like I was hoping you would." His eyes slid toward Alma as he added in a whisper, "No one else plays with me."

Nicholas's tone was heart wrenching. Maybe he was acting out because he wanted me to spend even more time with him; as far as I could tell, no one else bothered. Even now, when he was crying, Alma ignored him. She leaned back against the upholstery, eyes closed. I wasn't sure if she was his official nanny, but still; she'd known him since birth. She should be chastising me for upsetting him, not pretending she wasn't even in the car with us. Based on what I'd seen, it was hard to believe that she'd served as a second mother to Richard and my dad.

"Please don't be angry with me, Janie," Nicholas begged, grabbing my hand with his tiny ones. "I can't stand having you mad at me."

"I'm not mad," I reassured him, even though the way he said his sister's name always sent a tremor down my spine. I cast about for a solution that wouldn't involve barricading my door against him. "When we get back home, maybe you and I should have a talk with Eliza. If I make friends with her, she might not make you do stuff like that again. Does that sound okay?"

Nicholas shrank back against the seat. "I don't know," he murmured. "She doesn't like it when other people go in the attic."

Before I could suggest finding another place to talk to her, Alma's head snapped up. "No attic!"

My jaw dropped. *That's* what got her attention? "Listen, Nicholas is really upset. He thinks his sister—"

"You have bag?" Alma demanded, talking over me as if I wasn't even there.

Nicholas nodded and pulled something out from under his shirt. Seeing it, I frowned. It was a tiny pouch on a leather cord. "What's that?"

"It's for protection," Nicholas said solemnly. "If I wear it, Eliza is supposed to leave me alone."

"And does she?" I asked, keeping a steely gaze fixed on Alma. She had already settled back against the seat, her eyes firmly shut again.

Nicholas nodded vigorously. "Oh, yes. But sometimes I forget to put it back on after my bath." His face fell. "Like this morning. That's why it's my fault."

He looked utterly desolate. After a moment's hesitation, I wrapped my arms around him. *He's just a confused kid,* I reminded myself. Kissing the top of his head, I said, "It's okay, Nicholas. It's not your fault."

And it wasn't, not really. Nicholas tucked his little head under my chin and sighed gratefully. "Thanks, Janie. And don't worry. I won't forget the pouch again."

"Wear pouch," Alma muttered. "And no attic."

I glared at her over the top of his head, but her eyes remained closed. It was practically criminal, letting a grieving little boy think that if he didn't wear a magic necklace, his dead sister would make him do terrible things. Did his parents know about this? Maybe they were unable to admit that Nicholas really needed help. Not that I was about to tell them; I could just imagine Marion's reaction if I suggested hiring a shrink.

I was at a loss, though, and way out of my depth.

"Don't worry, kiddo," I said, trying to sound adult and reassuring. "We'll figure it out."

Nicholas twitched in my arms. He'd fallen asleep.

I cradled him as we drove the final half hour. We passed several vineyards, row after row of grapevines strapped to spindly posts. At a different time of year, when they were in bloom, it was probably beautiful. But in the stark wintry light, the barren, twisted vines looked menacing—like withered creatures trapped in perpetual agony. As the sun dropped below the hills, their shadows stretched long, grasping fingers toward the road. I held Nicholas a little tighter, grateful for the small, warm body in my lap.

Chapter V

At this moment a light gleamed on the wall. Was it, I asked myself, a ray from the moon penetrating some aperture in the blind? No; moonlight was still, and this stirred; while I gazed, it glided up to the ceiling and quivered over my head.

"Is it Henry's law?" I guessed.

"Hess's law. You keep getting those confused." Helen made a face at me. "What's with you today?"

"Just tired." I stifled another yawn. We were sitting in the library studying for tomorrow's chemistry test, and the heat was cranked to about a hundred degrees. That, combined with the fact that I hadn't clocked a full night's sleep since moving into the Rochesters' a month ago, made the temptation to put my head down on the desk nearly overwhelming. But if I failed this test, I was totally screwed.

Helen scrutinized me. "You know that losing sleep takes years off your life, right?"

"That's helpful," I groaned. "Something to obsess over tonight as I stare at the ceiling."

"Insomnia, huh?" she said. "My mom gets that sometimes. Have you tried melatonin?"

"Doesn't work," I said. Which was true—I'd tried every herbal treatment on the market, but none of them was equipped to handle "strange noises coming from a forbidden section of the house." In the end, they just left me feeling awake but groggy.

Helen chewed on the end of her pen while she scanned the rest of her homework. Watching her, I debated sharing the real reason I wasn't sleeping. But she'd probably think I was crazy, and I didn't want to risk losing the only friend I had here. *Aside from Daniel,* I reminded myself.

As if she'd read my mind, Helen asked, "So are you and Daniel still just surf buddies?"

"Basically, yeah." I rubbed at a pencil mark on the desk's surface. "I can't believe you two never met."

"Right, because I'm such a society girl," she snorted. Seeing my expression, she added, "My parents and Blanche are into that sort of thing. I'd rather be LARPing. If they institute that at the next Symphony Ball, I'm totally in."

"I'd do pretty much anything to see Marion in a troll costume," I grinned.

Helen mused, "She'd make a halfway decent Miraak, actually."

"Right." I'd learned that sometimes it was best to just pretend I knew what she was talking about. "Anyway, Daniel invited me to a bonfire on the beach this weekend. That sounds like a date, right?"

Helen's eyes danced. "Like I'd have a clue. The closest I've come to a date was flirting with an Orc in a Skyrim forum."

"Now that's just sad," I said.

Helen issued an exaggerated sigh. "Yup, I'll die a virgin for sure. And you'll flunk chemistry. Guess we're both doomed." I swatted her arm, and she shied away, laughing.

It was starting to feel like Daniel and I were never going to be anything more than friends, though. So far our "dates" had consisted of me yelling instructions as he tried to catch waves, followed by greasy diner food. He'd also text links to stuff he thought was funny. I knew this because he always wrote, "funny!," "hilarious!," or ":-P."

And that was pretty much it. Once he added, "xoD" below the

link, and I spent the entire day obsessing over whether or not it actually meant anything.

"A bonfire definitely sounds like a date," Helen said, noticing my discomfort. She wagged a finger at me and added, "And I want to hear all about it, so call or text if you don't get home too late."

"Okay, Mom," I said thoughtlessly, and then swallowed hard. The grief still occasionally caught me unawares. All it took was a familiar song pouring out of a café or a TV rerun; even seeing a Hawaiian Airlines ad could reduce me to tears.

I still hadn't deleted my parents' numbers from my phone; a few times, I'd actually dialed before realizing that no one on the other end would pick up. Sometimes I'd lay awake at night, going over old text threads.

don't forget to pick up milk on your way home from Kaila's

does that count toward my allowance?

it counts toward you having a roof over your head

love you too. Sheesh.

love you always and forever xo

No matter how mundane the texts were, reading them always made me dissolve in a puddle. I wish I'd said more, appreciated them more. I should have ended every single message with, *I love you always and forever, too.*

Part of me was grateful for the fact that everything here was so unfamiliar. If I were living back on the island, with constant reminders everywhere, I'd probably have lost my mind by now.

Helen's eyes softened, but she didn't say anything. She never gave me that pitying look; one of the many things I'd come to appreciate about her.

"Only ten more minutes of study hall," she observed. "So stop distracting me."

"Sure," I said gratefully. "Chemistry. Henry's Law."

"Hess's—"

"I know," I said with a grin. "Just seeing if you were paying attention."

I SQUINTED AT MYSELF in the mirror. *Ugh.* I looked like I was embarking on an arctic mission. Frustrated, I tugged off the black fleece jacket. Nights in San Francisco were cold; you couldn't risk exposing bare skin. And it was hard to be a temptress when you were dressed like the Michelin Man.

I bit my lip, weighing the options. Georgina had actually been going out of her way to be nice to me lately, at least when we weren't at school. Maybe she'd lend me something that managed to be slinky and warm simultaneously.

I set off for her bedroom. It was in the other wing of the house, down the hall from Richard and Marion's room. Georgina had dragged me in there once to help her decide which pair of jeans made her look skinniest. Since the correct answer was "all of the above," my stay was short-lived.

As I rounded the corner, my steps slowed. Someone was talking loudly and angrily; it sounded like Marion. *Who was in there with her?* I really hoped they weren't talking about me.

I drew in a deep breath and plastered a smile on my face. Not that it would make a difference. Unlike Georgina, Marion was never pleased to see me. Listening to her strident tone, I was tempted to abandon my mission. I really needed an outfit though; maybe if I was quick and quiet, Marion wouldn't notice me.

Both bedroom doors were ajar. I approached Georgina's room as silently as possible and peeped inside. No luck: the room was empty, the bedside lamp waging a futile battle against the wide pool of darkness surrounding it. Sighing, I started walking back down the hall; then the sound of my name stopped me in my tracks.

So Marion *was* talking about me.

I hesitated, then moved closer to hear what she was saying. Her voice rose and fell in a regular cadence. I realized with a jolt that she was actually alone and repeating the same phrase, over and over again. "She came back for him. We can't let her have him. Janie is a bad girl, very, very bad. But we need the money. She came back for him . . ."

I caught my breath as Marion suddenly moved into the doorframe. Seeing me, she stopped dead. Her face was cast in shadow, making it impossible to read her expression. Her hands hung by her sides. Her hair was mussed. Most startling of all, she was wearing a bathrobe; I'd never seen her in anything but a designer outfit before. Her shoulders rose and fell as if she was breathing heavily.

"I-I was looking for Georgina," I squeaked. Clearing my throat, I continued. "Um, have you seen her?"

Marion didn't respond; she just stood there. Something about her posture cued an alarm in me, like she was a predator poised to pounce. I took a step back. "I guess I'll just find her later!" I chirped.

Nothing. Marion was never friendly, but this was beyond strange, like she was sleepwalking or hypnotized. I backed away, the fake smile straining my cheeks. As soon as I rounded the corner, I bolted toward my room.

The black fleece would have to suffice. No way I was going back to that wing of the house—not ever if I could help it.

"LIKE WHAT KIND OF noises?" Daniel asked curiously.

"Really weird ones," I said.

We were walking down the beach, moving away from the bonfire. At a loss for something to say, I'd mentioned that I hadn't had a full night's sleep in almost a month. When he asked why, I'd admitted that something in the attic kept waking me up.

It was a relief to finally have a receptive audience. The few times I'd tried to talk to the Rochesters about it, they'd shut me down. They obviously thought it was all in my head, and I hadn't been able to prove them wrong. I'd tried to record the noises on my phone, but it was usually just a low hum, barely discernible. Occasionally I heard footsteps pattering back and forth: A raccoon, maybe? That would have explained some of the other noises, too. But when I'd asked about calling animal control, Marion had coldly informed me that would be absurd, since there was absolutely nothing up in the attic. And I had to admit, only an extremely brave or incredibly foolish animal would dare move into her home.

But *something* was up there. I was sick and tired of laying awake listening to it. The sleep deprivation was killing me.

"Weird how?" Daniel asked.

"It sounds like a person humming, usually." I repressed a shudder, remembering what had snapped me awake last night at 3 A.M. "Sometimes it sounds like nursery rhymes. You know, 'Jack and Jill,' 'Ring Around the Rosie.' That sort of thing. But just the tune, no words."

Daniel's eyes sparked. "Cool."

"Cool? Seriously?" I grabbed his arm to stop him, irritated. "How, exactly, is that cool?"

"It sounds like a ghost. How is that not cool?"

"Trust me, it isn't," I muttered. "You don't actually believe in that sort of thing, do you?"

"What else could it be? Raccoons aren't really known for their humming skills," he said with a grin.

I was starting to regret telling him. What if he thought I was going crazy, too? Hearing things didn't exactly attest to my sanity. Determined to change the subject, I said dismissively, "It's probably something totally normal and boring, like the kitchen radio coming up through the vents."

Daniel cocked his head to the side. "Who's hanging out in the kitchen in the middle of the night?"

"I don't know. Someone," I mumbled. I didn't admit that I'd snuck downstairs last night to test that theory and found the kitchen deserted and dead silent. By the time I got back upstairs, the noises had stopped.

I kept my head down and continued walking. "Well, you're in luck," Daniel said. "Because I happen to know a lot about ghosts."

"Seriously?" I raised an eyebrow.

Holding a hand up like he was taking an oath, Daniel said, "I'm a horror movie junkie."

I groaned. "I hate horror movies."

"Too bad," Daniel said blithely. "See, if you liked horror movies, you'd know exactly how to handle this."

"Really." I crossed my arms over my chest. The bonfire had been reduced to a faint flicker of red in the distance. When Daniel suggested taking a walk, I'd let myself imagine all sorts of things: him sweeping me into his arms and kissing me, or at least holding my hand. Instead, we were talking about ghosts. *Way to set the mood, Janie,* I berated myself.

Then again, I was exhausted; if Daniel really did have helpful suggestions, I'd love to hear them.

"All right, then. The first rule of ghosts is figuring out who it is," he said authoritatively.

I felt a pang of guilt; even though I'd never met Eliza, it felt wrong to talk about her. Also, more than a little dangerous, like I might accidentally summon her. *Ghosts aren't real,* I reminded myself. "A little girl died in the house about a year ago."

Daniel's face grew somber. He pulled on my arm, turning me to face him. "You're serious," he said, examining me.

I nodded, suddenly cold. "Eliza was Nicholas's twin sister. He keeps claiming that she talks to him, and makes him do things."

He breathed out hard and ran a hand through his hair. "Wow. I thought you were kidding about this, but . . . it's real, isn't it?"

"I wouldn't have said anything if it wasn't," I mumbled. "Why? What's wrong?"

"I never met her," he said quietly. "I didn't even know Nicholas had a twin."

"Why would you know that?"

"It's a pretty small social circle," Daniel said vaguely. Frowning, he added, "The Rochesters are a pretty big deal around here. I can't understand why everyone isn't talking about this."

"That is weird," I agreed. I'd been here long enough to get a sense of the high society crowd that the Rochesters and Daniel's family traveled in. It was a group that thrived on gossip, so why wasn't this being discussed?

Yet another mystery, I thought grimly. Growing up on an island where everyone knew each other's business, this level of secrecy was completely foreign to me.

"How did she die?" Daniel asked.

I shrugged, shivering in the frigid ocean wind. "They didn't tell me. And it feels weird to ask. They don't really like talking about it."

That was an understatement. It was as if Eliza had never existed. No one but Nicholas ever mentioned her. There were no photos of her in the house, either. In fact, the only publicly displayed portrait was from Marion and Richard's wedding. I'd assumed that since the others probably included Eliza, they'd been tucked away. "I guess I can ask Nicholas what happened to her."

"From what you've said, he's having a hard enough time as it is," Daniel stared out at the black ocean. "Poor kid."

"Yeah, he's definitely taking it hard." I hesitated, then added, "I'm pretty sure he's sneaking into my room and messing with my things."

"That's probably pretty innocent, though, right? I mean, I used to do that with my mom's stuff," Daniel said.

"Maybe," I grudgingly agreed. I still didn't like it, though.

One of my necklaces kept moving to different spots around the room, even though I made a point of memorizing where I'd left it. And just this past Tuesday I came home to find all my bureau drawers open. Nicholas claimed he didn't do it, although it was hard to imagine anyone else rooting through my things.

"There are a lot of rumors about the Rochesters," Daniel mused, still gazing out over the waves. "I never believed most of them, but maybe they really are true."

"Like what?" I asked warily.

Taking in my expression, he said, "Relax. It's just stuff about Marion throwing tantrums, or Richard drinking too much at a party. And—" Abruptly he stopped. "Man, listen to me. I'm just as bad as the rest of them. Anyway, if you want, I can come check it out."

"What, like . . . sleepover?" I asked, startled. I'd wanted to ask more about the rumors, but the thought of smuggling him into my bedroom swept my mind blank.

"Well, I was thinking we could check it out in the afternoon. But if you're offering . . ." Daniel waggled his eyebrows in a way that was more mocking than suggestive.

I tried to laugh it off, as if the thought of him sleeping over was hilarious. "Yeah, right. I never hear anything in the daytime anyway. And the attic door is always locked." I didn't add that the Rochesters would probably freak out if I had a guest over; even Georgina never brought friends home.

"I can get in," Daniel said, sounding surprisingly self-assured.

"You can?" I raised an eyebrow. "How, by picking the lock?"

"Something like that. So how about it? Think you can sneak me in tomorrow?"

I turned his offer over in my mind. The next day was Sunday, and Georgina was supposed to compete in an equestrian event up near Sacramento. When the family discussed it over breakfast, it definitely sounded like all the Rochesters would be going. Since the Napa fiasco, Marion didn't insist on my presence anymore, so it would be easy to beg off. Alma would still be lurking around as usual. But the rest of the staff was gone on Sundays.

"Okay," I finally said. "It's a plan."

"Awesome." Daniel gave me a once-over. "You look cold. Let's head back to the fire."

I walked as slowly as possible, dragging my heels. But he didn't even move closer to me. By the time we reached the bonfire, I was forced to conclude that in Daniel's eyes, we were just surf buddies. Surf buddies who went ghost hunting, apparently.

"SOUNDS QUIET UP THERE," Daniel said in a stage whisper, one ear pressed to the attic door.

I couldn't respond at first. My palms were sweating so badly, I kept having to wipe them on my jeans. We'd both taken our shoes off, and the cold seeped through my socks. I couldn't repress an overwhelming sense of foreboding. "Maybe this isn't such a great idea," I hissed.

Daniel dropped into a crouch to examine the lock. "Easy," he said, throwing me a grin. "I was hoping it would be an old door."

"Why is an old door easy?" I asked, perplexed.

"You'll see. It would be faster if we could use a hairdryer on it, though."

"Too loud," I said, shaking my head. I couldn't imagine explaining the situation to Alma if she stumbled across me and a strange boy in the hallway, giving a door a blowout.

"It'll take a little longer, but I think I can manage it."

My eyes widened as Daniel opened a small pouch and started sorting through the metal rods inside. "Are those lock picks?"

"Yup." He sounded completely nonchalant, like everyone carried around a set of breaking and entering tools.

My mind was reeling. "Um, okay. And why do you have those?"

"My grandfather was a locksmith," he explained. "I locked

myself in a closet once when I was eight—scared the hell out of me. So he gave me this set and taught me how to use them."

"I didn't know there were locksmiths in high society," I joked.

Daniel threw me a look. "That's why everyone thinks my mom was a gold digger."

"Oh." I cleared my throat. *I can't seem to stop saying the wrong things around him.* "Sorry."

Daniel didn't answer, but his jaw had tightened. He held up a long, narrow piece of metal appraisingly. "This is a half diamond pick, it usually does the trick."

I slid down the opposite wall until I was sitting on my heels. "I didn't realize locksmiths knew how to do this."

Daniel chuckled. "How did you think they got doors open?"

"I don't know," I said, feeling stupid. "I just figured they had some sort of skeleton key thing."

"A bump key works for modern doors, but something like this?" He patted the keyhole affectionately. "Gotta go old school."

"Of course," I mumbled. "Silly me." At least his voice didn't sound strained anymore. As he eased the metal rod into the lock and started methodically twisting it, I tried to ignore a swell of dread in my gut. Doors were kept locked for a reason, right? I flashed back to the time Kaila and I had snuck into a foreclosed house when we were eleven.

What's that? Kaila hissed, clutching my arm even tighter.

Ow! I said, shaking her fingers loose. The afternoon light in the bedroom shone on a pile of rags in the corner. I crept across the room to peer at it. *Looks like a body,* I commented. At the time I considered myself an expert, thanks to the *Law & Order* reruns my mom and I were obsessed with.

Ohmigod! She gasped.

I was kidding, but then the lump of clothing shifted slightly. Kaila spun and ran, but I was frozen in place. All I could do was stare as a small kitten poked its nose out, followed by another . . .

"WHAT'S SO FUNNY?" DANIEL demanded.

"Nothing." I shook my head. "Just remembering the last time I broke into a place."

"Former life of crime, huh?" He winked at me. "What happened?"

"My best friend ended up with a kitten." At his puzzled look, I laughed. "Never mind." At least the memory had shaken off some of my nerves. We probably wouldn't find anything but a raccoon's nest up there, and I'd have proof that I wasn't losing my mind.

A click, and the door slowly creaked open. It bumped lightly against Daniel, as if someone had pushed it from the other side. "Hey!" he exclaimed, jumping up.

"Wow. I didn't think it would be that quick. I'm impressed," I said.

"I don't think that was me. I hadn't even made it through twenty revolutions, and it usually takes a lot more." He stared down at the pick in his hand. "That was weird, right?"

"Really weird," I said, suddenly finding it hard to breathe.

We gazed at each other across the hall. Daniel said slowly, "This is starting to feel like that scene in a movie where you're screaming at everyone for being idiots."

"Because they're going somewhere that no one should ever go?" I nodded vehemently. "Definitely."

Daniel carefully rewrapped the picks and stuck them back in his pocket. He eyed the door, frowning. "So what do you want to do?"

That should have been an easy decision: Close the door. Go

downstairs and ply Daniel with leftover chocolate mousse. Or even better, we could go out for something to eat, somewhere far away. Like Los Angeles.

But I felt an inexorable pull toward the attic, like there was something up there that I desperately needed to see. "Maybe we should take a quick look."

"You're sure?" Daniel gazed into my eyes, and I felt the last shreds of resistance crumbling. *What's the worst that can happen? It's broad daylight, and there are two of us. Two teenagers, against what'll probably turn out to be a couple of raccoons.* I pictured Marion's face if I returned with a report of animal droppings; that clinched it. "Let's go."

Steeling myself, I mounted the stairs behind him. The staircase was reassuring in its banality: plain and unassuming, with a banister in desperate need of varnish. The wooden stairs had a slight groove worn down the center. I was struck again by how much older everything was in San Francisco; Richard Rochester had told me that this was one of the only houses to survive the 1906 earthquake and fires.

Judging by the dust, it had been nearly that long since someone cleaned up here. Our feet kicked up small clouds of it, making me sneeze.

"Huh," Daniel said, stopping at the top. "I gotta admit, it's a little disappointing."

I peeked around him: we were in a narrow hallway that mirrored the one downstairs. It extended in both directions, with doors lining either side. Light filtered in through dusty, cobwebbed skylights overhead.

"Which side?" he asked.

"Want to start with the left?" I suggested.

"You're the boss."

I repressed a nervous giggle. Creeping along behind Daniel, I nearly walked into his heels when he stopped in front of the first door. "Looks like this used to be the servants' quarters."

It was a tiny room, barely eight feet long and six feet wide, basically a windowless prison cell. And it was completely empty. The same with the room across the hall. We continued down the corridor, ducking our heads inside each room. They were all identical. "Well, we know one thing for sure," Daniel said when we reached the end of the hallway.

"What's that?"

"The Rochesters aren't hoarders. If my folks had this much space, it'd be filled top to bottom with labeled boxes."

"Labeled?"

"Oh, yeah." We headed back to where we started, our voices not quite as muted. "My mom loves to pack things away in plastic bins, then label them. Christmas, Easter, you name it. We have three whole boxes marked, 'Tiki Party Props.'"

"So your folks throw a lot of tiki parties?" I asked, feeling slightly giddy. I'd imagined a lot of terrible things up there, but in the end the attic had turned out to be like everything else: disappointingly mundane.

"Never. But you gotta be prepared, right? Never know when the urge for a volcano bowl might strike you." He jerked his head toward the right. "You want to check this side, too? Or should we head back down?"

Emboldened, I said, "Let's check it out."

We proceeded down the opposite end of the hallway—directly above the wing of the house I shared with Nicholas, I realized with a flutter of trepidation. Why Nicholas had been banished to the far reaches of the mansion was beyond me; I couldn't imagine waking up from a nightmare as a kid and being forced to trot down a long, dark hallway to reach my parents' bedroom. Then again, Marion was his mother. She wouldn't be anyone's first choice for comfort.

The thought sobered me. I had yet to see anyone coddle him the way my parents did when I was his age. He was never at the "family meals," and Alma walked him to and from school.

Georgina always referred to him as "the brat," and Richard and Marion never referred to him at all.

Ever since the doll incident I'd been avoiding him, claiming I had too much homework and couldn't play. From here on out, I resolved to spend more time with him. It wasn't his fault that he thought his dead twin was still hanging around. After all, I'd almost managed to convince myself of the same thing.

The rooms on this side were equally barren. By the time we reached the end of the passage, my eyes burned from the dust, and the back of my throat was coated with it. Cobwebs were tangled in my hair, and my socks were filthy.

"That's it," Daniel said, sounding deflated. "Empty. It doesn't even look like there are animals up here."

He was giving me an odd look, probably wondering if I'd made the whole thing up just to come across as more interesting. Or maybe he did think I was nuts. "I heard *something*," I insisted, immediately wishing the words hadn't come out sounding so shrill.

Daniel nodded sympathetically, which made it even worse. He scanned the hallway. "Which of these is above your bedroom?"

I mentally constructed a map of the house in my head. "I think it's that one," I said, pointing three doors down.

"All right. Let's take a look."

I stayed close as he marched toward the room. He stopped on the threshold and said, "Huh."

"Huh, what?" I asked, trying to see around him.

"There's less dust in here," he pointed out. "See?"

Daniel stepped inside, and I joined him. He was right; this room had been swept clean. There were grooves in the wood where a twin bed must have stood.

"What's that?"

I followed his pointing finger; something was scrawled on the wall in the far corner. I crossed the room and bent low to examine it. It was dark inside; the light from the hall barely penetrated. But I could make out two crude stick figures, drawn in what looked like bright red crayon. A girl and a boy. Their hands overlapped, and their mouths were small round *O*s, as if they were screaming.

A chill crept up my spine. "Maybe Nicholas plays up here sometimes."

"Maybe," Daniel said. "That could be why they keep it locked."

"Yeah, that's probably it." *Mystery solved*, I told myself firmly. It was just an empty, dust-filled, creepy-as-hell attic. But nothing to be scared of.

"Do you feel better?" Daniel asked. He was staring down at me, his brown eyes full of concern.

"Much," I said, trying to sound convincing.

"Good. Then we should probably—"

I held up a hand to silence him. "Do you hear that?"

He'd already frozen, head cocked to the side. The sound was unmistakable. And it was coming from the hallway right outside the room.

I scrambled to my feet, my heart in my throat. Daniel cast a quizzical glance at me, then stepped into the hall. I followed and froze, catching my breath.

It was a tiny pink rubber ball. As it bounced down the hall toward us, it picked up speed. But instead of continuing past, it skittered to a stop at our feet.

As I stared at it, the ball rolled in a slow circle, batting against my toes.

Chapter VI

"So I think: you have no ghost, then?"
"None that I have ever heard of," returned Mrs. Fairfax, smiling.
"Nor any traditions of one? No legends or ghost stories?"
"I believe not. And yet it is said the Rochesters have been rather a violent than a quiet race in their time . . ."

I slowly turned my head to look at Daniel; he appeared every bit as terrified as I felt. Without exchanging a word, we both tore toward the stairs. My feet were moving so fast, I stumbled and nearly went flying. Daniel, with his longer legs, made it down ahead of me. He came to a dead halt at the landing. I slammed into his back.

"No attic!" a shrill voice yelled. "Very bad!"

I edged around Daniel to discover Alma glaring at us, hands on her hips. Her features were twisted in rage.

"I'm sorry, we just—" The words tumbled out of my mouth, but Alma didn't seem to be listening. Muttering to herself, she pushed past us and slammed the door shut, then drew a key out of her pocket and locked it.

"What's going on, Alma?"

A boy came out of a room down the hall. He was nearly as tall as Daniel, with wavy blond hair. Square jaw, features straight off a Greek statue. He was dressed in jeans and a blue sweater that matched his eyes.

"Who the hell are *you*?" I blurted.

His eyebrows shot up. "Nice manners. I can see why Georgie likes you."

"Rochester," Daniel spat.

I turned to him, surprised. He was glaring at the boy, looking completely enraged.

"Hey, Fairfax," the boy replied coolly. "Looking for something else to steal?"

Daniel's whole body had gone rigid, and a flush extended down his neck. I put a hand on his arm. "Daniel. Chill."

"Yeah, *Daniel*," the kid mocked. "Wouldn't want to have to call the cops on you."

Alma snapped something in Filipino. Without taking his gaze off Daniel, the boy said, "Alma doesn't want us messing up her carpet. So it's probably time for you to go."

"I'm sorry, who are you, exactly?" I demanded, stepping forward. *He understood Filipino? What were the chances of that?*

"So sorry," he said with exaggerated formality. Extending a hand to shake mine, he continued, "I'm John Rochester. I'm guessing you haven't heard about me?"

"No," I said, ignoring his hand. "You live here?"

"Not very quick, are you." He tilted his head to the side. "Funny, Nicholas said you were smart."

I frowned at the insult, but was too dumbstruck to respond. What kind of family neglected to mention *by the way, we've got another kid.* Even Nicholas never talked about him. "So where have you been?"

"Boarding school, in New Hampshire."

"Got kicked out of another one, huh, Rochester?" Daniel snarled. The sweet wannabe-surfer with the easy laugh had vanished. Daniel's voice was thick, his hands curled into fists at his sides. I hadn't seen this side of him before. And I definitely didn't like it.

John shrugged. "What can I say? It wasn't for me."

Alma pushed past us, flapping her arms and speaking quickly.

John sighed and translated, "Alma wants me to tell you that she's very angry you went into the attic, and you're not to go up there again." He glanced at Daniel and added, "No strange boys in the house, either."

"That's okay. I'm going." Daniel stormed down the hall, shoving past John.

I hurried after him. "Daniel, wait . . ."

He didn't stop until he reached the front door. Even then, he wouldn't meet my eyes. Looking past me, back toward the stairs, he said, "Janie, you should stay away from him."

"I don't even know who he *is*. Will you please—"

"He's trouble," Daniel interrupted. "Just . . . trust me, okay? I'll call you later."

He headed for his car at a near sprint, and then pulled out of the driveway so fast he nearly clipped the curb.

"Well, that was certainly interesting," a smooth voice remarked over my shoulder.

I turned and scowled at John Rochester. Crossing my arms I asked, "Why does he hate you so much?"

"Jealous, maybe?" John flashed a cocky grin, then clapped his hands and said, "I'm starving. Why don't we get better acquainted over lunch?"

THE SILENCE ON THE other end of the phone had gone on for so long that I finally said, "Um, *hello*?"

"Still here," Kaila replied, but she sounded distracted.

"If you're busy, I can call you back," I said, disgruntled.

"No, it's cool. So . . . you and this Daniel guy saw something?"

"Yeah." I settled back against the pillows, my eyes inadvertently drawn back to the ceiling. Overhead, the attic remained silent, but that only made it feel more ominous. I half expected that pink ball to drop through the chandelier. "It was super creepy."

Another long pause, then Kaila said hesitantly, "A ghost? I mean, it just seems—"

"Crazy, I know," I groaned. "But trust me, it happened." I repressed a twinge of annoyance; she was acting like I was telling her about my chemistry test. How could she be so blasé?

Kaila and I had managed to talk every few days since I'd left, but the conversations felt strained. It was hard to hear about my friends doing all the stuff we used to do together, especially since I'd secretly hoped they wouldn't be able to carry on without me. But, of course, that hadn't been the case. Sometimes I wondered if they really missed me at all. "What?" I finally snapped.

"It's just . . . I mean, you've been through a lot. Do you think you might've imagined it?"

Kaila had adopted the sort of soothing tone you'd use with a mental patient, which really ticked me off. Defensively, I said, "Daniel saw the ball, too."

"Okay. So what does he think?"

"We haven't had a chance to talk about it yet. I told you, we ran downstairs, then John showed up and he took off."

"Uh-huh." Voices in the background. Kaila giggled and hissed, "Quit it!" under her breath.

"What's going on?" I demanded, exasperated. "Is Taka there?"

"No, it's Tommy. We were about to go grab an ice."

"Tommy Oliver? Seriously?"

"Yup," she said with forced nonchalance.

"Since when?" I asked. Kaila had fostered a hopeless crush on Tommy since the seventh grade. And despite the fact that he'd dated pretty much every other girl in our class, he'd never shown any interest in her before. *Must be her turn,* I thought uncharitably before catching myself. I should be happy for her. And I would be, except that I knew how things always ended with Tommy Oliver.

"We've been hanging out for a few weeks," she said vaguely. "Anyway, I should probably go. There's a Kona truck down the street."

"Yeah, sure," I said dispiritedly. Kona trucks served towering cones of shaved ice dripping with flavors like Orange Creamsicle (my favorite) and Wedding Cake (Kaila's, not surprisingly). My mouth watered just thinking about it. "I'll call you later," I said, and hung up before she could protest.

I drew in a deep shuddery breath. I'd been counting on Kaila to make me feel better about the way Daniel had raced out on me. Instead, I wound up feeling like an obligation she grudgingly accepted, like the weekly call to her grandma in the nursing home.

Which was totally unfair. I'd always been there for Kaila. I'd helped drown post-breakup tears in pints of ice cream. I'd cheered for her in every surf contest (even when she was my main opponent). I'd taught her how to ride a skateboard when we were eight, and how to sneak out of her house when we were fifteen. And now, when I needed her, she didn't have time for me?

Screw her, I thought angrily, checking my phone again. I'd sent three texts to Daniel, and he hadn't responded to any of them. *And screw him, too.* I tossed my phone to the other side of the bed and grabbed my laptop. I had an essay due this week on the clash of social classes in *Wuthering Heights*—eerily appropriate, considering my current situation. Shoving aside all the spooky events of the morning, I settled down and started writing.

"Oh my God, are you actually doing homework?"

Georgina flounced into the room and flopped down on my bed. I grabbed the laptop to steady it.

"Shocking, I know," I said acerbically. "Since it's due tomorrow."

"Oh, Janie." She sighed dramatically. "You don't actually have to *do* the homework. Haven't you learned that yet?"

"Personally, I'd like to graduate," I said, bristling at her tone. "And besides, I don't mind."

"Really?" she said dubiously.

"Really." I threw her a look. "Now I need to finish this paper—"

"So this is where the party is," John interrupted from the doorway. Sauntering in, he added, "What a ghastly room. I don't think I've ever been in it before."

"It was Marion's present room," Georgina said idly, rolling over on her side and propping her head on her hand. "Guess how thrilled she was to hand it over?"

"Oh, the horror," John gravely agreed. "Where *will* she keep the hostess gifts now?"

"The present room?" I asked, puzzled.

"Yes, our Marion is quite generous," John said as he settled into a chair by the fireplace. "She keeps a stack of presents on hand at all times."

"Well, I guess that's one way to get the jump on Christmas," I muttered, turning back to my computer.

They both burst into laughter.

"What?" I demanded.

"They're not for us, silly," Georgina said as soon as the giggles petered out.

"We get checks for Christmas," John explained. "Ten grand, just under the minimum that needs to be reported to the IRS."

"Wouldn't want them to come sniffing around, now would we, Johnny?" Georgina said, doing a dead-on impression of Marion.

"Those brutes, sullying my carpets? Never," John replied, matching her tone.

Watching them banter, it was hard to believe that John hadn't been here all along. I didn't understand why nobody had mentioned him. He was a conceited jerk, basically the male version of Georgina, but still—their comfortable familiarity gave me a pang. Maybe it would've been nice to have a sibling. At least then, I wouldn't be going through this alone.

"Ugh. She's making that face again," Georgina noted.

"She does that a lot?" John asked, squinting at me.

"Constantly."

"I'm right here, you know. I can hear you," I grumbled. I wanted to ask them to leave, but this was technically their house. They'd probably just ignore me anyway. Sighing, I shut my laptop and leaned back against the headboard. "What do you two want?"

"Testy, too," John said to his sister.

"You see what I have to deal with." Georgina sighed again.

I glared at her, but she pretended not to notice. Tossing a throw pillow to her brother, she said, "Lovely to have you back, Johnny. So what was it this time? Cheating? Stealing?"

He caught it with one hand and smiled. "Drinking."

"Really?" She frowned. "That shouldn't have been enough to get you kicked out. Especially not at St. Paul's."

John balanced the pillow on his palm and shrugged. "Not usually, but I accidentally mistook the headmaster's dog for a urinal. Right in front of him."

Georgina cracked up. I couldn't help but smile too, in spite of myself. John flashed us a genuine smile. For the first time since we'd met, he seemed like a real person.

Don't trust him, echoed Daniel's voice in my head. Annoyed, I pushed it away. Issuing a warning like that without explanation—who did Daniel think he was?

As if guessing my thoughts, John said slyly, "You missed some excitement today, Georgie. Alma caught Miss Janie here in the attic."

"No!" Georgina spun, regarding me with a mix of horror and awe. "Why?"

"You *know* why," I said, throwing her a glare. "I wanted to find out what was making the noises."

"What noises?" John asked, eyeing me with the same skepticism I'd gotten from everyone else.

"Weird noises," I said defensively. "Humming, footsteps, even screams sometimes—"

"Oh, that," he said dismissively.

"'Oh, that?'" I echoed. "Um, call me crazy, but that's not really normal."

Georgina had visibly relaxed, too. "He's right. It's just Alma."

"Alma?" I looked back and forth between them; they had to be putting me on. "What are you talking about?"

"She considers herself a bit of a witch," John said, as if it was the most natural thing in the world. Examining his fingernails, he continued, "Richard and Marion tolerate it because she's been with them for so long."

"It's so gross." Georgina wrinkled her nose. "Chicken bones and smoke and God knows what else."

"Now, now," John chided. "It's not nice to criticize other people's beliefs."

I opened my mouth to protest, then shut it again. Because what could I say? To suddenly bring up a bouncing pink ball seemed ridiculous—and maybe there was a plausible explanation for that, too. It could have been sitting in the shadows, stirred up by our footsteps. I flashed back on it bouncing toward us, as if it had been thrown . . . but was I completely sure that's what happened? I hadn't slept well in so long, I wasn't sure of anything anymore.

"I'll have Daddy Dearest tell her to cool it," Georgina said, suppressing a yawn. "If it's really bothering you."

"But seriously, it's no big deal," John chimed in. "Alma probably doesn't even realize you can hear it. Nicholas can sleep through anything, and there hasn't been anyone else in this wing of the house since—"

His mouth slammed shut, lips pressed together.

A look passed between him and Georgina, and the air was suddenly thick enough to cut with a knife.

Eliza, I thought. With a chill, I wondered which room had been hers. Surely not this one? Hopefully it had always been Marion's "present room."

"Well, that's a relief," I said awkwardly to break the silence. "I was starting to think I was losing my mind."

"Oh, you haven't been here nearly long enough yet," Georgina replied drolly.

"Takes at least six months for that," John agreed.

"Eight if you're lucky." Georgina got to her feet and stretched her arms above her head. "I'm famished."

As if on cue, the dinner bell rang. John bowed in my direction, extending an arm toward me. "M'lady, may I have the pleasure of escorting you to dinner?"

"You're both nuts," I said, rolling my eyes. But secretly, I experienced a small thrill. For the first time, it felt like maybe I could belong here.

BY NOW, I'D GROWN accustomed to the awful, stilted dinners at the Rochesters'. It seemed particularly bad tonight, however. Everyone's gaze remained fixed on their plates. As I sipped water, I wondered if they could all hear me swallowing.

"So, John," Richard Rochester said, making me jump. "You've been kicked out of another school."

John sat complacently, occupying the seat to Marion's right that until now had been vacant. "Six in three years," he said. "I'm kind of hoping that's some sort of record."

Richard set his wine glass down so hard it teetered. Marion's eyes narrowed at the drops of red wine that splashed out, sullying the pristine white tablecloth. "You think this is funny, young man?"

"A little, yeah," John said, but his voice wavered. Privately, I wondered why. Marion was the one who terrified me.

"Do you have any idea how much money I've lost? Tuition alone was more than forty grand," Richard growled. His low, measured voice made the words sound even more venomous. The chicken Kiev dried up in my mouth.

"It's just money," Georgina muttered weakly. Her face had gone pale, though.

"*Just* money?" Richard's face amped up another shade of red, matching his voice's rise in decibels. "Neither of you has a clue, do you? No idea what you cost me?"

After a weighted moment of silence, we all put our silverware down. I wondered if dropping to the floor and crawling out of the room was an option. I was glad that Nicholas ate in the kitchen, so he wasn't witnessing this.

"Riding lessons," Richard spat. "Fancy schools. A driver. God, what you waste on clothing alone—"

"Richard," Marion warned. "The staff."

"Screw the staff!" he slammed his palm down hard enough to make the tableware jump. The candles guttered, sending wispy black plumes toward the ceiling. "*None* of you understands the things I have to do to keep this family going. You think it's easy? Making all these decisions, knowing that if I screw up, it'll all just disappear?"

"We know how hard you work, dear," Marion soothed.

"Yeah, really hard. Great job." John said, so low I barely heard it.

Richard's eyes blazed. He slowly rose out of his seat, up to his full height. The vein in his temple throbbed alarmingly. "You," he said thickly. "All of you. You're nothing but vultures. You sicken me."

He stalked toward John, stopping behind his chair. I wasn't the only one holding my breath. Marion had gone rigid, although her gaze was still fixed on the plate in front of her. John didn't move, not even turning his head to look at his father. His shoulders had hunched protectively, as if braced for a blow. Time slowed to a crawl, marked off by the dolorous ticking of the grandfather clock in the corner. It suddenly chimed, each toll loud and resonant.

Without another word, Richard stalked from the room, leaving silence in his wake.

We all sat there, rooted in place. I felt shaky. *That* was an entirely different side of Richard, one I never could have imagined. And the way his family had reacted, as if preparing themselves for physical violence . . .

First Daniel, then Richard. Ever since John appeared.

"So I'm guessing the market crashed again," John said conversationally. "Did Dad lose another couple mill?"

"Shut up," Marion hissed, turning on him. "Why must you always make things worse for yourself?"

"Mother, you have to admit—"

"If you weren't my son, I'd throw you out myself," she said curtly.

John looked like he'd been slapped.

We all watched silently as Marion folded her napkin and set it to the side of her plate, then pushed back her chair.

"You should avoid your father until he's in a better frame of mind," Marion said without looking at us.

"Sobered up, you mean," John muttered, but she'd already left the room.

I stared at my plate, feeling sick to my stomach. I desperately wanted to retreat to the sanctuary of my room, but I'd rather not run into Marion or Richard on my way there. Pushing the mostly uneaten chicken breast around my plate, I decided to give the halls five minutes to clear.

"She's right, you shouldn't joke about it," Georgina snapped. "It's not funny."

"Just imagine if after all those years of hosting charity functions, Marion suddenly became a charity case," John said snidely. "It would almost be worth it."

"That's ridiculous," Georgina retorted, but there was a tremor in her voice. "Daddy would never let that happen."

"Sure he wouldn't. Hey, remember our ski house in Vail, and the Paris apartment? How long until he auctions off Napa, too?"

"Everyone has downsized," Georgina scoffed. "It's no big deal. We'll get it all back soon."

John laughed ruefully. "My dear sister, you're always such

an optimist where money is concerned. Anyway, thank God for Janie." He lifted his water glass in my direction. His hand shook slightly, making water bead along the sides. "Good to know that *something* keeps the old man in check."

If that was "in check," I'd hate to see Richard out of control, I thought. I'd come down to dinner with an arm linked through John's, feeling for the first time like maybe this family wasn't so bad. And now I realized they were so much worse than I'd ever imagined.

The fact that they'd been selling off houses was news to me, too, although they were still a long way from the financial troubles my family used to have.

Dad sat in front of a stack of bills, his hand hovering over the checkbook. A lot of them were bright red late notices.

Everything okay? I asked, grabbing orange juice from the fridge.

Fine, he said, but it wasn't very convincing. I knew business had been slow, half the time his helicopter sat idle on the landing pad.

I don't have to compete this weekend, I said, swishing the juice around my glass. *I mean, we could save the entry fee.*

Dad reached out for me. I went over, and he pulled me into a hug. *Don't worry, baby girl. We always find the money somewhere.*

"WHAT WERE YOUR PARENTS like?" Georgina suddenly asked.

"What?" I said, startled. It was as if she'd read my mind.

"Your parents," she said, with only a trace of her usual condescension. "What were they like?"

"Um, I don't know. Normal, I guess." My hands were clenched in my lap; I forced them to relax, wondering what she wanted to hear. Was she seeking reassurance that every family was like this behind closed doors?

"There's no such thing as normal," John mumbled.

The depth of emotion in his voice seemed utterly at odds with his persona. In fact, he sounded almost exactly like Nicholas, which gave me an odd twinge.

Georgina let out a short, brittle laugh. Stabbing a chunk of chicken viciously with her fork, she said, "Just wait until Thanksgiving. Richard's a ton of fun after a few whiskeys."

"Don't worry, though," John added. "He's careful not to leave any marks."

"Oh, he wouldn't hurt *her*." Georgina scowled down at her food as if it had offended her. "She's the golden goose, remember?"

John made a scoffing noise. "Thank God for that."

"What are you talking about?" I asked warily, looking back and forth between them.

"Nothing. Don't worry your pretty little head about it." John reached over and grabbed Marion's abandoned wine glass, draining it in one gulp. Then he got unsteadily to his feet, nearly knocking over his chair. "I'm out of here. If they ask, tell them I went to piss on a few more puppies."

Chapter VII

The light that long ago had struck me into syncope, recalled in this vision, seemed glidingly to mount the wall, and tremblingly to pause in the centre of the obscured ceiling.

The attic was blissfully quiet that night—so silent, in fact, that I figured either Georgina or John must have talked to Alma about curtailing her midnight rituals above my bed.

Which left me feeling foolish. Of course there had been a reasonable explanation. Just a month ago, I never would've believed there was a ghost tromping up and down an attic. It was the kind of ridiculous explanation a child Nicholas's age would come up with; and even when I was his age, I hadn't been that type of kid. As a four-year-old, I'd found the concept of the Tooth Fairy preposterous.

Yet I'd nearly convinced myself that my new house was haunted. Sure, I'd been through a lot: losing my parents, moving to a new city, changing schools. But that didn't totally excuse it.

Well, I was done with that nonsense now. And I felt more than a little embarrassed about getting Daniel involved.

I couldn't help but wonder if that was why he hadn't called last night. Had he written me off as a sad, crazy girl? Monday in school, I kept surreptitiously checking my phone for calls or texts.

But there was nothing. The total radio silence was starting to annoy me. If Daniel had decided that based on our little adventure he was done with me, the least he could do was let me know. Anything else was cowardly.

And what was up with him and John Rochester? Obviously they had some sort of history. I'd meant to ask this morning, but John hadn't been at breakfast. I sat with Richard and Georgina, dutifully devouring an omelet while we all avoided each other's eyes. It was as if John had never returned at all.

What a weird family, I thought again. And the fact that Daniel was ignoring me didn't say much for him, either.

Unfortunately, telling myself that didn't make it hurt any less.

SO WHEN I WALKED out of school with Helen and saw Daniel leaning against the hood of his car, I was conflicted. Part of me wanted to run over and throw myself in his arms; the other wanted to slap him. Of course, doing either in front of the entire Hamill carpool line would make me a topic of gossip for weeks. I slowly descended the stairs, trying to decide what to do.

"What's wrong?" Helen asked, taking in my expression. Following my gaze, she grabbed my elbow and said in a low voice, "Is that Daniel? Oh my God, you did *not* do him justice."

"Yeah, well. You should see how good he looks when he's running away from me," I muttered. But my traitorous heart had lurched into a skippy little dance in my chest. I slowed my pace even further, determined not to look like I was eager to see him.

Helen, on the other hand, practically set a land speed record crossing the street. "Hey, I'm Helen!" she chirped, jutting out her hand.

Daniel threw her a smile, identical to the one that had first gut-punched me. "Hi, Helen. Hasn't Janie told you how uncool it is to shake hands?"

"Oh, she has," Helen said serenely. "But my attempts to civilize her should kick in any day now."

Daniel burst into laughter and pumped Helen's hand with enthusiasm. "Nice, Helen. I like you already."

"You seem okay," Helen said, eyeing him skeptically. "But I'm reserving judgment for the moment."

"Really?" He cocked an eyebrow. "And why's that?"

"Because you're in the doghouse with Janie," Helen said matter-of-factly. "And honestly, you're too attractive to be one of the good guys."

Daniel's gaze shifted toward me. In a more serious tone, he said, "The doghouse, huh? That doesn't sound good."

I'd spent the entirety of their exchange praying that one of San Francisco's infamous earthquakes would strike, swallowing up me and, more importantly, Helen. My face burned with embarrassment. Throwing her a glare, I said, "Helen's exaggerating."

"No, I'm not," she retorted. "Better to get everything out in the open, isn't it? I think people should always be straight with each other. That way everyone knows where they stand."

"You know what, Helen? I totally agree." Daniel walked around his car and opened the passenger side door for me. "Want to go for a drive?"

"Sorry, I'm busy," Helen said blithely. "But I bet Janie would love to." She gave me a little push toward the car.

I bit my lip. The Town Car was in the shop, so I'd offered to walk home from school today. And it wasn't like I had anywhere else to be; Helen and I had knocked out most of our homework in the library during a free period.

Still, I threw her a final angry glare, muttering, "I'm seriously going to kill you for this."

"Please." Helen waved a hand disdainfully. "You're going to thank me. Text later, I'll be home." With a final wave, she trotted off.

Daniel was still holding the car door open. "Well?"

"Fine," I said, aggravated. "But I have to get home soon."

"Woof," he joked. I scowled through the windshield as he pulled away from the curb.

DANIEL DIDN'T BREAK THE silence until we were sitting on top of the dunes at Ocean Beach. "So . . . that was weird yesterday, huh?"

"Which part?" I asked, digging my toes into the sand. I'd taken off my loafers, and the sand was cold against my feet. "The ball in the attic, or when you basically ran out of my house?"

My house, I realized the second the words left my mouth. That was the first time I'd ever referred to it that way. It felt like a betrayal of the little cottage where I'd grown up. I stared out at the ocean.

In front of us, a perfect set was rolling in. The waves hurled themselves over at the last moment, exploding in a cascade of foam. My fingers itched for my surfboard. Wind whipped past us, tossing my hair. Shivering, I wrapped my school skirt tightly around my legs.

"Here," Daniel offered, taking off his coat.

"I'm fine," I replied curtly.

Daniel sighed. "I really am in the doghouse, huh?"

"I hate that term," I muttered.

"Well, whatever you want to call it, then." Crossing his arms around his legs, he stared past me, out to sea. "It just surprised me, seeing Rochester like that."

"You were in *his* house," I reminded him. "And, oh yeah, we've been friends for a month, and you never said anything about him." My voice caught a little on *friends*; I hoped he didn't notice.

Daniel's jaw twitched. "I didn't really want to get into it."

"Well, guess what? We're into it." Angrily, I plowed a furrow through the cold sand with my feet. "And it would've been nice if you'd given me a heads up. You two obviously have some sort of history."

After a beat, he said, "Yeah, we do. God, Janie, if you had any idea . . ."

"Any idea of what?" I pressed when he didn't continue.

"Just—the way I am now? I wasn't always this guy. I used to be . . . someone else."

"Someone more honest?" I said. His expression immediately made me wish I could take the words back.

His eyes clouded. "Less, actually. Sophomore year was kind of rough for me. I was hanging out a lot with John, and things got kind of out of control. Anyway, that's why I told you to stay away from him."

"Um, hello? Kind of hard to avoid someone who's living in the same house," I pointed out.

"I know. I guess what I mean is—" Daniel helplessly tossed up his hands. "I don't know. Try to keep your distance, as much as you can."

My eyes narrowed. "You're still being really vague."

"Yeah, well. This isn't stuff I'm proud of talking about. Especially not to you."

"Why not?" I asked.

"Because you're special," he blurted.

That hung in the air between us, heavy and charged. I said slowly, "So you don't want to be honest with me, because you're afraid I'll think less of you?"

"Exactly," he said.

"Okay, but when you ran away yesterday, and then ignored all my texts . . . that didn't exactly make me feel special."

I'd planned to say something much more casual and flippant. And I *really* hadn't intended to sound so wounded. I stared down at my legs as I tried to rub some warmth into them, avoiding his eyes.

"Janie," he said softly.

I couldn't face him, I just couldn't. I bit my lip and wished again for the ground to open up beneath us. A seagull flew overhead, screeching plaintively. I knew exactly how it felt. "I'm not special," I finally said. "Trust me. Maybe here I seem different, but back home I'm just like everyone else."

"I doubt it." Daniel gently cupped my chin, turning my face back toward him. And suddenly I didn't feel the cold, or the sand, or the mist peppering my cheeks. His hand was so warm and firm; it felt right. It rooted me to the spot and swept every other thought from my mind.

Daniel leaned closer, until his face hovered inches from mine. His thumb stroked my cheek, his eyelashes brushed my forehead. Then, finally, I felt the pressure of his lips against mine. They were soft, gentle. He tasted of mint gum and smelled like cinnamon. As he kissed me, I swear I stopped breathing; for the briefest of moments, all the grief and homesickness and loss were swept away. I felt a hundred pounds lighter, as if I'd awoken from a dream, and the world was recognizable again.

"I-I didn't think you liked me," I murmured as he pulled away.

His brown eyes softened. "Why not?"

I shrugged, not wanting to ruin the moment. Already, I could feel the weight descending again, bowing my shoulders. "I don't know."

"So you think I just happened to be at Ocean Beach that day?"

I frowned. "What are you talking about?"

He gave me a crooked smile. "I figured a girl from Hawaii would probably hit the waves the first chance she got. I didn't mean to crash into you, though. That almost blew the whole plan."

I struggled to process what he was saying. "You were hoping I'd be there? That seems a little . . ."

"Stalker-y? Yeah, that's why I didn't mention it earlier," he said ruefully. "But there wasn't going to be another mixer for months. And I really wanted to see you again."

My heart leapt. I'd waited so long for Daniel to say something like this, it was hard to believe it was finally happening. "So why didn't you just ask me out? We never really had any dates."

"Denny's doesn't count as a date?" he joked.

I shrugged, terrified that the moment was slipping away, desperate not to let it. "Those didn't feel like dates."

"You're right, they weren't." He gently scooped up some of my hair and slid his fingers down the length, making my breath catch again. "God, your hair is so soft. Ever since I first saw you, I've wanted to do that."

I shivered involuntarily. "So why didn't you?"

He didn't answer. Some sort of internal battle was playing out on his face. Finally, he said, "I'm in a program, and they have these rules. One of them is that you're not supposed to date for the first year."

"Oh," I said, suddenly understanding. "So is it AA, or—"

"Drugs," he said, cutting me off. "Pills, mostly."

"But, uh—you're okay now?" *Please be okay*, I thought desperately. Back on the island, I knew kids who smoked pot, but no one with a serious problem.

"Well, I'm a month short of a year, but, yeah. I think I'm good." His smile faded as he took in my expression. "Are you okay with this?"

Honestly, I didn't know what to say; I never would've guessed that he had a drug problem. It was an entire life experience that I couldn't really relate to. "I'm fine," I lied.

"That wasn't very convincing," he said. Picking up a stick, he drew a circle in the sand between our feet. "It's cool. I just figured I should explain, after what John said back at the house."

"Okay. Well, thanks for telling me." I remembered John's dig about calling the cops—had Daniel stolen things? Or worse?

But asking might just make him shut down even more. He'd already drawn away from me and was staring moodily out toward the water. If I couldn't find a way to be okay with this, we'd be over before we even got started. But was I ready to get involved with an addict? *What would Mom and Dad think?*

They'd admire him for getting into a program, I told myself firmly. They'd say he deserved a second chance. And he'd been clean for almost a year, so he'd definitely earned one.

I put a hand on his arm. "Look, I'm sorry. I just wasn't expecting this."

"It's cool, Janie. I get it." He shook his head. "Believe me, I didn't want to tell you, at least not like this."

"I'm glad you told me," I said, meaning it.

"Yeah?" He met my eyes again.

"Yeah." I cleared my throat and asked, "So, um . . . does this mean we can start dating in a few weeks?"

Daniel burst out laughing, tilting his head back toward the sky.

"It's not that funny," I said, miffed.

"It kind of is. I just like the way you said it." He grinned at me. "That's what makes you special, Janie. Around you, I feel like myself, but better—like the person I've been trying really hard to become. Does that make sense?"

"Yeah," I said, still fixating on the fact that he thought I was special. "But it doesn't really answer my question."

Without warning Daniel leaned in again, bringing his forehead to rest against mine. "I say we start now," he said in a low voice that sent shivers through me. "What do you think?"

"Sure—" I said weakly, but the word was cut off when he kissed me again.

I PRETTY MUCH FLOATED into the house after Daniel dropped me off. I could still feel the pressure of his lips, and the slight scratchiness of his cheek as it brushed against mine.

Best. Day. Ever. I told myself. *Well, at least since . . .*

But I didn't let myself go there. Nothing was allowed to ruin this mood.

Judging by the quiet, most of the Rochesters were out, so I

had the house largely to myself. Not that I planned on doing anything other than taking a nice, long bath, then calling Kaila and Helen. *The only thing better would be telling Mom,* I thought with a pang. I pictured her sitting on the living room couch with her legs tucked under her, sharing a bowl of popcorn while I gushed about a date.

She'd like Daniel. For once, thoughts of her didn't hurt. Instead of the void those memories usually elicited, I could almost sense her with me. Maybe the grief was finally transforming into something else.

Smiling, I pressed the button for the elevator, not trusting my wobbly legs to the stairs. The elevator descended slowly with the usual groans, like an old person getting out of bed. I'd grown acclimated to it by now, though. It was actually kind of awesome having an elevator in the house. Especially since the rest of the family never used it.

I stepped inside and pressed the button for the third floor, letting my backpack drop to the floor. I settled back against the rear handrail, watching the door slowly slide shut. The mirror above the panel reflected my face back at me, complete with goofy grin.

I thought of my parents again, the way my mom used to brush her palm across the small of my dad's back as she passed him in the kitchen. He'd reach back to return the gesture, and they'd share a private smile.

How they'd met was a long-running family joke. My father had made a game out of coming up with crazy stories, each more ridiculous than the last. I'd stopped expecting a real answer at an early age, and only kept asking because I loved how silly they were.

There I was, investigating a Mayan tomb, he'd say, pretending to peer through the gloom. *After dodging booby traps, I finally reached the treasure room, and your mother was sitting right there on a throne.*

Like in Indiana Jones? I'd asked, eyes wide.

Exactly like that, he'd said with a wink.

Another time, it was, *I was fishing . . .* He mimicked throwing a line into the water, then rocked wildly as he pretended to reel it in. *And your mother came up on the end, with seaweed tangled in her hair.*

So I was a mermaid? Mom asked, raising an eyebrow.

Yup. Which was a shame, because I'd been trying for tuna. He grinned as she rolled her eyes.

ONE THING WAS ALWAYS the same, though. As soon as he finished spinning the tale of whatever absurd circumstance had brought them together, my dad would get this look on his face. If my mother was in the room, he'd gaze at her, as if seeing her again for the first time. It was a look that used to make me jealous when I was younger, because on some deep level I understood that I wasn't a part of this story, not yet, anyway.

"Everything froze," he'd say. "Like when you're sitting at the top of a slide. It was quiet, and still, and as I stared at her a little voice in my head said, *This one. Only this one, for the rest of your life.*"

Usually at that point my mother would settle in his lap, and they'd kiss. I'd make the appropriate gagging sounds, secretly thrilled to witness something so mysterious.

"And then came you," he'd always say, smiling as he extended a hand to draw me into their circle. "And that's how I'll always know that little voice was right. Although sometimes, when she makes me clean the garage, I have my doubts."

My mom would bat him on the shoulder then, still smiling, and we'd all go about whatever we were doing.

The memory gouged me, but not too painfully. Because for the first time, I knew exactly what he meant. At the beach with Daniel, I'd heard that same voice. As soon as he kissed me, I realized this was it; he was my one. No matter what, we were meant to be together.

I sighed and let my fingers brush through my hair, lingering on a few strands the way his hands had earlier. Daniel thought I was special. Remembering the words, and the way he'd said them, made everything inside me trill.

The elevator moaned and jolted to a stop.

I frowned. "What—"

The lights went out.

"Hey!" I yelped, the good feelings chased away by panic. A moment passed, then another. Nothing happened. I took a step forward, and the elevator shifted, swinging on the cables. I froze, then moved more carefully toward the door. The lit panel that indicated the floors had gone dark, too. I fumbled for it with my hand, pressing buttons. Was there one for emergencies? I couldn't remember.

Light. I needed light. I dropped into a crouch and groped for my backpack. Digging my cell phone out, I turned on the screen. It flared brightly, and I heaved a sigh of relief. I tilted the phone toward the panel: no red one for emergencies, just the buttons for each floor.

And no phone.

That's okay, I thought. *I've got a phone right here.* Trying to still my shaking hands, I opened the phone app. Then I bit my lip, wondering whom to call. *911? Did they rescue people from elevators?* I pictured Marion's reaction to a battalion of firefighters storming through her house; surviving this would be pointless if she killed me afterward. I realized that I didn't have mobile numbers for her or Richard, though. Georgina, then? Or John?

I don't have their numbers, either, I realized with dismay. It was pretty messed up that I had no way of contacting the people I lived with. So instead I drew in a deep breath and hit the button to call Daniel.

The phone didn't ring. I frowned, examining it: no bars.

"Great," I muttered. I'd never had issues with cell reception in the house before; it figured that the signal would drop when I really needed it. A text would still send, though, right?

I typed, hey Daniel crazy story, I'm stuck

The screen went dead, hurling me back into darkness. I gasped, then frantically tried to turn the phone back on. It didn't respond. I realized with mounting panic that all of my obsessive checking for messages had drained the battery.

I closed my eyes, trying to calm down. *It's no big deal,* I told myself. *Someone will be home soon.*

But when? the small voice in my head countered. *Minutes? Hours?*

"Just relax," I said out loud. My voice echoed eerily, bouncing off the walls. The darkness felt oppressive and strangling. I drew a deep breath and held it for a count of three. *You've got a water bottle in your bag,* I reminded myself. I hadn't eaten much today, since I'd felt sick to my stomach ever since dinner last night. But it wasn't like I was going to starve to death.

Although of course as soon as I thought about the water, I realized that I had to pee. Desperately. And I wasn't about to do that in the elevator.

Getting up, I felt my way back to the door and pounded on it, yelling, "Hey! Is anyone home? I'm stuck!"

I could've sworn I heard footsteps. I pressed my ear against the door; it was cold enough to make me wince. I shouted again, "Is anyone out there?"

A long beat, then a tremulous voice said, "Janie?"

"Nicholas." I almost collapsed with relief. "Hey, listen. The elevator stopped working, and I'm trapped. Can you please go get Alma?"

Nicholas called back uncertainly, "Um, I'm not sure where she is."

I squeezed my eyes shut again, forcing myself to be patient; he was just a kid. "Could you go find her? This is really important, Nicholas."

It was silent for so long, I assumed he'd gone for help. But then he spoke again, sounding much closer; I was trapped between the second and third floors, so he must have come up a level. His voice shook slightly as he said, "She doesn't want me to."

"Who doesn't, Nicholas?" I demanded, rapidly running out of patience. "Did you find Alma?"

"No, it's Eliza."

Gritting my teeth, I said, "Nicholas, honey, you need to listen to *me* this time, not Eliza. Go get Alma. Now."

His feet slowly shuffled away. I collapsed against the door, pressing my cheek to it. Good. Someone would come soon. I kept my eyes closed; for some reason it made the situation less frightening.

At least, until I sensed a flicker that was bright enough to penetrate my closed eyelids. It was accompanied by a sudden chill that spiked goose bumps across my bare arms and legs. Slowly I opened my eyes.

There was a tiny light bobbing in the air. As I stared at it, transfixed, it darted up toward the ceiling, then lazily turned in a slow circle, tracing the perimeter of elevator. I shrank back as it came closer, weaving like a firefly. It stopped inches from my nose.

I had stopped breathing. My heart was pounding so hard it felt like it might burst free of my rib cage, and a roar filled my ears. The light hovered, quivering slightly, as if wafting on a breeze. Then it started to grow, increasing incrementally until it was as large as a tennis ball.

I reeled away from it and started pounding on the elevator door with both hands.

"Help! Someone, please!"

Without warning the lights snapped on, striking me blind. I fell back, reflexively raising my arm to shield my eyes. The ground beneath my feet quaked and shifted. Then, with a shudder, the elevator started moving upward.

Almost too frightened to look, I lowered my arm and turned around. The light was gone.

When the elevator doors slid open, I stumbled out, leaving my backpack behind. My whole body trembled, and I felt nauseous. Nicholas was standing there wide-eyed, gripping his bunny Bertha in a chokehold.

"Janie? Are you okay?" he asked uncertainly.

I dashed past him and raced down the hallway, barely making it into my bathroom in time. I bent over the toilet, heaving. Sweat beaded across my forehead and ran into my eyes, mingling with my tears.

"Janie?"

I swiped a hand across my mouth, my gut still churning. Nicholas stood in the doorway, regarding me somberly. "It's okay, Nicholas," I gasped. "I'm fine."

He glanced back over his shoulder as if checking for someone, then leaned toward me and whispered, "Don't take the elevator. Ever!"

Without waiting for a reply, he scurried away.

Chapter VIII

Reader, do you know, as I do, what terror those cold people can put into the ice of their questions? How much of the fall of the avalanche is in their anger? Of the breaking up of the frozen sea in their displeasure?

"That's terrible, Janie. We'll have a repairman check it as soon as possible."

Mr. Rochester shoveled another bite of lamb in his mouth, gazing at me with what appeared to be genuine sympathy. It was hard to reconcile this version of him with the monster that had terrorized us last night.

I pushed food around my plate, still too queasy to eat. Without much enthusiasm, I muttered, "Great, thanks," while thinking, *I'll never set foot in that deathtrap again.*

"It's never been an issue before," Marion said crisply.

"How would you know?" John demanded. "I've never seen you take the elevator."

Marion's spine stiffened, adding a half-inch to her already perfect posture. "Of course I take it," she said.

"I hate that thing," Georgina declared as she buttered a roll. "It's like a coffin."

My throat seized; that's exactly what it had felt like, a coffin. I saw the strange hovering light again. It was probably just my overactive imagination, but it had seemed to radiate malevolence.

Stop, Janie, I berated myself. *Just stop. You imagined the whole thing.*

John leaned in and said, "Hey, remember that time Nicholas got stuck—"

"Elbows off the table!" Marion snapped.

He glared at her. At the head of the table, Richard's eyes narrowed. Slowly, John drew back in his seat. "Sorry, *Mother.*" Coming out of his mouth, it sounded like a dirty word.

Marion's features were still taut. "Georgina, don't forget your appointment tomorrow for the fitting. I'm afraid you'll have to miss your riding lesson."

Georgina brightened. "Like I'd forget that."

"I really wish the two of you would speak properly," Marion scolded, but the corners of her mouth relaxed.

"You're taking Janie, too, right?" Richard asked. His tone was casual, but there were steel rods underpinning the words.

Marion jerked her head toward him. "Janie? Why?"

"Because she's a member of this family," Richard said slowly, glowering at her. Now that I knew what to watch for, I could see the storm clouds brewing. His cocktail had been refreshed twice already, and there were two high, bright dots of color in his cheeks. The rest of the family regarded him warily, like one would a dangerous dog.

"I'm sorry," I said hesitantly. "What are we talking about?"

Marion flashed me a look of contempt, and Georgina said with exasperation, "The cotillion next month. My dress just came in from London, and it's being altered."

"Oh." *Follow-up question,* I added silently. *What the hell is a cotillion?*

"It's a debutante ball," John explained, as if guessing my thoughts. "*The* social event of the season. And Georgina is being brought out this year. In white, ironically enough."

His sister scowled at him. "I wonder if they'll even let you in. Aren't you banned or something?"

"Like they'd dare keep a Rochester out," he scoffed.

"Enough." Richard's voice maintained the same low timbre, but the threat was clear. He shifted to look at Marion, who shrank from his gaze. "You'll make sure Janie is dressed appropriately for the occasion."

Marion opened her mouth as if to protest, then pressed her lips back into a thin line and nodded curtly. After folding her napkin, she started to rise from her chair.

"I didn't say you could leave," Richard growled.

Marion slowly sank back down.

Georgina and John stared at their plates. I was reminded of the way geckos freeze when you come upon them unexpectedly, attempting to hide in plain sight.

As much as I loathed Marion, I felt a flare of anger. Richard Rochester had no right to use me as an excuse to intimidate his family. My mom always said that bullies only have the power you give them. And I refused to be pushed around. After all, what was he going to do? Hit me? If that happened, I'd be on the phone to the cops and Mr. Briggs and whoever else would listen before he could lower his hand. "I really don't have to—"

"You're going," Mr. Rochester mumbled, moodily sloshing the nearly melted ice cubes in his tumbler.

I wanted to press the issue, but John caught my eye and subtly shook his head.

Fine, I thought. I was too tired and woozy for a fight, anyway. Probably better to discuss it another time anyway, preferably when he was sober.

We sat there as the clock tortuously ticked off the minutes. Richard Rochester polished off his dinner, ignoring the fact that the rest of us had stopped eating. When his plate was clean, he swiped a cloth napkin across his mouth, gulped down half of the fresh drink that had been set in front of him, and then abruptly got to his feet, saying, "I have work."

We all listened as he made his way toward the den. I caught

a few muffled curses, followed by the sound of heavy objects being jostled. Finally, the door slammed behind him. Everyone at the table sagged—myself, included—as if the strings holding us upright had been snipped.

Marion left next.

I rose to follow her.

"He'll make you go to the cotillion whether you want to or not," Georgina said without looking at me.

I turned. She was still pushing food around her plate. Now I understood how she managed to stay so skinny. "I don't get why he cares," I grumbled.

John snorted. "Are you kidding? You make the rest of their charity work look like nothing."

At that, something inside me snapped. "You know what?" I snarled. "You're all just . . . just . . . awful, miserable people. You think any of this matters? The parties? The special schools? It's all bullshit. The rest of the world could give a crap. The truth is, I feel sorry for you. Because at the end of the day, your lives suck. And being able to buy whatever you want doesn't change that."

Georgina gaped at me.

John, on the other hand, looked bemused. "You're right," he said. "We *are* all miserable. And you're one of us now."

"I'll *never* be one of you." I whipped around and practically ran from the room. Behind me, I could hear John laughing hollowly.

I tore up the stairs, my exhaustion forgotten, then pounded down the hall toward my room.

I stopped on the threshold.

Nicholas was sitting on my bed, clutching something in both hands. He raised a tear-streaked face to me.

I was about to yell at him to stay out of my room, but when I saw his expression the words died on my tongue. He looked like someone had just killed his best friend.

Stepping closer, I realized that wasn't too far off the mark. He clutched what remained of Bertha. The bunny had been shredded, every limb torn off. Stuffing spilled from dozens of rips. He was trying to clasp the pieces together, as if he could make her whole again by simply wishing it so.

"Eliza hurt Bertha," he wailed. "She's *so* angry at me for helping you."

I bit my tongue to keep from pointing out that he hadn't helped, not really. Instead, I settled on the bed beside him and gently took the mangled rabbit. The damage wasn't irreparable. "Nicholas, can you find me a needle and some thread?"

He nodded, still sniffling.

"Great. I'll sew her up."

"Good as new?" he asked, a thin sliver of hope in his voice.

"I'll do my best." Sewing wasn't one of my strong suits, but my mom had been amazing at it, and she'd taught me a few tricks.

"Right away?" he asked, eyeing the bunny doubtfully. "Because I need Bertha tonight. She watches over me while I sleep."

Crap. Now that my rage had dissipated, I barely had the strength to change into pajamas and brush my teeth. All I wanted was to bury myself in the covers; but Nicholas's big blue eyes shone bright with tears. And the look he was giving me, like I was a cross between a saint and a superhero . . . I sighed. "Yes, tonight. Now go get me that sewing kit."

"Okay, Janie!" He scurried from the room.

I fell back against the pillows and closed my eyes. Richard Rochester was a drunk. Marion was a shrew. Georgina was a narcissist. John was a creep. And Nicholas was so messed up that he destroyed his favorite toy, then convinced himself that his dead twin was responsible. "My new family," I said aloud. It suddenly struck me as funny.

Nicholas returned to discover me rolling around on the bed, consumed with hysterical laughter.

"THE COTILLION ISN'T SO bad," Daniel said, popping a fry in his mouth.

"You're kidding, right?" I said, cocking an eyebrow at him. "Because it sounds horrible."

We were sitting in a leather booth at Barney's, a burger place near school. I inhaled more of my coffee, still wiped out. Last night, it had taken nearly an hour to coax Bertha back into something that remotely resembled a rabbit. I'd fallen asleep fully clothed on top of my blankets, with Nicholas tucked against my shoulder like a sad puppy.

I'd forgotten to set the alarm, slept through breakfast, and barely made it to school on time. So I'd had to wait until my first free period to dig up information on the cotillion. What I'd discovered was pretty awful, at least as far as I was concerned. John hadn't been kidding; this was the ball to end all balls. Based on the photos (most of which came from a snooty local society paper, *The Nob Hill Gazette*), Cinderella would've been considered underdressed.

There were ranks of boys and men, their tuxedos stiff as straitjackets. They seemed to serve solely as a backdrop, like potted palms strategically placed to compliment the real finery.

The girls mainly wore white, although the variety was impressive considering the monochromatic palette. Ten-foot-long trains. Hairstyles that must've required a small army to assemble. Rigid smiles and coquettish head tilts and perfectly applied makeup. Despite their blatant attempts to outshine each other, I got the sense that layering the photos would form a single, perfectly bland girl.

As if to compensate for what I'd already decided to call "The Virgin Army," the older women wore startling shades of plumage. Their smiles were as fixed as their Botoxed foreheads, and their jewelry was insane. Necklaces with gemstones the size of babies' fists. Earrings so layered with diamonds, it was hard to believe their earlobes could handle the weight.

Bracelets and tiaras and, in one case, what appeared to be an actual crown.

Beneath the images were captions like, "Mrs. Sophia de Laurentis in vintage Versace" and "Miss Bitty Caldwell in a stunning sheath from Armani, accompanied by Sir Edward Brooks III."

And that was just the *people.* There were also gushing descriptions of the food and decor. One year, the event planner had set up a, "lush fairytale wonderland," complete with "vines spiraling down from the ceiling," and "more than 500,000 hydrangeas perfuming the air."

I'd pored through cotillion photos for the entire free period. When I finally closed my laptop, I'd felt the onset of a panic attack. Compared to this, the Country Day mixer was practically a barn dance. That was the minors; this was clearly the big leagues.

"You okay?" Daniel asked after a moment.

"Fine." I managed to smile at him. The one bright spot in my day had been a text he'd sent around lunchtime: thinking of u.

Every chance I'd gotten I'd looked at it, tracing my fingers over the words.

Daniel had been waiting for me again after school; I practically skipped to his car, my whole body singing. I wasn't hungry, but when he'd suggested grabbing a burger, I'd agreed. Anything to be sitting across from him, to feel his knees brush mine under the table, to see the studious concentration he devoted to every bite.

All the weirdness at the Rochesters' faded into the background. This was what mattered.

Daniel wiped the corner of his mouth with his napkin. For a boy, he was a very tidy eater; clearly he'd been raised with strict table manners, which made me a little self-conscious about my own chewing. "We can go together," he offered.

"Really?" The thought hadn't even occurred to me, but of course this was the type of event where you brought a date. I'd planned to beg off, telling the Rochesters that I'd come down with an unfortunate case of the plague or something. But the thought of walking in with Daniel changed everything. He'd look amazing in a tux, and I could find a more elaborate version of the dress from Saks. I could practically see the caption: "Miss Janie Mason in Vera Wang, accompanied by Mr. Daniel Fairfax." Like we were actually together. Like we belonged.

But then, Daniel *did* belong in this world.

A thought struck me. "So you've been before?"

"Oh, yeah." He laughed shortly. "It's pretty much a requirement once you hit fifteen. My sister came out that year."

In this world, coming out has a totally different meaning, I realized, amused. I teased, "Have you ever brought a date before?"

The minute the words left my mouth, I knew they were a mistake. I didn't want to know about his former girlfriends. Selfishly, I preferred to imagine that he'd entered my life fresh, his heart whole and undamaged, his lips pure.

But of course that was ridiculous; I already knew about his addiction problems. And someone as attractive as Daniel probably had a slew of exes.

Besides, I'd dated other boys; nothing serious, but I'd certainly been kissed. Yet I couldn't bear the thought that he'd ever looked at someone else the way he looked at me.

Daniel carefully set the burger back on his plate and cleared his throat. He looked nervous, and guilty; that sent a flicker of fear through me.

I said, "You don't have to—"

"It was Georgina," he said, cutting me off. "She was my date last year."

You know that saying, about all the air getting sucked from the room? I'd always thought it was an overwrought metaphor, an exaggeration. But I was suddenly gasping and gulping for air. Spots danced before my eyes—I was going to get sick again. I bolted for the bathroom.

Kneeling before the toilet, I tried not to think about what had made the floor so sticky. My breath shuddered as I fought back bile. I'd barely eaten all day, thankfully, so my stomach was empty. Closing my eyes, I forced myself to relax. My heartbeat pulsed in my throat, a constant cadence of *Georgina . . . Georgina . . .*

A knock at the door, followed by Daniel's voice. "Hey, Janie? You okay?" He sounded worried.

The picture in my mind shifted: instead of us, it was the two of them together. Georgina: gorgeous in a low-cut white dress, gripping Daniel's arm possessively. Her smile was even toothier than normal—the leer of a shark. Hot tears lurked behind my eyes, anxious to slip out . . .

"Janie?" Daniel called more urgently.

I tried to get a grip on my hurt and rage. *Daniel didn't do anything wrong,* I reminded myself. He hadn't even known me back then. I'd been thousands of miles away.

But he should've told me, I amended. First I find out he had some sort of secret past with John, and now Georgina? He knew that I lived with them; he should've said something right away. Another flash, of them dancing. Georgina smiling up at him, his hand encircling her waist. My stomach executed another sharp flip.

Seriously, of all the people he could have dated . . . Georgina?

And why hadn't *she* said anything?

I suddenly realized that she might not know we were dating; I certainly hadn't told her. It wasn't like we stayed up late gossiping and braiding each other's hair.

"I'm fine," I croaked. "Be right out."

I splashed water on my face and patted it dry, which only served to highlight the blotchiness. Regarding myself in the mirror, I ran wet fingers through my hair to tame the flyaway ends, overly aware of the fact that the image staring back at me didn't hold a candle to Georgina. I was okay-looking—some might even say pretty. But she was exquisite. Stand us side by side, and there was no comparison. I suddenly felt ridiculous for obsessing over the text Daniel had sent earlier. God only knew what he'd written to her when they were dating.

I drew in a deep breath and gave myself a nod, confirming that I was at least moderately in control. Then I went back outside.

Daniel was leaning against the wall in the narrow corridor, his features creased with worry. "Jeez, Janie, I'm so—"

"I'm fine," I repeated, cutting him off. The words came out sharper than I'd intended. "I just haven't felt very good all day."

"So that wasn't . . . I mean . . ." He ducked his head. "Sorry. I was going to tell you about Georgina sooner, but I was still sticking to the one-year thing, you know? And I figured, as long as we were still just friends . . ."

I stood against the opposite wall, unwilling to let him off the hook so easily. I remembered him dropping me off at the house that first day, the overly casual way in which he'd said, "Georgina lives here, right? Oh, yeah, everyone knows Georgie."

That should have tipped me off. Only her family called her Georgie. And, apparently, her boyfriends.

"So was it serious?" I asked.

He shuffled his feet. "Not really. I mean, we weren't, like, official or anything."

That sounded like the kind of thing Tommy Oliver would say, which didn't bode well. I scowled at him. "So what were you, exactly?"

"I don't know." Daniel looked up at me. "I didn't think of her as my girlfriend, if that's what you're asking."

I couldn't decide if that made it better or worse. Questions tumbled through my head, each worse than the last. *Had they kissed? Had they done more than just kiss? Who had broken it off? Did he still like her?*

Now I felt like an idiot; after a couple of kisses and a single text, I'd imagined us riding off into the sunset together. For all I knew, that's exactly what Georgina had thought a year ago.

"Listen, Janie," he said, stepping forward and reaching toward me.

I shrugged off his arm. "I should get home."

A mother escorting a small girl approached. "Are you two waiting for the bathroom?"

We both muttered no. She gave me a sympathetic smile as they eased past, shutting the door behind them. A wave of bleach from the bathroom mingled with the aroma of sizzling meat and fries. My stomach lurched again. "I really don't feel so good."

"Okay," Daniel said quietly. "Let's go."

In silence, we paid the bill, leaving our uneaten food behind. I walked to the car, holding my anorak closed against the chill. When he'd picked me up at school, Daniel had opened the door for me; this time, he continued on to the driver's side. I opened the door myself and climbed in.

I stared at my hands, waiting for him to start the car. Picturing the rest of my day only made it worse. The tense drive home. Being dumped on the Rochesters' doorstep. Dragging my backpack upstairs, trying to focus on homework. Another painful dinner with the Rochesters. That last thought nearly broke me; the tears clambered over each other in their eagerness to spill out.

But I wouldn't let them. I dug my nails into my palms and gritted my teeth, holding them at bay.

Daniel still hadn't started the car. I surreptitiously glanced over at him from beneath dropped eyelashes. He was staring pensively out the windshield.

"Our first fight," he said. "And we've only been dating for a day."

A laugh escaped me. He was right. "World's shortest relationship, huh?" I said ruefully.

"You're dumping me?" He sounded wounded.

"I don't know. I mean . . . I don't know what to do," I concluded helplessly. And I didn't. I'd had very little experience with dating before; most of my "boyfriends" had been friends who became something more for a while, then regressed to something less. Looking back, it was hard to pinpoint an actual breakup; it was more like both of us lost interest and drifted on to someone else. But I'd never felt like this about any of them. And that terrified me.

"Janie," Daniel said, twisting to face me. "It's like I said. Back then, I was a different person. I was high most of the time, I didn't care about anything but partying."

"So you didn't care about Georgina?" I asked in a small voice.

Emotions flitted across his face, too fast for me to read. But he said, "No. Not really. I mean, Georgie was cool, and fun. And we were hanging out a lot, so it just kind of happened."

"Oh." Should I believe him? I wanted to. It was hard to accept that he'd only dated Georgina because she was convenient. Most guys would probably sacrifice an arm to take her out for coffee.

"It wasn't like this," Daniel said more softly, reaching out to take my hand.

"Like what?" I asked, letting him. His fingers ensnared mine, warm and strong.

"When I'm with you, I feel like myself." He sounded embarrassed. I waited for him to continue, holding my breath. "Sometimes being a better person is just so much work. It's exhausting, like acting a part in a play. But I do it, because I know I have to."

"I'm sorry," I said. "That sounds awful."

"Yeah." Daniel laughed weakly. "Pretty awful. But with you . . ." his grip tightened on my hand, and he leaned in. "With you I'm just automatically that guy. I don't even have to try."

The look of raw need in his eyes was almost scary.

"Daniel," I finally said, "You can't lie to me again. Ever."

"I won't," he protested. "I didn't."

"Not telling me something is basically the same as lying," I pointed out. "I really need to be able to trust you."

He reached up and trailed the back of his hand down my cheek, sending a shudder through me. "Okay," he said. "I promise."

And then he kissed me. It was different from yesterday, deeper and more intense. I lost time in that kiss; I lost a small piece of myself. I felt it pass from me to him and realized that chances were, I'd never get it back.

And I didn't care. I claimed a similar piece of him and tucked it away, deep down inside me, somewhere dark and safe where no one would ever find it. *This is what love is,* I realized. Forsaking bits of yourself to the care of another person.

When he pulled away, it felt like I was being riven in two. I wanted to spend the rest of my life locked together like that. I wanted more. Suddenly, the fight seemed silly. This was Daniel. Even if he didn't know himself yet, I knew him. "So you'll be my date for the cotillion?"

He laughed and brushed a stray hair away from my eyes. "Of course."

"Good." I sighed and settled back against the car seat.

"Just wait until you see me in a tux," he said in a lighter tone. "Women have been known to faint."

"I'll try to prepare myself," I said wryly.

"Oh, there's no preparing yourself." He threw me a wink, suddenly back to normal. "But don't worry. I'll catch you."

It wasn't until after he dropped me off that I realized I'd forgotten to tell him about the elevator.

"THAT SOUNDS GREAT," KAILA said.

"I know, right?" I flopped over on my bed and stared up at the ceiling. "I'm thinking I might repaint my room orange. Do you think that would be too much?"

"Mmmm," she said.

"Or maybe neon green," I said with a frown. "Wouldn't that be awesome?"

"Totally awesome," Kaila said mechanically.

"Um, Earth to Kaila?"

"What?" she asked, in the same weary tone.

"What's up with you? We haven't talked in days! I finally have news, and it feels like you're barely paying attention." I kicked up to sitting and crossed my legs.

"Tommy dumped me," she said curtly.

"Oh. God, Kaila, I'm sorry."

"It's fine," she said, but it sounded hollow, like she was speaking down a long tube. "I'm fine."

"Well, you don't sound fine."

No wonder she hadn't shared my elation about Daniel, I realized, feeling guilty.

"I'm bummed, yeah," she acknowledged. "I mean, you know how long I've liked him."

"Years," I commiserated.

"Right. I'm an idiot." Her voice dropped another notch as she continued, "I still can't believe he asked me out in the first place."

"Hey," I said firmly. "Tommy Oliver is the idiot. You know that, right?"

She made an indeterminate noise.

"I'm serious, Kaila." I squeezed my eyes shut, debating how to frame this. In our old school, Tommy Oliver had always been unofficially ranked as the hottest guy, with his sun-bleached hair, ice-blue eyes, dark tan, and insane body. And he was a damn good surfer; even I had to admit that.

The biggest problem was that he knew it, too.

Tommy was notorious for keeping surfboards around longer than girlfriends, and he generally went through one of those a month. I'd always found him kind of gross. When he'd asked me out last year, I'd basically laughed in his face. I'd also made sure that Kaila never found out about it.

The fact that she'd just become his latest casualty was hardly a surprise, at least not to me.

"He said he really liked me." Kaila's voice cracked as she continued, "That it was different with us. That I was special."

I swallowed, hearing Daniel's exact words parroted back to me. *Daniel's not like that, though,* I reassured myself. "This totally sucks. I feel awful that I'm not there for the ritual."

"Me, too," Kaila agreed.

When a relationship went south, we always did the same thing: matching pints of ice cream consumed in front of *The Princess Bride.* It was a foolproof recipe my mom had recommended that never failed us.

"Tell you what," I said, suddenly inspired. "I'll go grab a pint and cue up PB on my computer. We can Skype while we're watching it."

"Yeah?" Kaila said, sniffling.

"Absolutely," I said firmly, even though a glance at my laptop confirmed that it was nearly 11 P.M., and I had school the next day. *What the hell,* I thought. I'd pretty much adapted to five hours of sleep a night anyway. With any luck the attic would remain quiet, and I wouldn't be awakened at 3 A.M.

"Thanks, Janie," Kaila said, sounding relieved.

"Are you kidding? Any excuse to spend a few hours with Westley," I said cavalierly. "Just let me go grab the ice cream. Back in five."

I padded downstairs as quietly as possible. The rest of the house was dark and still, reminding me of my first night here. I repressed a shiver and hurried down the servant's staircase that led to the kitchen. The light on the exhaust fan barely illuminated the room; the tile was cold against my bare feet. I dug a pint out of the freezer compartment without even checking to see what it was, grabbed a spoon and napkin, and practically ran back upstairs.

As I turned down the hall that led to my room, I stopped dead.

A light bobbed at waist level ten feet away. I squeezed my eyes shut, thinking, *it's all in your head.* My eyes were still adjusting to the darkness, that's all it was.

When I opened my eyes again, it was gone.

My shoulders relaxed. The ice cream container sweated against my palm, the contents softening.

Kaila's waiting, I reminded myself.

I kept to the sides of the hall, skirting the spot where I'd seen the floating light even though I knew that was silly. I practically ran the final twenty feet, hurling myself into the room. I was gasping for breath, as if I'd run a far greater distance. It took a second to process what I was seeing.

In my brief absence, the room had been tampered with. The chairs that had been huddled by the fireplace were now on either side of my bed, facing it as if invisible guests were keeping watch. My bedside tables sat in the space the chairs had just occupied. The pile of stuff that was usually shoved in a corner had been neatly tiered in the center of room.

And Bessie, the mutilated doll that had been buried at the bottom of a box, sat on top of the pyramid. She stared at me with those gaping, bleeding eye sockets.

I was too startled to scream. I stared at the rearrangement, trying to make sense of it.

When a voice behind me said, "Good. I was hoping you'd still be up," I nearly jumped out of my skin.

Whipping around, I discovered John standing in my doorway. He was wearing dark jeans, a button-down shirt, and a cocky grin. "Did you do this?" I demanded.

"Do what?" he asked. "Oh, you redecorated. Kind of creepy, but I like it."

I glared at him, trying to determine if he was messing with me. Showing up like this was too much of a coincidence. Aside from the day he'd arrived, I hadn't even seen him in this wing of the house. But why would he mess with my furniture? Why would anyone?

"Ice cream, huh?" John said brightly. "Can I have some?"

He exuded wide-eyed innocence; again, I was struck by how much he resembled Nicholas. I made an exasperated noise and asked, "What do you want?"

"Nothing," he said, holding up both hands. "Just coming to hang out."

"Well, I'm busy." Kaila had to be wondering what was taking so long. A dollop of ice cream escaped the top of the container and slid over my hand. I switched hands and licked it off, then caught John staring at me. I grimaced at him.

"Seriously, I've got to call my friend back."

"Suit yourself," John said, tucking his hands back in his pockets. "Later."

After he was gone, I stared at the door for a few beats. Then I shut it and turned the bolt. Cutting a wide swath around the stacked boxes, I made my way to the bed and woke up my laptop. There were five missed Skype calls. I sighed and hit the button to call her back.

"Well, that took forever," Kaila grumbled.

"Long story," I said, debating how much to tell her. Her face looked red, her eyes raw. I sighed and said, "One sec."

Ignoring the string of complaints issuing through the speakers, I pushed back off the bed and walked to the pile. I carefully reached for Bessie, then held the doll like it was contaminated. Opening the bottom drawer of my bureau, I dropped her inside, then slammed it shut with my foot.

"All right," I said, feeling moderately better as I settled back down. Raising a dripping spoonful of ice cream toward the camera, I said, "Cheers."

Chapter IX

"I wonder with what feelings you came to me tonight," she said, when she had examined me a while. "I wonder what thoughts are busy in your heart during all the hours you sit in yonder room with the fine people flitting before you like shapes in a magic lantern."

"Ugh," Georgina said, putting a hand on her stomach. "I'm getting so disgustingly fat."

I didn't bother acknowledging the comment; Georgina calling herself "fat" was like a butterfly describing itself as hideous. We were lounging in the fitting room of an upscale boutique. It was nearly the size of my new bedroom, and almost as elaborately furnished. A family of five could live relatively comfortably in the space between the mirrors and the chaise.

"No more carbs," she said decisively.

"Does that include booze?" I asked, raising an eyebrow.

"Don't be ridiculous." Georgina cast a sideways glance at me. "Champagne hardly has any, anyway."

"Right," I agreed, lounging back on the chaise. In a weird way, Georgina was growing on me. At least with her, you knew what you were getting: namely, lots of navel-gazing. As long as you were willing to serve as an appreciative audience, she was delighted to be your friend. She still avoided me at school, but I was fine with that, too. I had no interest in joining the posse of mean girls who stalked the halls with her.

"So did you find anything?" she asked, with at best mild interest.

"I haven't really looked." A glance at the price tags had nearly made my heart stop. Even though Richard was paying, it just seemed wrong to waste that much money on a few lengths of taffeta and silk.

Besides, I'm busy, I thought with a smile, sending another text to Daniel.

They actually offered us champagne.

So u r drunk?

Please

I wrote, sipping more water from my crystal flute.

I think the water is actually baby tears, though.

Ha! How about Georgina?

On her third glass.

Awesome. Can I come by l8r?

I paused. As far as I knew I was allowed to invite friends over, but it felt like a really bad idea. Plus, even though we were able to joke about Georgina now, the thought of them under the same roof still made me twitchy. Not that I wanted to admit that to Daniel, at least not outright. So I typed,

Not too scared of bouncing rubber balls?

Terrified. But I want 2 c the freaky doll.

He attached a photo of Chucky from the horror movies. In spite of myself, I smiled.

"Who are you texting?"

I looked up guiltily. This was the longest I'd seen Georgina go without a phone in her hand; as soon as they started surgically implanting them, she'd be first in line. "No one."

"You don't look like you're texting no one," she observed archly. Breaking into a wicked smile, she asked, "All right, what's his name?"

My stomach clenched. All things considered, I'd rather not tell her yet. "Someone from home," I finally said.

"Oh." Georgina swiveled back around; apparently if it wasn't someone she knew, it wasn't gossip-worthy. "Hey, do you think a tiara would be too much with this?"

I eyed the gown. It was long and white with a three-foot train. Low cut in the back, high-necked in the front. Stunning.

"Kate Middleton could've gotten married in that gown," I observed. "So, yeah, I think a tiara works."

"It was made by the same designer," Georgina said, tilting her head to catch her reflection from the side. "But this one's a little sexier, don't you think?"

"Definitely." Three dots indicated that another text was coming through.

Come 2 a party then? @8?

I bit my lip. It was already nearly six o'clock. "Hey, are we all eating together tonight?"

"Why?" Georgina asked, eyeing me again. "Do you have a date?"

"Helen wants to grab dinner," I lied.

Georgina made the noise that expressed her general displeasure with anything Helen-related. "There's a benefit at the Hermès store tonight. So no family dinner."

"I can't even begin to pick apart all the things that are wrong with that sentence," I muttered.

"What?"

"Nothing."

Without warning, Marion swept into the room. "Girls," she said, the same way another person might say, "Slugs."

Georgina broke into a wide, fake smile and executed a small twirl. "What do you think, Mother?"

Marion's lips pursed, and she gingerly cupped her chin with long, manicured fingers. "Still too tight. And that low back makes you look like a prostitute."

Georgina's mouth tightened. She drew her shoulders back and said, "Well, I like it. And we already had this fight."

"Yes, we did," Marion acknowledged dryly. "And I believe that in the end, we agreed to have Mrs. Fitzsimmons incorporate some lace."

"But that'll ruin it!" Georgina wailed.

I sat perfectly still.

"It's not me, Georgina," Marion said. "When your father sees this—"

Georgina made a noise and flounced across the room, throwing herself onto the chaise. I hurriedly shifted to make room. Marion's eyes narrowed, as if she'd just noticed me sitting there.

"And you," she said, with distaste. "What will *you* be wearing?"

I stammered, "Um, I haven't really had a chance to look yet."

"Really, Jane. We don't have all day." Marion clapped her hands twice, and a chic salesgirl scurried in.

Without looking at her, Marion said, "I need to find something for her, too."

They both scrutinized me. The salesgirl donned a helpless expression, as if she'd just been handed a lost cause. "In white?"

"No," Marion scoffed, as if the very suggestion was absurd. "She won't be coming out this year. Any color will do."

The salesgirl fled back into the store. My phone buzzed, and Marion's attention snapped back to me. I didn't dare glance down at the screen. As she continued the death glare, I sipped water, desperate to ease my dry mouth.

The salesgirl rushed back in, holding a tier of dresses that reached nearly to her chin. Her hands shook as she hung them on the rack. Marion was a regular, clearly.

The girl was still disentangling the dresses when Marion started sorting through them. She grabbed each dress and yanked it left; the sound of hangers scraping the bar was sharp and staccato. "No, no, no . . ." she muttered, jerking them aside one by one.

The salesgirl finished hanging the last dress and stood back, hands clasped protectively in front of her.

"She can pick her own dress, Mother," Georgina said with irritation. "I mean, seriously."

Marion ignored her. I tried to fight a mounting sense of dread. I hadn't seen any ugly dresses in the store, but then, I hadn't really been paying attention; I'd been too focused on my texts. If there was one, I had no doubt Marion would find it.

"Uh, would you like some help?" I offered weakly.

But she was already whipping a hanger off the rack. "This one," she said decisively.

The dress was simple but elegant. A long length of scarlet with thin spaghetti straps, a crisscrossed bodice, and a flowing skirt. It was pretty much the most beautiful thing I'd ever seen. "Really?"

Marion's eyebrow lifted a fraction of an inch. "Put it on behind the curtain."

Meekly, I crossed the room and took the dress from her. I undressed fast behind the privacy screen, nearly toppling over as I removed my shoes. After a moment of confusion, I figured out the complicated straps and managed to get the dress over my head, squirming slightly until it slid over my hips. The salesgirl appeared on cue to zip it up.

It was too long, but then I was barefoot; this was obviously another dress that would require towering heels. I suddenly understood what they meant about something fitting like a glove. That's what this felt like: a second skin that had been crafted for me and me alone.

I stepped out from behind the curtain.

Marion's expression didn't change, but Georgina's jaw dropped.

"Holy crap," she said. "You look amazing. Now *I* want to wear red!"

As I slowly approached the mirror, the salesgirl unobtrusively helped with the train so I wouldn't stumble. I barely recognized myself. The color made my skin shimmer. My hair shone jet black against the crimson, and the wrap of the bodice emphasized my slight curves. *I actually look like a Bond girl,* I thought.

"Excellent choice," the salesgirl said approvingly.

Marion threw her a withering look and said, "It needs to be hemmed. Please send Mrs. Fitzsimmons back in."

Looking equal parts contrite and relieved, the salesgirl left.

"Thank you, Marion," I said with genuine gratitude. "This is perfect."

Unless I was mistaken, her eyes softened slightly. But all she said was, "I hope this won't take long. We have plans this evening."

Georgina changed back into her uniform while Mrs. Fitzsimmons buzzed around my feet, periodically sticking me with pins. She wasn't gentle, but she was quick; within five minutes, we were done. I actually experienced a small pang of regret as I pulled my hideous uniform back on.

When I came back around the screen, Marion was gone.

Georgina stood rigidly by the doorway, arms crossed over her chest and an expression of pure rage on her face.

"Hey," I said cautiously. "Is your mom—"

She threw my phone at me; I lunged, catching it right before it hit the floor. "Daniel Fairfax," she spat accusingly.

I gulped. "Georgina, listen—"

"How could you?" she demanded, her face going as scarlet as my dress. "You little bitch!"

"But, I didn't know that you'd dated. I just found out—"

"Don't you dare deny it," she growled, a crazed glint in her eyes.

I shrank back. *Definitely her father's daughter*, I thought—from zero to rage in less than a minute. "I'm sorry. I didn't know it would be such a big deal."

That was apparently the wrong thing to say. Georgina drew herself up, like a cobra poised to strike. She glared down the length of her perfect nose at me and hissed, "I will ruin you. Just wait. From now on, your life will be a living hell."

She whirled around and stalked out of the room.

It took a few seconds to get my breathing under control. The phone felt abnormally heavy in my hand. I hit the ON button, and saw what had set her off:

DANIEL FAIRFAX: awesome, sweetheart. C u soon xo.

"Crap." Even though I murmured it, the word seemed to echo off the walls. "Why isn't anything ever easy here?"

I NEARLY BOWLED OVER Alma as I charged out of my bedroom and into the gloom. I don't know if the Rochesters were closet environmentalists, or if they just preferred a creepy atmosphere, but the hall lights were never turned on.

Hand to my chest, I gasped, "Alma, you scared me."

She blinked, her face as inscrutable as ever. "I wait for you," she accused, as if we'd had a date or something.

I checked my phone: it was a quarter past eight, I was already late. It wasn't totally my fault, though. I'd come home to discover that my clothing had been tossed all over the room again. A shirt had been shredded, too. Luckily it wasn't one of my favorites, but it renewed my resolve to get a better lock installed ASAP—and to have another chat with Nicholas.

I ran a hand through my hair, still wet from the shower. "Do you need something, Alma? Because I'm in kind of a hurry."

"Here." Alma thrust something at me. I squinted down at it.

It was a small leather pouch, tied closed with a long red string. Just like the one Nicholas wore.

"Oh," I said doubtfully. *Like I wasn't having enough trouble fitting in without wearing the world's ugliest necklace.* "Thanks, but I really don't—"

"You take!" she insisted as I tried to hand it back. "Keep on neck."

"Right," I said. There wasn't time to argue; I just needed her to get out of my way. "Okay, thanks."

I started to tuck it in my pocket. Alma shook her head so vigorously it knocked her wig askew; I had to resist the urge to reach out and straighten it for her. "Neck!"

Resistance was clearly futile. Rolling my eyes, I slipped it over my head, wincing as I caught a whiff. "Ugh. What's in this, anyway?"

"It keep you safe," she said. As if to underscore the point, Alma tapped it, releasing a foul-smelling cloud.

I nearly gagged as the particles drifted up my nasal cavity. "Thanks again," I wheezed. "Gotta go!"

I felt Alma's eyes on me as I trotted down the hall. I took the stairs two at a time and bolted outside, pausing briefly on the front stoop to yank the disgusting thing off. I held it up to the overhead light: there were strange characters carved in the leather.

"Thanks, but no thanks, Alma," I muttered, chucking the bag into the hedge. "I've got enough crazy in my life already."

"YOU SHOULD'VE KEPT IT," Daniel said.

"You didn't smell it," I replied, my nose wrinkling up at the memory. "Trust me, no one would've wanted to come within ten feet of me."

"Maybe that was the point," Helen said.

"Exactly," Daniel agreed. "Ghost-repellent."

"Everyone-repellant, more like," I scoffed, taking another sip of soda. From the look of things, the three of us were the only ones not drinking. Most of the crowd was huddled around the liquor table in the kitchen, leaving the "conservatory" largely to us. And yes, it was an actual conservatory, filled with towering palms and a baby grand that was currently seeing more use as a cup holder.

I wasn't clear on who was hosting this party, but their house was nearly as impressive as the Rochesters'. The decor was modern, though, with a preponderance of white: white sofas, white drapes, white carpeting. Judging by the amount of beer and red wine sloshing out of plastic cups, it wouldn't stay that way for long. The teen who lived here was either really brave or incredibly stupid; I could imagine my parents' reaction if I'd ever thrown a party like this.

A twinge at the thought, but just a small one. The grief was lessening, becoming more manageable every day. And the rush of memories had slowed, too. Which was probably good, although it felt disconcertingly like a betrayal.

"I should get going," Helen said, frowning at two guys who were play-wrestling in the opposite corner.

"Not yet!" I protested. "It's still so early!"

Helen was scanning the room nervously, like a deer surrounded by camo-clad hunters. Bringing her might've been a mistake, but I'd thought it would be nice for her to deal with real live people for a change. Daniel was being very sweet, keeping the conversation going with lots of funny anecdotes about the other people at the party. But we weren't exactly mingling.

A girl I'd never seen before—blonde and tall and pretty—suddenly stumbled over to us and draped an arm across Daniel's shoulder, slurring, "Danny Fairfax. I've missed you, baby."

I bristled. She was a slightly less attractive version of Georgina. I noted with pleasure that lipstick was smeared across her front teeth.

"Classy," Helen murmured.

Daniel gingerly extricated himself and said, "Sadie, this is Helen. And my girlfriend, Janie."

I'm not sure which of us was more shocked by the word "girlfriend." Sadie's eyes widened, and I felt a surge of glee. Trying to act casual about it, I said, "Lovely to meet you, Sadie," in a frosty voice that would've done Marion proud.

"Uh, yeah," she said, weaving slightly. "You, too. Enjoy the party. There's a fortune-teller upstairs, she's totally kick-ass."

And with that, she was gone.

"A fortune-teller?" Helen asked dubiously. "At a high school party?"

"Sadie's mom is really into that sort of thing," Daniel explained. "Crystals, Tarot, the works."

My glee dissipated. "So she's another ex-girlfriend?"

Daniel's expression said it all. I muttered, "Maybe we should get going."

"Hey." Daniel slid his hand down my bare arm until he caught my fingers. He said in a low voice, "Different time, different guy. Remember?"

"Wow," Helen commented into the rim of her red cup. "I'm not uncomfortable at all. So happy I signed on to be the third wheel."

"Right. Sorry." Daniel gave my hand a reassuring squeeze, then released it and put some space between us. "So, fortune-teller?"

"Sure." Helen sighed. "It's not like I have an entire season of *Battlestar Galactica* waiting for me at home, after all."

Daniel raised his eyebrows at me.

I shrugged. "I started the night with creepy. Might as well end it that way, too."

I FOLLOWED THEM UPSTAIRS, feeling sullen. I was having a hard time adjusting to the emotional rollercoaster of our relationship: total highs (*he called me his girlfriend!*) to devastating lows (*apparently he'd called a lot of other girls that, too, including my new sort-of sister*).

On the landing, we were pushed aside by a giggling girl

running away from a tall kid. The boy caught up and pushed her against the wall, holding her there as he kissed her.

"Lovely," Helen said, easing past them with an expression of distaste. "And to think I've been missing out on all this."

I shot her a look, but she was right; this wasn't my kind of scene, either. Parties in Hawaii were more like the bonfire Daniel had brought me to: a bunch of kids hanging out on the beach, someone playing a guitar, everyone chilling and laughing. When people hooked up, they slunk away to do it in private.

This party had a weird edge to it, like there was something hungry at its core waiting for the right moment to open wide and swallow us whole. At least there didn't appear to be anyone else up here; aside from the lovebirds, we had the hall to ourselves.

At the end of the corridor, there was an open door. Candlelight seeped across the threshold. A handwritten sign liberally speckled with glitter proclaimed: *Madame Garland, Seer of the ages!*

It stood in stark contrast to the opulent surroundings, like a girl wearing a ball gown and sneakers.

"O-kay," Helen said. "Who's first?"

"I'll go," Daniel offered.

"Thank God." Helen sounded relieved. "I really didn't want to be the sacrificial lamb."

He smiled at her, then leaned in and brushed his lips across my forehead. Looking into my eyes, he said softly, "You good?"

"Couldn't be better," I said, even though I was still getting flashes of Sadie draped over him.

He ran a hand through my hair, then cupped my cheek. In spite of everything, I leaned into it. "So you're not going to run away on me?"

"Of course not," I protested, even though I'd been considering doing just that.

"Still here," Helen muttered. "Still uncomfortable."

"Don't let her sneak out," Daniel said, wagging a finger at her. "I'm holding you personally responsible."

"Yeah, yeah." Helen waved a hand dismissively at him. "Now get in there. If we hurry, I'll still have time to watch an episode when I get home."

With a final grin, Daniel slipped inside the room and closed the door. I slid down the wall until my butt rested on my heels. Helen joined me, crossing her legs.

"So," she said. "There's a catch with Mr. Perfect?"

"I don't know." I worried at a cuticle with my thumbnail. "I mean, he says that's all in the past. But I guess the past was pretty crazy."

"Crazy how?" Helen's eyes narrowed. "Drugs?"

I shifted uncomfortably, not sure how much to share. It was his secret, after all. "Yeah."

"But he's clean now?"

"One year," I said. "But I guess it was bad. Like, really bad."

Helen blew out a puff of air and said, "You realize I have, like, zero experience with this sort of thing?"

"I know," I said. "Trust me, I don't, either."

"I was waiting for the bathroom downstairs," Helen continued. "*For-ev-er.* And finally, three girls came out. I don't think they were all checking their makeup in there."

I nodded. "I know. This isn't what I'm used to at all."

"And you don't want any part of it?" She was examining me closely, a hint of skepticism in her eyes.

I shook my head vigorously. "No. Definitely not."

"So why are we here?" Helen asked, throwing her hands up. "Why did Daniel want to come, if he's trying to stay clean?"

I opened my mouth to respond, and then shut it again. She had a point. He'd brought us to just the sort of crazy party he claimed to be done with. At one of his ex's houses, no less.

Why would he do that?

Helen laid a hand on my arm and said, "Listen. He seems pretty great, all in all. Just be careful."

The door flew open. Filling the frame, Daniel threw his arms wide and announced, "I'm going to be President!" Taking in our expressions, he frowned. "What'd I miss?"

"Nothing." Helen scrambled to her feet. "Might as well get this over with."

She closed the door, casting us in shadows.

Daniel hunkered down. "So? Everything cool?"

I shrugged. "Not really. Why are we here?"

His forehead wrinkled. "What do you mean?"

"I mean, why did you take me to this party? I thought you weren't into this sort of thing anymore."

"I'm not," he protested, looking around as if noticing our surroundings for the first time. "I just figured . . . I don't know. Bobby told me about it today, and I thought it could be fun."

"Not so much," I said dryly.

"Yeah, you're right," he said ruefully. "Look, I'm sorry, I wasn't thinking. I guess I just kind of slipped into autopilot." He shifted closer, until his shoulder touched mine. "Forgive me?"

I didn't answer. He smelled like aftershave and mint and cinnamon, which I'd recently decided was the best combination of aromas in the world. Those gorgeous brown eyes were so wide and beseeching . . . I sighed. It was incredibly difficult to stay annoyed with him.

"Fine," I said, lightly punching his arm. "But if you take me to another ex's party, no guarantees. This is your one get-out-of-jail-free card."

He held up a hand. "I swear, never again. Not even if they're serving pigs in a blanket."

"Well, I actually might be able make an exception for those. And mini quiches are pretty awesome, too—"

He cut me off, bending down and covering my mouth with his. I was still drowning in the kiss when light flooded over us.

Helen groaned. "Seriously?"

"I like you, Helen, but you have terrible timing," Daniel murmured good-naturedly.

"Your turn," Helen said, pointing at me. "And hurry up. It's nearly my curfew."

"What'd the fortune-teller say?" I asked as I got to my feet.

"I'm going to be president, too," Helen said drily. "Now go!" She gave me a little shove, propelling me through the door.

It was tiny, more of a closet than a bedroom. The only light came from a candle set on top of a card table covered with a black cloth. And behind it loomed an enormous woman who pretty much epitomized my mental image of a fortune-teller, down to the minutest degree. Large purple turban. Flowing emerald green robes. Lots of makeup, especially around her pouched, dark eyes. Blood red fingernails. And a scruff of . . . wait a minute. As I slowly settled into the seat, I peered closely at her. The fortune-teller was either a trans woman or a man in drag. But since she was going as "Madame," female pronouns seemed the safest bet.

"So," she said in a slow drawl, peering at me through the gloom. I tried to place the accent—Louisiana with a touch of Brooklyn? "What do you want to know?"

I blurted out the question thoughtlessly. "Am I being haunted?"

Her eyebrows shot up. "My, my. The night finally gets interesting."

"It's just . . ." I struggled to explain. "Weird things keep happening, and I think there has to be a rational explanation for it, but—"

"But some things defy reason," she said, her voice dropping an octave. She leaned back in her chair and crossed her arms. I suddenly felt silly. This was all just a party trick, after all. She'd told both Daniel and Helen that they were destined for the Oval Office. So what kind of reassurance could she possibly offer me?

"Sorry," I said, getting up. "I should just—"

"Sit," she thundered.

Taken aback, I dropped into the chair. She reached beneath

the table and took out a deck of cards: Tarot, identical to the set I gave Kaila for her thirteenth birthday.

I sighed again. This was a waste of time. I should politely excuse myself, and get home.

"Don't worry, hon," the fortune-teller said without looking up from the cards she was shuffling. "I've got something special for you."

"That sounds ominous," I muttered.

She chuckled. "Oh, I believe you've seen your fair share of ominous." She set the cards down with a loud slap and ordered, "Cut."

I cut the deck. She did some sort of elaborate shuffling, her hands moving so fast it was hard to follow. Then she started flipping the cards over, one at a time.

When she'd laid out five, she leaned in, lips pursed as she examined them. "Well, well," she mused. "You *are* a special case."

"Special how?" I asked, not liking how that sounded.

"Lots of loss here," she said, jabbing at the top card. "People close to you. And not long ago."

I bit my lip, wondering if either Daniel or Helen had let that slip. She met my eyes. "And no, your friends didn't tell me. It's written right here. And this one . . ." She motioned to another card. "There's someone after you, all right. Someone close." She looked up sharply. "In your house, I think."

I shifted uncomfortably in the chair. None of this was a stretch, I told myself. After all, I was the idiot who had walked in blathering about a ghost. Of course that implied a recent loss, and trouble at home.

"There's more, though," she said pensively. "Much more."

Without warning, she reached across the table and grabbed my hand. I tried to wrench free, but her grip was iron, nearly crushing my knuckles. Madame Garland's breathing deepened, and her eyes rolled back in her head.

"Hey!" I protested. "You're hurting me!"

She didn't seem to hear. The voice that came out of her was chilling, the bizarre accent gone.

"You will die," she hissed. "You're already dead, you just don't know it yet."

A well of panic surged inside me. I yanked as hard as I could, tearing my hand free. The fortune-teller splayed across the table. She blinked up at me, an expression of confusion on her face. Her eyes cleared, and in a deep bass she said, "What the hell—"

I was already scrambling for the door, struggling to open it with shaky hands.

"Wait!" she cried after me. "Please, I have more to tell you. I saw something!"

I couldn't answer, couldn't speak. I dashed past Helen and Daniel, who stared after me, agape. I could hear them scrambling to follow, calling my name.

But I was deaf to their pleas. The only thing that penetrated was the voice screaming at me to run, as far and fast as I could . . . because when she'd clenched my hand, I'd seen something, too.

Standing right behind her chair, I'd glimpsed a small, pale child dressed all in white. My ruined doll dangled from her right hand, and her left was a ball of fire. As I stared at the girl, horrified, her mouth yawed open, wider than humanly possible. Inside was a deep, dark chasm filled with terror and screams and the things nightmares are made of.

And without a shadow of a doubt I knew what she wanted. Me, dead. And nothing would stop her.

Chapter X

In an instant, I was within the chamber. Tongues of flame darted round the bed: the curtains were on fire. In the midst of blaze and vapour, Mr. Rochester lay stretched motionless, in deep sleep.

I fled downstairs, nearly tripping over two kids sharing a joint on the landing. Their protests barely registered. Helen and Daniel finally caught up to me by the front door.

"Jesus, Janie," Daniel gasped, extending an arm to steady me. "Are you okay? What the hell happened?"

"I'm guessing she didn't say you'd be president someday?" Helen said, but her tone belied the words.

I struggled to breathe; it felt like my lungs had solidified into stone. "It's . . . I'm . . ."

"Just catch your breath," Daniel said gently.

"I need some air." I struggled for the doorknob.

Before I could turn it, the door was thrown open from the other side. I found myself staring at Georgina, who gaped back with an equally shocked expression. Her eyes flitted to Daniel, still clutching my elbow, and her gaze darkened.

"So," she said coldly. "Guess I'm late to the party."

"Not now, Georgina," I muttered, pushing past her. I stopped a few feet away from the stoop, rubbing my arms to try and warm them. The night was cold; a thick mist coated everything.

On top of my terror, I was struck by an overwhelming pang of homesickness. I yearned for the familiar smell of close-cut grass, hints of jasmine, and salt on a warm breeze. Blinking back tears, I stared up at the moon. It glowed orange through a veil of fog.

"Here." Helen draped her jacket around my shoulders.

I gratefully drew it close, the wool scratchy against my skin. "Thanks," I croaked.

"So are you going to tell us what happened in there?" Daniel asked.

I shook my head, still too unnerved to talk about it. Besides, I must have imagined the girl, right? Just like the lights in the elevator and hallway: all by-products of a hyperactive imagination fueled by lack of sleep.

I was having a hard time convincing myself, though. The girl I'd seen had looked eerily like Nicholas. And how could my brain have come up with that on its own? Plus, the way the fortune-teller had gone all *The Exorcist* on me . . .

No, I told myself. *None of this is real. You just need to forget about it.*

The cold was grounding, the sound of a siren in the distance oddly consoling. This was tangible: the city encircling me, my anxious friends hovering by my side. And judging by the expression on Georgina's face, I had much bigger problems to contend with.

"I'm fine," I said, fighting the quaver in my voice. "Really. I just want to go home."

SLEEP ELUDED ME THAT night for longer than usual. Every time I closed my eyes, the ghostly image of the girl snapped into focus. I'd taken care to lock my door from the inside. Tomorrow, I'd see if Daniel could install a better deadbolt to barricade it against whoever kept messing with my stuff.

Unless it's someone who doesn't need a door.

The thought popped unbidden into my mind. Angrily,

I forced it away. Any rational person knew that seeing ghosts equaled crazy, and I had no intention of skipping down the path toward a padded room.

Sixteen months, I reminded myself. In just under five hundred days, I'd turn eighteen and could go wherever I wanted, whenever I wanted. I could move back to Hawaii and finish my senior year there. And then I'd never have to think about the Rochesters again. I glared up at the ceiling, as if daring sounds to emanate from it. If the humming started, I'd storm up there and confront whomever—or whatever—was responsible.

Or I'd run out of the house screaming. Really, it could go either way.

WELL PAST MIDNIGHT, I finally drifted off. In my dreams, I wandered through dark hallways. It was the Rochesters' house, and at the same time, it wasn't. A small, cold hand gripped mine. Looking down, I discovered Nicholas gazing up at me.

"You won't let her hurt me anymore, will you, Janie?"

Before I could answer, a light appeared in front of us. It was much larger than the others, the size of a basketball. It bounced off the walls, spewing sparks. Nicholas screamed as flames erupted; explosions shattered the glass in the picture frames, and the gloomy faces inside melted as if they were made of wax.

I ran, keeping a firm grip on his hand, but at every turn we encountered another endless hallway, another taunting ball of throbbing white light. And when I looked again, the child I was dragging along wasn't Nicholas. It was the girl. She leered up at me, dark fluid oozing from her mouth.

I shot upright in bed, coughing and choking. For a minute, I thought I was still dreaming.

But no. The fire was real.

One whole side of my room was an inferno. The red drapes were roiling with dark smoke. The stack of cardboard boxes had turned into a pyre; flames danced around the top of it, licking the ceiling.

I rolled off the bed and dropped to all fours. The smoke was so thick I could barely see. It was disorienting; for a few panicked moments I couldn't figure out where the door was. Everywhere I looked, darting flames were claiming another piece of furniture.

If I didn't get out of here, I'd suffer the same fate. I heard people shouting and pounding on my door; it was locked, I remembered blearily. They couldn't get in, which meant help wasn't coming. I had to get out.

A crash behind me as something huge toppled to the ground. Beads of sweat coursed into my eyes, melding with smoke-induced tears. It was so unbearably hot. I couldn't see, couldn't breathe. Couldn't even gather enough oxygen to scream for help.

I crawled across the floor, praying that I'd reach the door before passing out. The smoke clawed its way down my throat and into my lungs like a malevolent beast. After what felt like an eternity, my fingertips finally encountered the edge of the carpet. With a renewed burst of strength, I scrambled the final few feet to the door. I reached up and fumbled for the lock, managing to turn the bolt on the third try.

The door flew open, nearly knocking me backwards. John and Mr. Rochester stood there in navy pajamas, their eyes wild.

"Janie!" John grabbed my arm and hauled me into the hallway. "What the hell?"

Alma flew past us, a fire extinguisher gripped in both hands. Despite the fact that it was nearly as big as her, she manned it like a pro, shooting a stream of white chemicals in a circle. The flames hissed as they fought back, smoke drifting past us like grasping tendrils.

John dragged me farther down the hallway.

I was still doubled over coughing. There was the shrill shriek of sirens outside. Heavy boots pounded up the stairs. Marion and Georgina stood at the end of the hall, glaring at me with identical expressions of condemnation. Behind them, Nicholas cowered, looking bewildered and afraid.

And in the shadows, for just a second, I caught a glimpse of a pale head. When I blinked, it was gone.

"What," Marion demanded, "did you do to my house?"

DESPITE THE BLANKET JOHN had thrown across my shoulders, I couldn't stop shivering.

We were clustered in the downstairs living room. I'd christened it the ebony palace; the dark, heavy furniture rendered it dark in the daytime, and positively oppressive at night. Richard had ordered us to wait here while the firefighters tamped down the final embers. He was still upstairs dealing with them.

Flashing back on the raw heat lapping at my hair, I shuddered again.

John was perched on the edge of the chair facing me, his eyes grave, the usual mocking smile gone. Marion and Georgina sat rigidly by the fireplace, wearing matching silk robes and icy glares. I had no idea where Nicholas was; Alma had probably taken him back to bed.

"You were smoking." Marion said it as a statement of fact.

"No, I wasn't," I muttered. "I don't smoke."

She snorted. "All you people smoke."

That penetrated the fog encasing in my head. "What do you mean, 'you people'?"

"Yes, Mother," John said, getting to his feet. "What exactly is that supposed to mean?"

Marion avoided his eyes. "Teenagers from Hawaii. Everyone knows they smoke marijuana."

"Well, I never have," I snapped. "And I'm pretty sure you weren't talking about 'teenagers from Hawaii,' anyway."

Marion cocked an eyebrow. "Then how did the fire start? Please, I'd love to know why my house has been destroyed!"

"It's not your house," Richard Rochester said from the

doorway. Tufts of his hair jutted out, as if he'd been tugging on it; his eyes were red and weary. "It's my house," he continued somberly. "I just let the rest of you live in it."

Marion's eyes flicked to me, then back to him. She rose, crossed the room, and laid a hand on his arm. "Richard, listen to me," she pleaded. "I told you this was too much of a risk. It isn't worth it. I can't have the safety of our children jeopardized by the likes of her."

John made a disgusted noise. "As if you care about us."

"Shut up, John," Georgina growled from her chair.

"This is a load of crap." John stepped forward and jabbed at the air with his finger. "And you all know it. This has Nicholas written all over it."

"Nicholas?" I said, confused.

"He's quite the little firebug," John said. "Didn't anyone tell you?"

"That's ridiculous," Marion said stiffly. "He promised to never do that again."

John returned her glare. "Yeah, like that means anything."

"But the door was locked," I said confused. "It couldn't have been Nicholas." *Unless he has a key*, I thought. But recalling his terrified gaze, I dismissed the idea outright. He wouldn't try to hurt me like that.

Would he?

"So you admit to being alone in there," Marion said triumphantly. "Then *obviously* you were the one responsible."

"Where's she going to sleep?" Georgina interjected. "That's what I want to know."

Until that moment, my relief at surviving the inferno had dwarfed every other concern. Now my heart sank as I realized that I no longer had a room. And everything I owned was probably ruined. Including every photo of my parents, and the few possessions of theirs I'd held on to. At the thought, something inside me started to crumble.

"Maybe you should stick her in the attic," Georgina suggested nastily. "She deserves it, after all."

"Georgina!" Marion said sharply.

Georgina's face shifted, as if she realized she'd gone too far.

"Don't be such a bitch," John snarled. "You've got plenty of room."

"She is *not* sleeping with me."

I was with her on that. Confined to a small space with Georgina, it might never feel safe to shut my eyes again.

"We'll call the Fairmont and book a room," Marion said decisively. "That way the rest of us will be able to sleep more securely."

"You'd send her to a hotel?" John scoffed. "Wow, that's low, even for—"

"Enough!" Richard boomed.

The room fell silent.

"Janie," he continued in a strained voice, "You're not going to a hotel."

Marion opened her mouth; but he threw her a look, and she clamped it shut again.

"We'll figure something out," he said. "At least a temporary solution."

"Well, then. I'm going to attempt to get some sleep," Marion said stiffly. "I have a big day tomorrow. Apparently I'll be trying to get this house back in some sort of order." With a final withering glare, she swept from the room.

Richard looked at his kids. "Georgina and John. Bed, now."

His tone didn't brook argument. John glanced at me then went to the door, keeping his head down as he passed his father. Georgina was next. As she passed by, she glowered from beneath her lashes and hissed, "Bitch."

The adrenaline had dissipated, and I was left feeling shaky and weak. If I leaned back against the cushions, I'd probably fall asleep sitting up.

Richard lumbered across the room and collapsed in the chair opposite me. He ran both hands over his face, like he was trying to scrub it clean. It only served to smudge the ash into his cheeks. "You're okay?" he finally asked.

I nodded, although in truth I felt very far from okay.

"Good." He sighed. "That's good." Grimacing, he continued, "We don't have another guest room."

That was hard to imagine in a house this size, but he was probably right. Marion had appropriated most of the vacant rooms for "salons," "dressing rooms," and various other equally senseless uses. "I can just crash in here," I offered. "It's fine, really."

"It's not fine." His frown deepened. "I suppose you *could* sleep in Georgina's room; there's a daybed in there."

"That's okay," I said hurriedly. "Really, I'd prefer—"

"She sleep with me," Alma barked from the doorway.

Startled, we both turned. She wasn't wearing her wig; strands of thin white hair barely covered her scalp. She was also coated with soot, which only added to the impression that a tiny troll had entered the room.

"That's a great idea," Richard exclaimed. "Thank you, Alma."

"Wait, I—"

He held up a hand and said firmly, "Alma has a very comfortable apartment. You'll be fine there."

The night just kept getting worse. But considering the alternative, at least I didn't have to worry about Alma trying to murder me in my sleep. Probably.

MUTELY, I FOLLOWED ALMA down a back corridor. I'd never been in this part of the house; I'd just assumed that the door behind the kitchen led to the basement.

Instead, it opened on a tiny hallway with a ceiling so low I could reach up and brush it with my hand. It was dark, the wooden floorboards cold beneath my bare feet. Alma led the way, padding silently in her slippers. I couldn't repress the sense that she was leading me into some alternate dimension from which I'd never emerge.

She opened the door at the end of the hall and beckoned for me to come inside.

I'm not sure what I'd expected; a tiny closet, maybe? Or an actual witch's lair, with a dirt floor and roots dangling from the ceiling? Instead, I was surprised to discover that Richard had been telling the truth. The room was simple, but cozy. Cheerier than the rest of the house. It was furnished with a plush red sectional, a squat blue chair, and a thick carpet in a rich shade of orange; all the contrasting colors should've been fighting each other, but instead it looked an interior designer's idea of shabby chic.

A battered table along one wall held an electric teakettle and a hot plate; the rest of the room was filled with low bookshelves, charmingly mismatched end tables, and all sorts of knickknacks. The overhead light cast everything in a warm glow. Matching doors on the other side of the room were painted a faded yellow.

My shoulders dropped as I relaxed. *Home,* I thought, then caught myself, startled. It was true, though; something about the shabbiness and clutter reminded me of our little beach cottage.

Alma was blinking up at me, her eyes huge behind her glasses. Unless I was mistaken, the slight crease in her lips was a smile.

"Thank you," I said. "I really appreciate this."

She nodded, then shuffled across to one of the yellow doors. "You sleep here."

Hesitantly, I followed; but the bedroom was even more charming. A four-poster bed, covered with a quilt and stacks of throw pillows. The rest of the room was relatively plain: a bureau and bedside table, both made of wood polished to a high gleam.

I picked up a framed picture from the table: a black and white image of a tall, thin man with his arm wrapped around a tiny woman. He wore a uniform, and she was extremely pregnant. Both of them beamed at the camera. It took a minute to realize this was a younger version of Alma.

"Wow," I said appreciatively. "You were gorgeous."

Alma made an indeterminate noise in the back of her throat

and took the photo from me, setting it back on the table. Then she crossed to the bureau and rooted through it, pulling out a set of flannel pajamas. Handing them to me, she ordered, "Change."

I wanted to protest that there was no way they'd fit; but holding them up, I realized they were nearly my size.

She went back into the other room, and I peeled off my clothes. They smelled terrible. I did, too, but the thought of showering was too exhausting to contemplate. I slipped into the pajamas and a pair of cotton socks; they were unbelievably soft and comfy. Alma reappeared clasping a mug in both hands. She set it on the bedside table, pulled back the sheets, and motioned for me to get in.

"I'm fine now," I said. "Thanks. I can just—"

"Lie down," she ordered. "And drink."

I was too tired to protest. I climbed into bed, the springs groaning slightly as I shifted to get comfortable. When I was propped up against the pillows, she handed me the mug. I sniffed it skeptically. "What's in it?"

"It make you calm," she explained. "Good for throat."

I took a tentative sip: chamomile tea with honey. Relieved, I drank half of it in one long gulp. Fatigue seeped through my bones, and my eyes started to droop.

I barely registered Alma taking the mug. She helped me ease down the bed, and tucked the blankets into a comforting cocoon. As I drifted off, she did the most startling thing of all.

In a voice so soft it was barely audible, she sang to me.

I couldn't understand the words, but the tune was oddly familiar. The verses elicited images of a strange land, vibrantly green and overgrown. Brightly colored birds and peculiar plants. A broad expanse of water, with waves the same shade of blue I'd grown up with.

As the last bit of consciousness slipped through my grasp, I felt Alma's warm, withered hand on mine. She breathed a single word, but I was already fast asleep.

Chapter XI

Circumstances knit themselves, fitted themselves, shot into order: the chain that had been lying hitherto a formless lump of links, was drawn out straight—every ring was perfect, the connection complete.

When I awoke, Alma was gone. Bright sunlight streamed through the filmy white curtains. I didn't want to leave. I was having a hard time reconciling this charming apartment with the brusque, cold woman I'd come to know. Of course, I never would've guessed that she'd sing me to sleep, either.

I peeked into the other bedroom: it was nearly identical to mine, but the air was pungent with tiger balm and jasmine. I was happy to have the place to myself for the moment. It was quiet in here, a less weighted version of the silence that constrained the rest of the house.

My throat was sore and raw from the smoke, but otherwise I felt okay. A small clock on the wall read 12:20 P.M. Wow, I'd seriously overslept. So much for school. Of course, my uniform was gone. Along with everything else I owned, probably. I could hardly bear the thought of going upstairs to see what was left.

Breakfast first, I decided.

I made my way down the hall to the kitchen: also empty, I discovered with relief. I ate a bowl of cereal and cleaned up after myself.

Now what? I thought.

Face the disaster of what used to be my room? Call Kaila, and Daniel? But I couldn't; my phone had been on the bedside table, there was no way it had survived. The same went for my laptop. As the list of what I'd lost mounted, my legs faltered. I dropped back into a seat at the kitchen table and clutched my head, fighting the urge to cry. *That won't accomplish anything,* I reminded myself fiercely. Everything important was already gone anyway.

"And I thought I was a late sleeper."

John looked immaculate as always, dressed in jeans and a cashmere sweater, his blond hair falling in perfect waves. There was no outward sign that he'd been awakened in the middle of the night by a raging fire.

I, on the other hand, looked every bit as ravaged as I felt. "Where is everyone?" I asked wearily.

He ticked them off on his fingers. "School for Georgie and Nick. Dad is at the club. And Marion is holding court at one of her luncheons, of course." He eyed me. "You look like hell."

"Gee, I wonder why," I said.

"You didn't set the fire, did you?"

I scowled at him. "Of course not."

"It would be understandable," he said.

Only then did I see what he was implying. "Yes, John. I tried to burn myself alive. That was my genius plan."

He shrugged. "That, or you *were* getting high. And if so, I'm highly offended that you didn't offer to share."

"I don't smoke pot," I said sullenly.

"Kind of strange that it only damaged your room, though," he said, an odd expression on his face.

"Why is it strange?"

"No reason," he said vaguely. "Anyway, what's the plan?"

"The plan?"

"For today." He waved at my outfit. "Will this be your new look?"

"My clothes were destroyed," I reminded him.

"Right. I'd take you to Saks, but despite our frequent buyer status, shopping in pajamas might raise a few eyebrows." John raised a hand to his chin and considered me. "I have an idea."

"It better not involve me running around naked," I muttered.

He flashed a grin. "You said it, not me."

"I'm not wearing any of Georgina's stuff, either," I warned.

"She'd skin us both," he scoffed. "No, something else. Back in a bit."

Five minutes later, he returned and tossed me a pile of clothes.

"Where are these from?" I asked suspiciously, sorting through them. Jeans, a long-sleeved cotton shirt, and a fleece jacket.

"They're mine," he said. "Might be a little big, but they should fit all right."

I held them up: he was right, the jeans would be a few inches long, but the shirt would fit fine. "How old are these?"

He shrugged. "From when I was twelve or so."

"And you still have them?"

"Don't tell Marion," he said with a wink. "She'd be horrified to know there was anything vintage in the house."

I wondered why he'd kept them; John didn't strike me as the sentimental type. Still, I was grateful to have something clean that didn't reek of smoke.

I showered and changed, then wandered back through the house. I found John in the media room, absorbed in a first-person shooter game. Cartoon violence raged across the widescreen TV.

"Welcome to the Rochester Academy," he said without looking up, his fingers flying across the controller. "Best home school in town."

"So this is what you do all day?" I asked.

"Not all day," he said defensively. "But Richard and Marion don't really approve of my other activities."

I decided I didn't really want to know what those were, either, so I didn't ask. I settled on the other end of the couch and watched. The game was oddly mesmerizing, although I couldn't repress a wince when his avatar brandished a flamethrower against the oncoming zombie horde.

"Too close to home?" he asked, noticing my discomfort.

I shifted. "Not a big fan of fire at the moment."

"Have you checked out your room yet?" When I shook my head, he said soberly, "I wouldn't. It's bad."

"Great." I ran a hand through my wet hair. Right now, I felt incapable of tears, like I'd been wrung out and had no moisture left to spare. Shock, probably.

"Georgie has you in her sights, too," he warned. "Better be careful."

"I know." I pulled my knees up to my chest and wrapped my arms around them. "You think she'll get over it?"

He laughed shortly. "Doubtful. Hailey Gardiner stole her boyfriend in eighth grade, and Georgie made her life miserable for years afterwards; I'm pretty sure the poor girl's still committed to an institution somewhere. Danny Fairfax, huh?"

"Yeah. Why?"

He shook his head, eyes still fixed on the game. "Watch out for him. He's trouble."

"Funny, he said the same thing about you," I snorted. "What's the deal with you guys, anyway?"

"He hasn't told you?" John shot me a quick glance.

I shrugged, not sure how much to reveal. "I know about the drugs."

"Good for Danny boy, trying honesty for a change," John said. "Did he happen to mention how he paid for them?"

He hadn't, actually. But did it matter? Like Daniel said, that was in his past. Plus I didn't like John's tone. Forcefully, I said, "He's different now."

"Sure he is." John chuckled, then added, "I gotta say, Janie. For a smart girl, sometimes you can be awfully naïve."

I pushed off the couch. "Go to hell."

"Whoa, easy," he said, setting down the controller. A wave of zombies washed over his avatar, and it vanished in a spurt of red. The screams emanating from the speakers reverberated through the room. "C'mon, I didn't mean it. I was being a jerk. Sorry."

The plaintiveness in his voice made me hesitate. Plus, the alternative was going to face the ruins of my room, and I wasn't up for that yet. Might never be, in fact. With a sigh, I moodily stalked back to the couch. "Fine. But if you say anything else about Daniel, I'm out of here."

"Don't worry. I'm done shattering your illusions, at least for the moment." John reset the game. As his fingers tapped buttons on the controller, he eyed me. "You've lost weight."

Self-consciously, I tugged at the jeans that had slipped down my hips. "Yeah, well. I've been a little stressed lately."

"A word of advice?" he said, while mowing down another row of zombies. "Eat out more."

"Why?" I asked suspiciously.

"Just trust me. It'll help with the nausea."

I stared at him, perplexed. Before I could question him further, he said, "Be grateful that you can afford a whole new wardrobe. All that potential shopping might make Georgie even more jealous, now that I think about it."

I laughed at that. "Please. I can probably barely afford another school uniform."

John hit the pause button and swiveled to face me with a frown. "You really don't know, do you?"

"Know what?"

He held my gaze for a few beats, then said, "Let's go for a walk."

"A walk? Why?"

He was already getting to his feet. "We're taking a little field trip. Don't worry, it's not far."

"THERE IT IS," JOHN said with a wave.

"There *what* is?" We were standing in front of a mansion a block away from the Rochesters. I'd noticed it frequently on the way to school, mainly because it was impossible not to; the place was nearly twice the size of the houses flanking it, and that was saying something. Behind an iron gate, a wide circular driveway led to a neoclassical monstrosity. It was like a slightly smaller version of the White House.

"Your dad grew up here," John said, regarding it appreciatively. "It stretches around to the other side of the block. There's even a pool with a retractable roof."

"What?" I gripped the bars and gaped up at the place. The thought of my father walking through that front door was preposterous. "No way."

"It was in the Mason family for generations," John continued, as if I hadn't spoken. "They bought it before the quake; one of the few families who actually got rich off the Gold Rush. They're the real old money. We're just nouveau riche upstarts."

I was having a hard time wrapping my head around what he was saying. "You're kidding, right?"

"Nope. This could've been yours." He swept his hand in a wide arc. "There's even a helipad up on the roof. Your grandfather was a pilot, he used to shuttle the family to Napa every weekend."

A helicopter, I thought with a start. My father had never explained how he learned to fly; I'd just assumed he'd taken lessons. But maybe his father had taught him. Which meant that what John was saying might actually be true. A wind whipped up, chasing stray leaves along the pavement. As they skittered past, I asked, "Who owns it now?"

John laughed. "Oh, that's the best part. After your grandmother died, it was bought by a couple who made a fortune with their Silicon Valley start-up. It drives Marion nuts. She always calls them, "Those horrible young people who wear jeans to galas. Listening to her, you'd never guess that she grew up in a split level ranch in Novato."

I had no idea where Novato was, but the thought of Marion in anything less than a mansion was even more preposterous than my dad spending his childhood here. "I still think you're putting me on."

"Why would I do that?" he asked, sounding genuinely offended. "But hey, you know how tech money is. They'll go broke in a few years, and you can buy it back."

I laughed. "With what money?"

"You really don't get it, do you?" John turned me to face him. Acutely aware of his hand on my arm, I flushed involuntarily. "Your grandparents were worth more than half the people in this city put together."

"Yeah, but they didn't leave it to me," I said.

"From what I hear, they did," he insisted. "Some sort of blind trust. They were still pissed at your dad for leaving, but your grandfather felt strongly that the money should stay in the Mason family line."

None of what he was saying made any sense. "How do you know all this?" I demanded.

"I overhear things. It's pretty much all Richard and Marion talk about, when you're not in the room." John waved up at the house. "Trust me. You could buy and sell these people ten times over."

My head was spinning. Grandparents I'd never met, leaving me some insane fortune? There was no way that was true.

"You honestly didn't think my parents took you in out of the goodness of their hearts, did you?" John asked.

"They were my back-up guardians," I said. "My parents made the will years ago, before my grandparents died, and they never updated it. Back then, our dads were best friends."

John laughed bitterly. "Right. They could have refused and sent you into foster care. Marion wouldn't have given it a second thought."

"So why'd they say yes?" I demanded.

He gazed at the passing cars without seeming to see them. "Let's just say that the Rochester family fortune hasn't been handled as competently as yours."

"What are you talking about? You guys are loaded."

"Appearances can be deceiving," John said darkly. "Dear old Dad made some bad investments. Really bad. We were basically running on fumes until you came along." He smiled wanly at me. "Saved by a Filipina surfer girl. You can imagine how Marion feels about that."

I was having a hard time processing all this information. Part of me was still struggling to picture my dad in this mansion. But like Richard said, he and my father were best friends. They'd gone to the same schools, lived the same life. My dad had probably been to cotillions. I was starting to wonder if I'd really known him at all.

You did, a little voice in my head insisted. *You knew the real him.* He must have felt just as out of place in this world as I did. That's why he'd left it all behind.

But were the Rochesters really living off my trust? Was that even legal? I had to get in touch with Mr. Briggs and find out what the hell was going on.

John was watching me guardedly. I wondered why he was really telling me all this; he wasn't the type to do something out of the goodness of his heart.

Be careful with that one, my mom's voice whispered in my ear.

"So I could've had a swimming pool?" I finally said. "That would've been awesome."

A look of relief swept across John's face, and he laughed. "Just imagine the raging parties we could've thrown."

"Sure," I said awkwardly. It felt like a gulf had opened between us, and I wasn't certain how to bridge it, or if I even wanted to. This turned everything on its head. All along, I'd been feeling like a burden, the pauper mouse barely tolerated by wealthy distant relatives. But if John was telling the truth, I was their benefactor.

"We should get back," I suggested. "It's cold out here."

We walked in silence back to the house. John's face was unreadable, making me wonder if he regretted telling me all this. I wasn't sure how I felt about it, either. An unfamiliar feeling churned in my gut, one that took time to identify: a sensation of power. I could suddenly envision Marion and Georgina at my mercy, forced to beg for pocket money. The thought was both thrilling and terrifying.

I spotted Daniel's car as soon as we turned into the driveway. He was sitting on the front stoop in his school uniform. Seeing me, he got to his feet, a look of relief on his face. "Janie! Thank God—"

Spotting John, he froze. His features settled into a furious scowl.

"Fairfax," John said, keeping his hands tucked in his pockets.

"Why aren't you in school?" I asked.

"I was worried," Daniel said, an edge to his voice. "I heard about the fire and cut my last class. I wanted to make sure you were okay." He looked pointedly at John. "But I guess you're just fine."

I really didn't have the energy to deal with their male posturing right now. "Enough, you two. Let's go inside."

"I actually have somewhere to be," John said lightly. "Later, Janie."

He turned and stalked back toward the street. As soon as he was out of sight, Daniel glared at me. "What were you doing with him?"

"It's a long story," I said. "And honestly, I'm freezing. If we're going to fight again, can we at least do it inside?"

SEEING THE STATE OF my room softened Daniel's mood. It hardened mine, though. I stood helplessly by the fireplace, my feet sinking into the soaking wet carpet, surveying my surroundings with despair. It was even worse than I'd imagined; the few things spared by the fire had been destroyed by the firefighter's zeal. It would be a miracle if I managed to salvage anything at all.

"Crap," I said.

"Man." Daniel's eyes were wide as he took in the wreckage. "It must've been a huge fire."

"It was," I said with a shudder. The lingering pall of smoke sharpened the memory of waking up to discover my room engulfed by flames.

"God, I'm so glad you're okay." He crossed the room and wrapped his arms around me. I buried my face in his chest and inhaled deeply. I wished I could just take his hand, walk out of here, and never come back. We'd go live on a beach somewhere, leaving this house and all its madness far behind.

"I'm sorry I snapped at you," he murmured into my hair. "I just hate seeing you with that creep."

I stiffened. Not that John *wasn't* a creep; in fact, he seemed to work pretty hard at sustaining that image. But I'd seen another side to him. He'd stood up for me last night, which was actually pretty remarkable. In a weird way, he'd become one of my only allies.

But telling Daniel that would only provoke another fight. Instead, I said, "He actually told me something really strange today . . ."

It tumbled out of my mouth in a rush: the will, the house, the blind trust. Daniel's frown deepened when I got to the part about Richard and Marion only taking me in for my money.

"Have you called that lawyer yet?" he asked.

I shook my head. "I haven't had a chance. My phone burned up, too."

"There must be a landline here," Daniel mused. "But you might not want a record of the call, in case they check. You can use mine if you want."

I laughed. "Wow. And I thought *I* was paranoid."

His eyes filled with concern. "Think about it, Janie. All this weird stuff has been happening, then you almost die in a fire. And you're sick to your stomach, like, all the time."

I flashed back on John's advice to eat out more. "What, you think they're poisoning me?"

He shrugged. "I know, it sounds nuts. But trust me; I've heard some pretty bad stuff about them. If something happens to you, who gets the money?"

I dropped heavily into a chair and instantly regretted it; water soaked the back of my pants. Cursing, I leapt to my feet. *Could the Rochesters really be that evil?* Trying to kill me seemed beyond the pale, even for Marion. And none of them had looked happy about the damage to their house.

On the other hand, it was confined to my room, which as John had pointed out was kind of weird.

"I'd call your parents' lawyer right away," Daniel advised. "John might've been lying about the trust anyway."

"I don't think he was," I said slowly. "I mean, why would he?"

Daniel grunted. "Because he's John Rochester, and he's a dick."

I chose not to respond. We stood in an uneasy silence for a few beats, then Daniel said, "So should we check the closet and drawers? Maybe some of your clothes are okay."

I nodded, and we set to work. Over the next half hour, we sorted my belongings into three piles: ruined, potentially salvageable, and mostly unscathed.

Almost everything went in the ruined pile. My insides went tight as I took stock; and I hadn't even dealt with the boxes yet. The cardboard stack had caved in on itself, looking like the lumpy remains of a sand castle after the tide had swept in. I wasn't hopeful that anything inside had survived the deluge.

"Hey!" Daniel exclaimed, pulling a hanger out of the closet. "Look what made it!"

It was the dress I'd worn the night of the mixer. I shrugged; it was soot-free, but drooped from the hanger. "It's silk. The water probably damaged it."

"Nah, I've got a great dry cleaner. He can definitely work with this." Daniel smiled at me. "Man, you looked amazing that night. I was almost too scared to talk to you."

"Really?"

"Oh yeah. Fortunately for me, you started choking to death on a quiche."

"Not one of my better moments," I said wryly.

"I was a little bummed that I didn't get to practice the Heimlich," he teased. "I was getting ready to grab you for it."

"Like how you dragged me out of the surf?"

"Exactly. So I've basically saved your life twice now."

"Real-ly," I drawled.

"Yup. You're a total damsel in distress."

I threw a pair of sodden socks at him. He dodged them, then held up the dress. "Hey! Don't make it any worse!"

I laughed and threw another pair, then another. He parried with the dress, batting the socks back toward me. There was a hysterical edge to our banter; the giggles bursting out of me sounded high and strained.

"Janie?"

I turned to find Nicholas standing uncertainly at the door.

"Hey, kiddo," Daniel said, composing himself. "What's up?

"Nothing," Nicholas murmured, eyeing him distrustfully. "Who are you?"

"I'm Daniel. Janie's friend."

Friend, I noted. Not boyfriend. But maybe he just didn't want to confuse the kid. "Hey, Nicholas," I said. "Did you get back to sleep last night?"

He shook his head mournfully. "No. I was crying. I know you think I started the fire, Janie. But I didn't, promise!"

I frowned, startled by the raw emotion in his voice. "Nicholas, I know that."

Tears coursed down his cheeks. "Everyone thinks I did. But it wasn't me this time, it really wasn't!" He spoke in shuddery hiccups.

I crouched down and pulled him into a hug. "Shh, it's okay. No one thinks that."

Over his shoulder, I saw Daniel eyeing us thoughtfully. When I raised my eyebrows at him, he gave a small shake of his head.

"Listen," I said. "Why don't we go downstairs and get some hot cocoa and a snack. Does that sound okay?"

He nodded. I straightened and turned to Daniel.

"Go ahead," he said. "I'll keep sorting through stuff."

I hesitated, picturing him stumbling across my collection of My Little Ponies. But they'd probably melted, anyway.

"All right," I agreed. "I'll be back soon."

I hustled Nicholas downstairs and got him settled at the table with a mug of steaming hot chocolate and a plate of cookies. As I watched him eat an Oreo with studied intensity, Alma appeared. Taking in his tear-streaked face, she waved me away. Yesterday, I would've hesitated at leaving them alone when he was in such a state; but the glimpse of a kinder, gentler Alma was still fresh in my mind.

I hurried back upstairs.

When I came in, Daniel triumphantly held something up to the light. "Look what I found!"

It was Bessie, my ruined doll. I scowled. "Of course *that* survived."

"So what do you want to do with her?" he asked.

The way he was holding her by the leg bothered me more than I liked to admit. Despite how she'd been damaged, I still associated her with some of my happiest childhood memories. Holding her high in the air as I went down a slide, making funny hats for her, clutching her to my chest as my mother tucked me in. Without any siblings to play with, Bessie had been an honored guest at every tea party I'd ever thrown. Now she was just another unwelcome reminder of how much my life had changed.

Decisively, I took Bessie from him and tossed her on top of the ruined pile.

"You're sure?" he asked, examining my expression.

"Yes," I said. "Now can I borrow your phone? I've got a call to make."

Chapter XII

Jane, you are mistaken: probably not one in the school either despises or dislikes you: many, I am sure, pity you much.

I spent another night in Alma's apartment. She didn't sing me to sleep this time, but after dinner we sat together in companionable silence. Alma crocheted an afghan; I labored over my homework. A stack of replacement textbooks and a uniform had been left on the kitchen table. I wondered briefly if Georgina had been charged with bringing them back, then immediately decided that was unlikely. Bob had probably been ordered to collect them.

Included was a handwritten note from Ms. Temple:

Janie—

I was so sorry to hear about what happened! Thank God you're okay. Obviously, I don't expect you to hand in the Virginia Woolf paper on Friday; take as much time as you need with it. And please, let me know if there's anything I can do!

Best,
Maria Temple

It was a sweet offer, but unless she could convince the battle-axes at Hamill to be as understanding, I was pretty much guaranteed to fail this semester. All of my homework had been in the bedroom, either in binders or on my laptop; and none of that was salvageable. Which meant that in a few classes, I'd have to start over from scratch.

Georgina's voice echoed through my mind, dripping with disdain. *Please, Janie. No one actually does the homework.* Guess it was time to test that theory, I thought grimly.

Mr. Briggs, Esq., hadn't been in the office when I'd called; his secretary informed me that he'd be out all week, attending to personal business. When she asked if it was urgent, I'd hesitated, then said no. Daniel had pressed me to call back for his cell number, but I'd refused. Even though I was dying to know if John had been telling the truth, what then? Confront the Rochesters about only taking me in for my money? Accuse them of trying to kill me?

I definitely wasn't eager to have that conversation. It could wait a week.

I got through as much homework as I could, then put the books away.

"Bed?" Alma asked, looking up.

"Yup," I said, stretching my arms above my head and yawning. It was only nine-thirty, but I was wiped out; it felt like I could sleep for days.

She set her knitting needles in her lap and tilted her head. "Good night."

"Good night, Alma. And thanks again." As if by mutual consent, dinner had been a haphazard affair that night: Richard and Marion went out; John, Nicholas, and I ate in the kitchen; and Georgina never showed up at all. I was kind of hoping this would be our new model, and I'd be able to avoid any more tense, multicourse family dramas.

"I'll probably be out of your hair tomorrow," I told her. "Richard said they're working on getting a new room ready for me upstairs."

The wrinkles in Alma's forehead deepened, and she said firmly, "You stay here now. Not upstairs."

"Um . . ." I hedged. I was pretty sure that Marion would have something to say about me sleeping in the maid's quarters, whether she wanted me in her house or not. "Thanks so much, that's really kind of you. But I think—"

"Here," Alma barked. Then she set back to work with her needles, signaling the end of the discussion.

Up until last night, I'd have ranked Alma alongside Marion as the least likely to let me onto a lifeboat. Her abrupt turnaround was perplexing, but I was too tired to argue. I went into her spare room and changed into the pajamas, which I noticed she'd laundered for me. I climbed between the sheets and fluffed the pillows.

My fingers brushed against something tucked against the headboard. Frowning, I drew it out: another of Alma's pouches, although this one smelled marginally less offensive. I regarded it for a minute, debating. Then I slipped it back under the pillow and shut off the light.

WHEN I ENTERED THE kitchen the next morning, Richard was perched on a barstool shoveling scrambled eggs into his mouth.

"Janie!" he exclaimed cheerfully. "I was hoping we'd get the chance to have breakfast together."

"Great," I said cautiously, setting down my new backpack as I pulled out the barstool beside him. Grace, the cook—an obese woman with a halo of frizzy brown hair and a permanent frown—scraped eggs onto a plate and set it in front of me.

Eat out more, John's voice warned.

Even though I was starving, I just pushed the eggs around. If I hurried, I could grab something in the cafeteria before class. And that would spare me from having to make awkward conversation with Richard, too.

On closer examination, his eyes were bloodshot, his skin

riddled with burst capillaries: sure signs of an alcoholic. I wondered if there was more than juice in his glass.

"Mmm, yummy," I said unconvincingly. "But I better get going. I'm really behind after missing school yesterday."

Richard frowned. "You've barely touched your eggs."

"That's okay. I'm not really hungry."

He sipped from his glass, smacked his lips, then said, "We should take a minute to discuss your sleeping arrangements."

"Oh, yeah. Actually, Alma invited me to use her spare bedroom," I said. "I think it's perfect." *And far away from the attic,* I added silently.

"You want to stay with Alma?" he said quizzically, as if he'd forgotten I'd been sleeping there.

"Sure. I mean, if that's okay with you."

Richard squinted at me, as if trying to determine whether or not I was serious. "You really don't mind?"

"No," I said truthfully. "It's perfect."

"All right, then," he said. "I guess that's settled."

"Great."

"Oh, and this is for you." He pulled something out of his pocket and slid it across the counter toward me: a black credit card, identical to the one Georgina used. It had my name printed on it, directly above "The Rochester Family Trust."

"Wow," I said without picking it up. "That's really nice of you."

"Of course," Richard said expansively. "I meant to get it for you before, but it slipped my mind. Now you'll need it, to replace your clothing and such." He covered my hand with his and continued, "And Janie, don't feel obligated to stay within a budget. You buy whatever you want. I insist."

"That's awesome," I said without conviction. "Really, really great. Thanks again."

Richard nodded, but there was uncertainty in his eyes. He'd probably expected more enthusiasm; Georgina would be gushing and simpering. My lackluster response was clearly off-putting.

As I tucked the card in the outer pocket of my backpack, all I could think was, *Thanks for giving me access to my own money. Big of you.* I slung the pack over my shoulder and started to leave, but a sudden swell of rage stopped me. I hesitated on the threshold, then said with forced casualness, "This is from my trust, right?"

Richard stiffened. He drew himself up and asked, "What trust would that be?"

"The one my grandparents left me," I said, meeting his gaze.

He regarded me intently for a minute, and then said, "I suppose your lawyer discussed that with you."

I didn't respond; no need to sell out John unless I had to. And Briggs probably *had* said something; it just hadn't penetrated my veil of grief at the time.

"Well," Richard finally continued. "Yes, I believe your card is linked to that account."

"Good to know," I said breezily. "Hopefully it's the only one."

"What's that supposed to mean?" Richard asked, looking taken aback.

"Nothing. I was just thinking, it's kind of weird that I haven't seen any statements yet. Maybe I'll call the bank after school to make sure everything is cool. Anyway, have a great day!"

As I climbed into the Town Car, Richard's expression still hovered in the air before me: a mix of surprise, rage, and fear.

I might have just made another enemy, I thought, biting my lip. Maybe it had been stupid, confronting him like that. After all, despite the way he treated the rest of his family, Richard was always nice to me.

Well, it's not like it could get any worse, I decided, settling back against the seats.

Had I only known then how wrong I was.

I CHEWED ON A bagel as I hurried down the hall toward chemistry class. Miss Scatcherd had threatened to give me detention if I showed up late again, and I wasn't about to spend a minute longer than necessary at Hamill. I skidded to a stop inside the lab with a minute to spare. Miss Scatcherd frowned at my stuffed cheeks, but she didn't say anything. I hustled to my desk at the back of the room.

Diana Reed, my lab partner, was already sitting at the table we shared.

"Phew," I whispered as I sat down. "Barely made it. Hope we don't have anything tough today."

Diana didn't answer. In fact, she made a big show of getting up and sliding her stool away.

I eyed her, puzzled. We weren't exactly besties, but we'd always gotten along well enough. But Diana studiously avoided my gaze, as if I'd offended her somehow. I shrugged it off. Thankfully, we didn't have any experiments in class that day; Miss Scatcherd spent the entire period scratching out formulas on the whiteboard while droning on about catalysts.

Diana practically ran from the room as soon as the bell rang. I followed slowly, clutching my books to my chest. Was it my imagination, or was everyone staring at me as I made my way down the hall? Frankly, I much preferred them acting like I was invisible.

"Janie!" Helen appeared at my elbow and tugged on my sleeve. "We need to talk."

"I'm late for class," I said.

"It can't wait," Helen insisted, dragging me into a corner. The crowd around us dispersed as the bell rang; lockers slammed shut, and loafers squeaked against tile.

"What is it?" I asked. My math teacher wasn't quite as horrible as Miss Scatcherd, but close.

"Listen," she said, speaking quickly. "Georgina is spreading all sorts of terrible rumors about you."

I snorted. "Shocking. That's not exactly a surprise, right?"

Helen hesitated, biting her lip. "They're like really, *really* terrible though."

My stomach started churning, making me regret eating the bagel. "You might as well tell me. It can't be worse than what I'm imagining, right?"

"That depends on your imagination."

The last bell rang; I was officially late. "Let me guess, she's claiming I started the fire."

"Worse than that," Helen said in an anxious whisper. "She's saying that you tried to kill yourself."

"What!" I gasped. A storm started to build in my chest.

"She's telling everyone that you're trailer trash, that you were basically a crack baby and her parents took you on as a charity case. But you've been suicidal, because . . ." She swallowed, seeing my expression. "You're sure you want to know?"

"Tell me," I said. "All of it."

In a rush, Helen continued, "She's saying that your addict parents blew up in a meth lab explosion."

I leaned against the wall, breathing hard. A tide of red rose before my eyes. It was one thing for Georgina to spread rumors about me; that I'd been prepared for. But maligning my wonderful, sweet, hardworking parents?

I was barely aware that my feet were moving. Helen said something, but the words sounded far away, and I couldn't make sense of them. The backpack slid from my shoulders and landed on the ground; I left it.

I didn't get angry often. I was like my dad that way; most things slid off me like water. But when something incited my rage, I went to a whole other place.

Helen caught up and trotted alongside me, but the roar in my ears continued to drown her out.

I found Georgina sitting on a bench in the courtyard, surrounded by three other girls. She looked up, her eyes narrowing at the sight of me.

"Janie, I really think—" Helen pleaded with me.

I brushed off her arm and kept marching forward. When

I was a foot away, Georgina sneered, "Well, if it isn't crazy Janie."

My hands clenched into fists at my sides. Fiercely, I said, "You're going to tell everyone it's not true."

Georgina casually sipped her diet soda. "Why, Janie, you can't expect me to keep lying to protect you."

"Say whatever you want about me," I spat. "But don't you *dare* talk about my parents."

"It's a shame, really," Georgina said to her friends, as if I weren't there. "I heard her dad was pretty hot. Can't believe he threw his life away on that whore. Guess he was too high to care."

From far away, I heard her friends laughing. Helen still beseeching me. But the whole world had narrowed to a pinpoint, just Georgina and me. More than anything, I wanted to wipe the smirk off her face.

So I slapped her, hard.

The sound of it rang out like a gunshot. The imprint of my hand on her cheek was bright red. Georgina's eyes went wide, and she reached up to touch her face.

I'd never been in a fight before, had never hit anyone. The shock of slapping her had quelled my rage, and I reeled back, stunned by what I'd done.

But it was too late. Georgina's features twisted and she lunged to her feet. She shoved me hard with both hands, sending me flying into the wall. Then she grabbed a clump of my hair, making me howl in pain. As I tried to bat her away, her nails raked my cheek.

Desperately, I fought back, but she was stronger than I would ever have imagined. Screeching like a creature possessed, she slammed my head against the wall so hard it rang from the impact.

From across a great void, I could hear the other girls' voices, shrill with panic. She grabbed my head again, and I frantically reached out, trying to block her. My hands locked around her throat. Georgina tried to shake me off, but I tightened my grip. I was consumed by one thought: I needed to make her stop hurting me.

"You're . . . choking . . . me . . ." she gasped.

The tide in my ears receded, and I became aware of the clamor of people around us. Just as I was releasing my grip, someone yanked me from behind. I flew backwards and landed hard.

"Off!" a voice below me growled.

I rolled to my side and discovered Miss Scatcherd beneath me, her face tight with pain and anger. I scrambled to my feet.

"I told you she was crazy!" Georgina screamed. Two girls stood on either side supporting her. She was bent double, clutching her throat with one hand and pointing at me with the other, tears streaming down her face. "She tried to kill me!"

I turned in a slow circle. A half dozen girls stood around us in shocked silence. Helen was among them, looking stunned.

"I—I'm sorry," I stammered. "But she—"

"You'll be even sorrier, young lady," Miss Scatcherd interrupted, lumbering to her feet. Stray hairs exploded from her bun, and her skirt was crooked. She straightened it, glowering. "That is *not* how a Hamill girl behaves."

"Janie? What's going on?" Ms. Temple appeared on the periphery of the group. Two girls parted to let her through. Her brow knit as she took in the scene. "Is everything all right?"

"Everything is most certainly *not* all right." Miss Scatcherd snapped. "She attacked Georgina! If I hadn't shown up when I did, who knows what would have happened?"

Ms. Temple searched my eyes.

"It was her, too!" I protested. "I didn't—"

"She should be arrested!" Georgina sobbed, cutting me off. "I want her arrested!"

"We need to inform Mr. Brocklehurst," Miss Scatcherd said. "Young lady, go to his office immediately."

"I'll take her in a few minutes, after she calms down," Ms. Temple said, wrapping an arm around my shoulders. "Come with me, Janie."

"That is not acceptable," Miss Scatcherd protested. "Maria, this girl is dangerous."

Ms. Temple drew herself up and said, "I very much doubt that. Tell Mr. Brocklehurst that we'll be in my office."

She led me away. Everyone studiously avoided my eyes as I walked past, including Helen. I stumbled slightly, and Ms. Temple's hand tightened on my shoulder, steadying me. Now that the storm had dissipated, a sense of calm settled over me. I probably *would* be expelled over this; Georgina would see to that. She might be able to have me arrested, too; after all, I'd started it.

"Easy, Janie," Ms. Temple said in a low voice. "We're almost there."

I realized that tears were streaming down my cheeks, making the scratches smart. I wiped them away with my hand, stiffly following her into a tiny office. Ms. Temple shut the door behind us and plugged in an electric kettle.

"I'm sorry," I croaked. "I didn't mean to hit her. But she said all these terrible things about my mom and dad, and I just . . . I went a little crazy."

Sobs wracked my body. Ms. Temple sat across from me and rubbed my forearms, consoling me. "Poor Janie," she said sympathetically. "I know this has been a difficult transition for you."

In my mind's eye I saw Georgina's face again, that sly smirk. I started crying harder.

"Here." Ms. Temple handed me a mug of tea. My hands were shaking badly, though; the tea spilled out and burned my hand, making me wince. She quickly took it back. "In a minute, then. After you calm down."

"What are they going to do to me?" I asked in a low voice, once I'd summoned a modicum of control.

Ms. Temple didn't answer immediately; the concern in her eyes was clear. "Honestly, I don't know. Nothing like this has ever happened here, at least not during my tenure."

I sank farther into the chair.

"Can I offer some advice, Janie?" Ms. Temple asked. She was leaning forward with an earnest expression. "Granted, I don't know you well. But based on your writing, it's clear that you're a sensitive person who's been through a lot. Losing your parents, moving in with strangers, and then surviving a fire; those are all extremely traumatic events."

I drew in a deep, shuddering breath. She didn't know the half of it. "I shouldn't have hurt her, though."

"No, you shouldn't have," she agreed. "But given the circumstances, I believe it's understandable."

"Thank you," I said in a small voice.

"I also believe that you're stronger than this. And in the end, you're going to be just fine." She took my hand and squeezed it.

I wanted to share her optimism, but at the moment, I felt a long way from fine.

The door popped open.

Mr. Brocklehurst, the headmaster, blocked the opening with his wide girth. I could see Miss Scatcherd peering hungrily over his shoulder.

"Janie Mason," he said sharply. "Come with me, right now."

"Could she just wait until she's had her tea?" Ms. Temple asked. "It might help—"

"Now."

Shakily, I got to my feet. He waited at the door, as if worried that I'd bolt.

"Thank you. For everything," I said.

Ms. Temple nodded, her face creased with worry. "Of course, Janie. I'm here if you need me."

As Mr. Brocklehurst frog-marched me down the hall, he said, "We've called your guardians. They're coming to collect you."

"Am I expelled?" I asked in a meek voice.

"That will be decided later," he said. "But I think it's best that you spend the next few days at home."

Miss Scatcherd was still scurrying in our wake; I heard her cluck reprovingly. My feet dragged as we approached his office. *Jail might actually be preferable,* I thought. At least there, I'd have a chance to get some sleep.

Chapter XIII

Something of vengeance I had tasted for the first time; as aromatic wine it seemed, on swallowing, warm and racy: its after-flavour, metallic and corroding, gave me a sensation as if I had been poisoned.

Marion sat as far from me in the car as possible without actually being outside of it. She hadn't said a word since "collecting" me from Mr. Brocklehurst. They'd spent ten minutes together behind closed doors. Then she'd swept out, her high heels clacking loudly against the parquet floors. She motioned for me to follow as she led the way to the Town Car.

I was feeling resentful that Georgina hadn't been punished, too. Sure, I'd started the fight, but she was the one who'd gone for blood. Bob kept shooting me sympathetic glances in the rear-view mirror. I sank down in the seat, arms crossed over my chest. Waiting for Marion to say something was wearing at my nerves.

Finally, unable to bear the tense silence a moment longer, I said, "I'm really sorry."

The thin line of Marion's lips stretched tauter, but she didn't respond. She continued gazing out the window, clearly set on ignoring me. As always, she was immaculately dressed in navy and white, her nails painted to match her beige purse.

I sighed and tilted my head back. Well, at least the cops hadn't shown up. Yet.

When we passed our street, I sat up straight. "We're not going home?"

Marion made a noise in the back of her throat, but maintained the silent treatment. Bob kept driving. After a few minutes, we passed the limits of Pacific Heights, leaving behind the regal homes that lorded over the rest of the city. Bob turned left, heading downtown, and I frowned. "Where are we going?"

"I should've done this years ago," Marion said quietly, as if to herself. "Years."

"Years?" I asked, confused. "But I haven't even known you—"

Her head snapped toward me. "You were always a problem. I didn't want you, but Richard insisted. His house, his child, his rules. What I wanted was irrelevant. Did he care about my feelings? How it made me look? The things that people said. They thought I couldn't hear them, but I could. I've always known what they were saying about me."

I stared back at her, spooked. Marion had a deranged look in her eyes. I remembered how she'd stared at me in the hallway a couple of weeks ago, that weird mantra she'd been repeating. Since then, she'd seemed normal, mostly. But maybe she was just good at feigning sanity.

"Almost there, ma'am," Bob said from the front seat. "Unless you've changed your mind?"

"Bob, where are we going?" I asked, edging toward the front seat.

His eyes flicked to me; he looked worried. But he didn't respond.

"Marion, what's happening?" I said, my voice rising.

"Ask Richard," she said, as her fingers tapped out an agitated rhythm on her purse strap. "Richard always has all the answers. My opinion doesn't matter. It never has."

"What answers?" I demanded.

"Too many questions," Marion muttered. "You ask too many questions. We need to take care of that."

A seed of fear sprouted in my gut. I flashed back on Richard's reaction when I'd grilled him about the trust. Was this some sort of retaliation for that?

The car swept up a wide driveway, coming to a stop in front of a squat, red brick building. I squinted at the sign posted by the entrance. "SF General? Why are we at the hospital?"

Marion had turned away, staring off into the distance. When Bob opened the door, she climbed out and beckoned for me to follow.

She must be dragging me to some charity event. Although it was weird that she wouldn't make me wait in the car with Bob. My steps slowed as we approached the entrance. A young man in white scrubs held the door open. I hesitated on the threshold, suddenly filled with foreboding.

"Come!" Marion ordered impatiently, as if I were a misbehaving lapdog.

The dread increased as I followed her inside. It was a standard waiting room, with uncomfortable-looking plastic chairs, a drooping ficus, and a reception desk behind a glass window. Two other men in white scrubs stood in the center of the room, flanking a goateed man in a tweed suit. Clasping a clipboard to his chest, he smiled and said deferentially, "Mrs. Rochester. I wanted to be here to greet you personally."

"This is her," Marion said, waving a hand back without looking in my direction. "What do you need me to sign?"

He handed her the clipboard. She skimmed the contents, then held out her hand for a pen.

"Um, what's happening here?" I asked warily.

Unless I was mistaken, the men in white had inched closer, forming a human wall.

No one answered; they acted as if I wasn't even there.

"Is that all?" Marion asked imperiously.

The goateed man bowed his head, then said, "Of course, if you have a few minutes, we were hoping to discuss our annual fund with you—"

"Send me the prospectus," she interjected, cutting him off.

Then she turned and headed toward the door without a backward glance.

"Wait!" I said, moving to follow. "Marion, what's—hey!"

One of the men had grabbed my arm to stop me from leaving. I tried to shake him off, but he clenched it tightly, glaring down at me.

"Stay calm, miss," he said in a low voice. "We don't want to have a problem."

"Get off me!" I protested. "Marion, what's happening?"

But she was gone, the door already shutting behind her.

"Miss Rochester?"

I turned. The goateed man was bent forward slightly at the waist, regarding me with a wan smile. "Who are you?"

"I'm Dr. Lloyd. Do you know where you are?"

"SF General," I said, still trying to shake off the creep's hand. "And so far I'm not loving it."

"You're here to get better," he said, using the sort of tone you'd employ to calm a small child.

"Oh my God," I said, realization dawning. "Is this a nuthouse?"

Dr. Lloyd frowned at that. He cleared his throat and said, "Don't worry, Eliza. We're going to take very good care of you."

IN MY WORST NIGHTMARES, I'd never imagined a place like this. When I thought of asylums, I pictured battered green doors, the air constantly rent by shrieks and babbling.

In reality, the silence was so much worse.

After Marion left, I did go a little crazy. It took all three orderlies to drag me kicking and screaming into the ward. Dr. Lloyd followed at a safe distance, brandishing his clipboard as if it were a shield. I was forcibly escorted into a tiny room where they held me down and injected me with something.

Instantly, numbness seeped through my veins. The tingling

sensation spread, wrapping my body in a tight cocoon. My head suddenly weighed a hundred pounds; it was almost impossible to hold it upright.

"There, now. Isn't that better?" Dr. Lloyd said soothingly, leaning over me. "We're here to help you, Eliza."

"I'm not Eliza." The words came out thick and slurred.

He patted my knee and said, "Why don't you get some rest. We'll have plenty of time to talk later."

The rest of the day took place underwater. I was dimly aware of being wheeled down a seemingly endless corridor. We stopped in front of a slate gray door with a thin, narrow window above the handle. One of the orderlies opened it, and another wheeled me inside.

A plain room: literally just a mattress on a molded plastic platform. No windows, no other doors. They helped me onto the bed. I lay there stiffly, unable to protest; it felt as if my tongue had swollen to several times the normal size. I pictured it protruding from my mouth, continuing to grow until it lay on top of my chest, flapping there. The thought struck me as funny, but I couldn't laugh, either. It was like they'd bottled up everything inside me and screwed the stopper shut.

The events of the past few months swirled past. It was like being on a carousel that was spinning too fast: I saw the fortune-teller and Nicholas, the beach and Georgina twirling in front of a mirror. Daniel and the little rubber ball. Every time I tried to latch onto an image, it vanished, and another swept into view.

I must have slept, because when I awoke the lights had dimmed. So either it was nighttime, or they did this to keep people calm.

Mental patients, I told myself. *And they think* I'm *one of them.*

At least my mind had cleared somewhat. I cautiously sat up. It took a minute for the room to stop spinning. My head throbbed, and my throat was dry and parched. I was no longer wearing my Hamill uniform; I was in a plain smock and thick cotton socks.

Someone had stripped off my clothing. I visualized the orderlies putting their hands all over me and shuddered.

I was dying for some water. I shuffled slowly toward the door, one hand against the wall to steady myself. Once there, I cupped both hands around my eyes and peered through the tiny window; the corridor outside was dim, too, and there was no one in sight. It was so quiet, my breathing sounded abnormally loud. It felt like I was the last person on earth, like I'd been forgotten here, abandoned.

Suddenly consumed by a wave of terror, I rapped on the window with my fist. After a minute of pounding, a young nurse hurried down the corridor wearing scrubs; at the sight of her, my knees nearly gave out with relief.

"Step back from the door, please," she said in a muffled voice. The room must be soundproofed; that's why it was so quiet.

An orderly appeared past her shoulder, looming threateningly. Obediently I stepped back, determined to prove my sanity.

The nurse opened the door and stepped inside. She was pretty, with dark hair and light eyes. She handed me two small cups: one held two pills, the other was filled with water.

"Meds," she said in a business-like tone.

"There's been a mistake." My voice came out raspy and harsh. "I'm not crazy."

She nodded as if expecting that response, and motioned toward the pills. "These will help you sleep."

"I don't need to sleep!" As my voice rose, the orderly edged closer. I forced some control into the words as I said, "Please, you have to understand. There's been a mistake. Marion, the woman who dropped me off? *She's* crazy. My name isn't even Eliza."

The nurse sighed and crossed her arms over her chest. "Listen, honey. If you don't take the pills, we give you a shot instead. Your choice."

I stared at her, but she just watched me impassively. After a minute, I tilted the dixie cup, dumping the contents into my mouth: the pills tasted chalky. I grimaced, tucking them under my tongue as I sipped the water.

"Open," she ordered.

I hesitated, then opened my mouth.

"Lift your tongue." The nurse sounded bored, like this was a task she was forced to repeat far too frequently. Begrudgingly, I lifted my tongue, revealing the pills. She raised an eyebrow and tilted her head. "So the shot, then?"

I shook my head and sipped more water. Opened my mouth wide and lolled my tongue defiantly back and forth to show that I'd swallowed them.

"Good," she said approvingly. "Now get some rest."

"Could I get some more water?" I pleaded. "I'm so thirsty. And I have to pee."

The nurse grumbled under her breath, but led me down a corridor. Humiliated, I went to the bathroom while she stood over me, eyes averted. I washed my hands in the sink and splashed water on my face: no mirror, which was probably a good thing; I really didn't want to see how I looked right now.

I drank three glasses of water, refilling my cup from the faucet. "This is the last bathroom break of the night," the nurse warned. "I hope you don't have a small bladder."

"I'll be fine," I said, although my legs had gone wobbly again.

The nurse called for the orderly, and the two of them helped me back to bed.

As I drifted off to sleep, I could've sworn that someone was huddled beside me, rocking back and forth as she hummed.

"Alma," I whispered. "Is that you?"

But nobody answered.

"YOUR MOTHER TOLD ME that you've been trying to hurt your twin brother. Is that true, Eliza?" Dr. Lloyd asked.

I rolled my eyes. This would almost be funny if it wasn't so horribly real and terrifying. We were sitting in my room. While it wasn't padded, it was definitely a cell. When I woke up, they'd forced me to take two more of the pills that inflated my tongue and wrapped my brain in wool; then Dr. Lloyd had appeared, with his clipboard and ridiculous questions. "I don't have a brother."

He nodded as his pen scratched across a legal pad. "What about sisters?"

"No. Listen, Dr. Lloyd. Marion is the one who's crazy. Her daughter Eliza is dead. She died last year, when she was five years old."

Scratch scratch. I wondered what he was writing. I was caught in a weird catch-22; in order to convince him I wasn't crazy, I'd have to make him believe that everything Marion had told him was a lie. And based on the reception she'd gotten yesterday, he was probably more interested in her checkbook than anything I had to say.

Her checkbook that was filled with *my* money.

At the thought, a surge of rage punched through the fog, and I clenched my fists. Apparently noticing, Dr. Lloyd's eyes flicked to the orderly standing guard at the door. I drew a deep breath and forced myself to relax. I had to get out of here. Then I'd deal with Marion. Mr. Briggs was going to get an earful when he got back from vacation.

"You've been hearing things?" he asked, scrutinizing me.

"Well, yes," I acknowledged. "But I found out what that was—"

"Was it voices?"

I shook my head forcefully; telling him about the attic noises, and the balls of light, would only serve to make me a permanent resident here. I had to come up with a way to convince him this was all a mistake. "Listen. Do I *look* like I could possibly be Marion's daughter? She and Richard are both white."

He sat back and put his pen down. The flicker of doubt in his eyes spurred me on. "My name is Janie Mason. I only met the Rochesters a few months ago, when my parents were killed in a helicopter crash in Hawaii. Marion Rochester is not my mother, and she had no right to bring me here."

Dr. Lloyd tapped the pen against his pad, eyeing me reflectively. He didn't say a word.

"You can look it up!" I said, desperation in my voice. "Eliza's death, and the chopper accident. All you have to do is search the Internet. Or call Richard . . ."

At that, my voice trailed off. It was possible that Richard was involved in all this; he might have given his approval. And if so, where did that leave me? Could they keep me here, drugged into a stupor, indefinitely?

What would happen to the money then?

Maybe this was the plan all along; they'd just been waiting for an opportunity to present itself. And attacking Georgina had provided the perfect excuse. I wondered if anyone would even bother to look for me; and if they did, could I be found? Committing me under the name "Eliza Rochester" had actually been a stroke of brilliance. Maybe Marion wasn't so crazy after all.

Daniel and Helen would ask questions, but they were just a couple of teenagers. Kaila, maybe, or her mom? But what could they do from the Big Island? I'd been living here for months, yet I was still completely alone in every way that mattered.

"Is there something else, Eliza?" Dr. Lloyd asked gently.

"Stop calling me that," I muttered, examining my hands. "I told you, my name is *Janie.*"

Dr. Lloyd blinked at me. Finally, he said, "We can talk more later. You should get some rest."

After he left the room, I curled up in a ball on the bed.

Once again, I found myself incapable of tears, but this time it was thanks to the medication. *How was I supposed to prove that I wasn't crazy?*

I wrapped my arms around the pillow, hugging it to my chest. I wanted my parents. Both of them, alive and well. I wanted them to show up at the door and take me home, where we'd eat a pizza and watch a stupid movie and then sit outside and stare at the stars until it was time to go to bed. We'd spent hundreds of nights like that, and I hadn't really appreciated any of them. I thought of all the times I'd rushed through dinner, in a hurry to meet up with my friends. My parents would stand at the front door waving as I climbed into a car and drove away.

I wish I'd never left them. If I could go back, I'd spend every waking moment with them; I'd tell them every day how much I loved them, and that I never wanted to be without them again.

I MUST'VE DOZED OFF at some point, although I couldn't say for how long. I was awakened by the sound of the door opening. I closed my eyes, feigning sleep; was it already time for another dose? I was so tired of the pills. I'd never felt so heavy and deadened before in my entire life.

"Janie?" A voice asked uncertainly.

I jerked upright; Richard Rochester was standing in the doorway, flanked by orderlies. He had a wool coat slung over his arm, and looked hopelessly out of place. Even more incongruously, Alma was peeking around him. She frowned at the sight of me and muttered something in Filipino.

"Oh, thank God!" I exclaimed, jumping to my feet. The room spun, and I nearly toppled forward. Gripping my head with both hands, I carefully sat back down and said, "Marion went totally nuts and checked me in here!"

Richard's expression was unreadable.

All at once I was afraid; was he here to save me? Or to slam the door shut forever?

"Marion overreacted," he finally said. "She's very upset by what you did to Georgina. And frankly, so am I."

I wilted a little at his stern tone. "I'm really sorry about that. She was spreading rumors about my parents, and I just . . . freaked out."

He grunted but didn't move from the door.

"She tried to hurt me, too." My hands moved to the scratches on my cheek. They were covered in ointment; someone must have treated them while I was unconscious. "See? She did this."

"I'm sure Georgie was just defending herself," Richard said dismissively.

My spirits sank further; it didn't sound like he was here to save the day.

Alma pushed past him. She crossed to the bed and took my chin in her hand, turning my head from one side to the other. "They hurt you?"

I shook my head and said in a small voice, "No. But they keep making me take drugs." Finally, the tears came. I let them course down my cheeks, sniffling as I said, "I'm so scared. I can't stay here. Please, take me home."

I sounded pathetic, reduced to begging, but I didn't care. Anything to get out of this place.

Richard seemed discomfited by my tears. He looked past me at the blank wall, and said, "Well, it's a little tricky, Janie. I can't just walk you out of here."

"Why not?" I demanded, panic rising in my chest.

"Once someone has been committed, there's a lengthy legal process to get them released." He patted his jacket, still avoiding my eyes. "I've been in touch with our lawyer, and he's assured me that he's doing all he can."

"But . . . wait!" I protested as he turned to go. Alma stayed where she was, her hand on my arm. "There has to be something you can do!"

"I'm sorry," he said. "But this will take some time."

"How much time? Days?" When he didn't respond, I said incredulously, "Weeks?"

"I'm sure it won't be too long." He glanced around the room. "And this place doesn't seem so bad. Think of it as a little vacation. Hell, we could probably all use some therapy, right?"

"But, Richard—"

"This might actually be for the best," he interrupted brusquely. "Give things a chance to settle down at home. And you'll have some time to think."

He started pulling his jacket on. A fresh wave of terror consumed me. I scrambled to my feet and crossed the room quickly, grabbing hold of his arm. "Please!" I pleaded. "If you leave me here for that long, I really might go nuts."

There was an odd gleam in Richard's eyes. I suddenly realized that he was enjoying this; he liked having complete power over me. I let go of his arm and stepped back. He wasn't here to help me; he was here to gloat.

Which meant it was up to me. I willfully ignored the sensation that the walls were closing in, fighting back the claustrophobia. My brain still felt sluggish and slow; I knew I was missing something important, but it bobbed just out of reach. I squeezed my eyes shut, trying to focus.

Finally, it came to me. "Have you met my doctor yet?"

"Dr. Lloyd? Yes. He seems very competent."

"Could we talk to him together, before you leave?"

Richard frowned, but I could see him wavering. Touching his arm again, I said in the most plaintive voice I could muster, "Please, Richard? It would mean so much to me."

That gleam again. He nodded curtly and said, "Of course, Janie. If it would make you feel better."

I perched on the edge of the bed, plastering a pathetic expression on my face while we waited. The three of us made an odd tableau: Alma frowning at the floor, me staring at a wall, Richard eyeing the door.

Fortunately, we didn't have to wait long; Dr. Lloyd appeared less than five minutes after we sent an orderly to find him. Sounding slightly out of breath, he said, "So sorry for the delay, Mr. Rochester. I was with another patient."

"Of course, Jim," Richard said with an easy smile. "Thanks for joining us. Janie has some questions for you." Glancing at his watch, he added, "We'll have to make it quick, though. I have dinner plans."

I held my breath, praying that he'd caught it. *There:* a flicker in Dr. Lloyd's eye, and a sudden tightness at the corners of his mouth.

Hesitantly, he asked, "I'm sorry, did you just say *Janie?*"

Richard looked puzzled. "Of course. Jane Mason. We're her legal guardians. But that should all have been in the paperwork that Marion . . ." As his eyes widened with understanding, I felt a surge of smug satisfaction.

Before he could cover with an explanation, I jumped in. "See? I wasn't lying. My name isn't Eliza."

"Well, I'm not entirely sure that's relevant," Richard said hastily.

"This is Janie," Alma said forcefully, stepping toward Dr. Lloyd. "Janie Mason. Now let her go."

"I'm sorry, I'm confused." Dr. Lloyd was blinking rapidly, like someone pulled abruptly from a dream. He was probably picturing a huge donation retreating in the distance. "*Why* was she committed under a different name?"

"A silly mistake," Richard growled. "But it shouldn't—"

"It certainly does." A note of righteous indignation entered Lloyd's voice. "A patient *must* enter under their legal name. This is very serious—"

"My driver's license," I interrupted. "It's in my wallet, in that backpack you took from me. It has my name and picture on it. My school ID is in there, too."

They both stared at me for a second. Dr. Lloyd motioned to an orderly and said something in a voice too low for me to hear. I reflexively clenched and released my hands at my sides, praying that they wouldn't find a loophole.

Five minutes later the orderly returned, holding my backpack by one strap.

At the sight of it, I released all the air in my chest.

"It's in the front pouch," I said.

Still looking put out, Dr. Lloyd opened the pack and removed my wallet. His eyes narrowed as he held my license up to the light, tilting it as though he doubted the authenticity. After a close examination, he turned to Richard Rochester and said accusingly, "According to her license, this is Jane Mason."

Richard returned the doctor's glare. "I never said it wasn't."

"Your wife did," Dr. Lloyd said pointedly. "On every document she signed, this patient is listed as Eliza Rochester. There are severe penalties for falsifying those documents, Mr. Rochester."

I felt giddy; was it possible that I'd walk out of here? Alma seemed to think so. Picking her purse up off the bed, she said firmly, "We go now."

Dr. Lloyd's eyes flicked to her, then me. He didn't look pleased.

"Get Miss Mason's clothes," he told the orderly. "And bring me the papers. We'll process her release immediately."

I let out a choked laugh of relief. "Oh, my God. Thank you."

"I want to extend my deepest apologies," Dr. Lloyd said in a completely different tone, stepping toward me. "Miss Mason, this has obviously been a tremendous mistake."

The fear was plain in his eyes, and I suddenly realized that this was probably grounds for a huge lawsuit. I ignored the hand he was extending and said coldly, "I'm glad you finally decided to listen to me."

"Yes, well, patients usually don't think they belong here . . . I couldn't have known," he stammered, "Nothing like this has *ever* happened before. If there's anything we can do—"

"There is. Make sure I'm walking out of here in less than five minutes."

Richard Rochester hadn't moved. In a voice thick with suppressed rage, he said, "Well, Janie. Looks like you'll be coming back with us after all."

While it would have felt really good to scream at him, I didn't want to give them an excuse to keep me here. Instead I said stiffly, "I just want to get changed and go home."

"Of course," Dr. Lloyd said, with the same cloying obsequiousness. "Right this way."

I walked down the corridor rigidly, trying to control the tremors in my legs. Now that freedom was so close, I was terrified that it would be snatched away again if I didn't hurry. I changed quickly in the same bathroom I'd used the night before. Back in the corridor, I found them all waiting in stilted silence. After Richard and I signed some papers, Dr. Lloyd led us out through a double set of locked doors.

Standing at the top of a small flight of stairs, I inhaled deeply. It was early evening, and the moon was a flaming orange ball on the horizon. It was hard to trust that I was actually free of that horrible place. Alma took my arm, helping me to the waiting car. Bob caught my eye as he opened the rear passenger door and threw me a wink.

I ignored him. He'd driven me here, and had done nothing to stop Marion. Which put him on the list of people I didn't trust.

Richard sat in the front passenger seat. As the car pulled out of the driveway, he said gruffly, "We still have to decide what to do with you. After what happened, I'm not entirely comfortable with having you stay at the house."

"She sleep with me," Alma piped up.

Richard shifted in his seat but didn't turn to look at us. "Georgina won't be happy."

"I'll apologize," I said. Not that it would make a difference, but still; I regretted attacking her. And I had bigger enemies to worry about now. As I'd just learned, Marion and Richard could do a lot more damage.

"That might not be enough," Richard grumbled.

I almost laughed. They'd committed me to a mental institution, and *my* apology wouldn't suffice?

As the car maneuvered through traffic, headed back uptown,

we lapsed into silence. My senses felt oddly heightened; my eyes hungrily scanned the buildings and streets, taking in the world I'd been abruptly removed from.

My mind still felt wooly at the edges, but as we drew closer to the house, it shifted into another gear. Daniel was right; these were some truly scary people. If the Rochesters had their way, I might not last another month.

Now that their initial plan had failed, they'd be scrambling to come up with an alternative. Remembering the fire, I shuddered; now I didn't have any doubt that they'd torched their own house. Maybe the elevator incident had been an attempt on my life, too.

It was probably a bad idea to go back there at all.

I eyed Richard Rochester's profile. *How far would he go to get his hands on my money?* I needed to get in touch with Mr. Briggs and tell him what was going on; there had to be *something* he could do.

As the house rose up before us, I felt myself quail. I really didn't want to go back inside. The sense of a malevolent presence was back, and this time I couldn't dismiss it. This was a dangerous place, filled with people who wanted to do me harm. And I felt hopelessly incapable of stopping them.

It was almost funny that up until now, I'd been afraid that something supernatural was out to get me. In reality, the flesh and blood people were much more dangerous.

It'll be okay, I told myself. *Now that you know what's going on, they won't get the best of you again.*

If only I could believe that.

Chapter XIV

Glorious discovery to a lonely wretch! This was wealth indeed!—wealth to the heart!—a mine of pure, genial affections.

The house was dark when we pulled into the driveway. I climbed out and waited for Alma. Being held in a room without windows, I'd lost all sense of time. I'd attacked Georgina on a Thursday, so this was . . . Friday night? Or Saturday?

"What day is it?" I asked.

"Friday. The rest of the family is in Napa," Richard said gruffly.

A wave of relief; I wouldn't have to face Georgina or Marion until Sunday night. And Richard probably wouldn't come after me again so soon, especially not alone. Which gave me a two-day window: time I intended to put to good use.

Wordlessly, I followed Richard into the house. He mounted the stairs without a backward glance, not even bothering to say goodnight. He was probably looking forward to a stiff drink.

Alma took me by the hand, as if I were a small child, and led me back to our tiny apartment. She bolted the door behind her, something she hadn't done the other two nights I'd stayed here. I hesitated, then grabbed the desk chair and moved it across the room, jamming it against the handle. I expected Alma to protest, but she merely gave me a thoughtful look, then nodded, as if barricading ourselves inside was perfectly sensible.

Locks wouldn't keep out another fire; but we were on the ground floor. At the first whiff of smoke, we could go through a window.

That decided, I collapsed on the overstuffed sofa and closed my eyes. I was emotionally exhausted, but physically charged to the point where it felt like my body was buzzing.

Alma brewed a pot of tea and brought over a mug. We drank it in silence.

"You can go to bed," I offered. I wasn't tired; after all, I'd spent most of the past two days asleep. "I might stay up reading."

Alma blinked at me. Then she rose and slowly went over to the armoire at the far end of the room. She carefully withdrew a photo album and brought it back. Holding it on her lap, she ran a wrinkled hand over the cover. I waited, watching her. It looked like she was barely holding herself together, which was weird; even during the fire she'd seemed almost preternaturally calm. So how could a photo album unnerve her so badly?

When she handed it to me, I hesitated, half afraid of what I'd find.

"Open," she insisted.

I turned to the first page and muffled a cry of surprise.

It was a photo of a young girl in pigtails and a flouncy white dress, standing in front of the Rochesters' house. She was around six years old, grinning widely at the camera. A younger version of Alma was holding her hand and smiling.

The little girl was my mother.

Alma was focused on the picture. With a faint smile, she ran her hand over it and murmured something in Filipino.

"What is this?" I asked in a small voice.

Instead of responding, she reached out and flipped to the next page, then the next. I watched my mother grow. Teeth vanished, then reappeared in later photos. Her haircut shifted between braids and ponytails and long, curled waves. Her face narrowed as her cheeks shed their baby fat.

In the final one, she was probably about my age. My mother was wearing a Hamill School uniform. Her expression was confident, and she had a familiar glint in her eyes.

"Why do you have these?" I asked thickly. But I already knew the answer.

Alma patted her chest with one hand and said, "Lola." When I stared at her, not comprehending, she translated softly, "Grandmother."

I was at a complete loss for words.

My mother had never mentioned her parents. She'd fended off all my queries, claiming they'd died when she was young. "Why didn't you tell me?" I asked, in a voice barely above a whisper.

The corners of Alma's mouth drew down. She plucked at her polyester knit pants and said, "Your mother . . . she leave. Very angry with me."

"Why?" I asked in a strained voice. "Why was she angry?"

Alma sighed heavily and muttered something in Filipino. I shared her frustration. The language barrier between us rendered something that was already difficult nearly impossible. She took the album and withdrew a folded piece of paper from the back. It was old and creased, worn thin by repeated handling. Opening it, I recognized my mother's handwriting.

I read it through twice.

Dear Ina,

I wanted to let you know that John and I have had a little girl. We named her Janie. Dad said that neither of you ever wanted to see or hear from me again, that I was dead to you both, but I'm hoping you'll be able to change his mind. This isn't the old world anymore. I know he has a hard time with that, but I was never going to marry a Filipino man. I've loved John ever since I can remember. I would never have been able to love anyone else, not even to make you happy.

I miss you, Ina. I love you. I'm sorry you didn't approve of our marriage, but we're happy. And maybe, now that you have a grandchild, you'll be able to convince Ama to change his mind. I hope that someday we can see each other again, and you can meet your granddaughter.

Love always,
Halina

I looked up. Alma was sitting rigidly in the chair, her tiny hands clenched in her lap. Tears rolled from behind her glasses, dampening her cheeks.

I sucked in a deep breath of air, feeling dizzy. I didn't have any letters from my mother, and the fire had destroyed everything with her handwriting on it. Holding this thing that she had not only touched but poured her soul onto . . . it was like having her in the room with us. I could practically hear her saying the words.

When I spoke, my voice trembled. "So you didn't want to meet me?"

Alma's wrinkles deepened. She reached out for my hand, but I drew back. It had been sixteen years since she'd received this letter; in all that time, she hadn't contacted us. She'd shut us out, to the extent that when my parents made their will, she wasn't included as a potential guardian. My father's parents hadn't bothered to meet me, either, but they'd still been listed first. Followed by virtual strangers.

Alma cleared her throat and said, "I want to, but your grandfather . . . he very angry with your mother. Wouldn't let me."

"You could have come anyway," I argued. "You could have told him to go to hell."

She was already shaking her head. "Your grandfather say no." After a long beat, she added, "So sorry. So very sorry."

I shook my head. "I don't know what you expect me to do with this. Why didn't you tell me right away?"

It suddenly dawned on me that the Rochesters must have known, right from the start. Richard had been my father's best friend; he'd said that Alma practically raised them. So my mother had grown up here, too.

Slowly, I turned my head toward the bedroom where I'd been sleeping. "That was her room."

Alma nodded, and I closed my eyes. No wonder it had seemed so familiar; when she'd decorated my room in Hawaii, my mother had given it a similar feel. A bed like the one she'd slept in. A bureau, in the same spot on the opposite wall. It must have been painful for her; but she'd probably missed home as much as I did. Her home here.

I was having trouble sorting through the flood of emotions. Sadness, because the letter made the heartbreak of losing my mother feel fresh. Anger, because she'd reached out to try to bridge the divide, and her own mother hadn't responded. Hurt, since my own grandmother had refused to meet me. And humiliation, because for months the people I'd been living with had kept the truth from me.

Including Alma.

"I can't stay here," I said, rising to my feet.

"Please." Alma placed a hand on my arm, but I shook it off.

"No," I said flatly. "If you didn't want me then, I don't want you now."

"Not safe!" Alma insisted, raising her voice.

My eyes went to the chair blocking the door; she was right, it wasn't safe out there. And I couldn't exactly bed down in Georgina's room, a dozen feet from Richard.

It was comical: Here we were, in an enormous house, and there was nowhere for me to sleep.

"Janie," Alma said tremulously. "Please—"

"Leave me alone."

I stormed into the bedroom—my *mother's* room—and slammed the door. Now that I knew, I saw the signs of her everywhere. Even the quilt on the bed was nearly identical to my old one.

My knees started to give. I stumbled to the bed and collapsed on it. Clutching a pillow to my chest, I stared up at the ceiling. I lay there for hours, wide-awake. I heard Alma's bedroom door open, then close. The creak of bedsprings. Eventually, muffled snoring.

Turning on my side, I curled into a ball. I was tempted to tiptoe back into the other room and get the letter, run my hands over it, memorize every word. But I couldn't bring myself to do it. It was only a pale vestige of her, like trying to grasp a shadow. My mother was gone—really, truly gone. And she'd died thinking that her own mother hated her.

I felt a surge of rage toward Alma. What kind of person turned her back on her only child? It was no wonder Mom had always looked pained when I asked about her parents. And how unfair that my sweet, loving, generous mother was dead, and this cruel woman was still alive.

I swore an oath to never speak to Alma again.

Tomorrow, I'd gather up my things and go somewhere else; maybe Helen's family would take me in. If not, a hotel. I'd get in touch with Mr. Briggs and tell him what had been going on. I'd let Kaila and her mom know, too. Then if anything happened to me, at least there would be people asking questions.

As I finally drifted off to sleep, I felt fingers stroking my arm, then my hair. Humming, close by my ear. My eyes flew open, and I practically launched out of bed, ready to scream at Alma.

But no one was there. Suddenly wide-awake, I sat up in bed. Was it my imagination, or had the room grown even colder? I scrambled for the pouch tucked under the pillow. Finding it, I held it up in front of me like a shield.

"Leave me alone," I said sternly. "I just want to be left alone!"

I held my breath, ears straining. The room was silent. I finally lay back down and closed my eyes, still clutching the pouch in both hands. But I was unable to fall asleep.

AS THE FIRST RAYS of sunlight peeped beneath the curtains, I finally gave up. I felt hollowed out, and ravenously hungry; the hospital Jell-O hadn't exactly been filling.

I crept out of the apartment and made my way to the kitchen, wincing every time a floorboard creaked. I made a fresh pot of coffee, and boiled some eggs on the stove. After devouring them with three slices of toast, I felt moderately human again.

My hunger sated, I sank down in a chair and put my head in my hands. My temples throbbed in time to my heartbeat, probably an aftereffect of the drugs. Maybe that's why I'd thought there was someone in the room with me last night. It was actually kind of surprising that I wasn't imagining worse things than someone petting my hair.

"We've got to stop meeting like this."

I raised my head. John was standing in the doorway. "I thought you were all in Napa," I muttered.

"I decided to skip it this weekend," he said casually. "Wasn't in the mood for a party."

"That makes two of us."

He crossed the room and sat beside me. "So. How was the loony bin?"

I made a strangled noise and said, "Not funny."

He regarded me thoughtfully. "Guess you discovered the sad truth about Mother Dearest."

I looked at him. It was hard to know if John was really on my side; better not to trust any of the Rochesters. "I think she actually believed I was Eliza," I said, watching closely to gauge his reaction. "She's completely insane."

"Well, not *completely*," he said with a faint sneer. "Mostly, though."

"She said a weird thing on the drive over, too," I added with forced nonchalance.

"Really?" he asked, matching my tone. "What was that?"

"She said she should've done this years ago. But she only just met me. So why would she say that?"

John didn't answer for a few minutes. We sat in silence, listening to the kitchen clock tick off the minutes. I'd started to think he wasn't going to answer, but abruptly he said, "Let's just say you don't know the whole story about Eliza."

"Of course I don't," I grumbled. "Because none of you tell me anything."

"Every family has secrets, Janie." He leaned forward on his elbows, glaring at the countertop.

"Yeah, well . . . since *your* family's secrets always seem to mess up my life, if you really want to be my friend, maybe you can fill me in," I retorted.

His face looked pained. "You think you want to see what's behind the curtain, but trust me, you don't."

"Try me," I said, crossing my arms. He must've known about Alma, too, and he hadn't said anything. I clenched my jaw. It was really hard not to go off on him about it, but so far John had been the only Rochester to tell me anything at all. This was probably my last chance to find out what the hell was going on; I couldn't blow it. Not yet, at least.

After another long pause, John said, "Let's just say that Eliza's death wasn't mourned as deeply as it might have been otherwise."

An image of the girl with white hair flashed through my mind, and I repressed a shudder. "That doesn't explain anything," I grumbled. "Who didn't mourn her? And what does that have to do with anything, anyway?"

John's lips were clamped tightly shut, as if he'd already said too much. "It's complicated."

"Complicated how?" I said, throwing up my hands. "Let's see:

apparently your mom is insane, Nicholas starts fires, your entire family is stealing my money, and, oh yeah, you and Daniel did something horrible. Is that it?"

With his usual bemused grin, John said, "That's not even half of it, Janie."

I made an exasperated noise. "Seriously? Oh my God, I'm so sick of all of you."

"Sometimes secrets can keep you safe," he said in a flat voice.

I couldn't help myself; that remark hit too close to home. "Sure," I scoffed. "Like no one mentioning that I have a grandmother? And by the way, she lives here?"

John looked surprised. "So Alma finally told you?"

"Yeah." I could still feel the letter in my hands. "And *finally* is kind of an understatement, don't you think?"

"It wasn't our place," he said, suddenly sounding much older than his years. "Look, I heard that when your parents ran off together, it pissed off a lot of people. Especially their parents, and my dad."

"That's stupid," I grumbled. "They were in love. Why shouldn't they have gotten married?"

"The heir to one of the oldest fortunes in town, eloping with the maid's daughter?" John snorted. "Scandalous. It was all society talked about for years. We feed on that sort of thing, Janie. It's like caviar for us."

"Oh, the horror," I said sarcastically. "Not the maid's daughter." The way he'd said it implied that my mother was some sort of gold digger. I remembered her pulling double shifts at the island hospital, not only because we needed the money, but also because she genuinely adored the work. She loved helping people, and people loved her. The other nurses had affectionately nicknamed her "Saint Halina." Someone like Marion could never hold a candle to her. Neither could John, for that matter.

I rubbed my throbbing temples; my headache was growing

by the minute. Arguing with him was a waste of time, though; his worldview was so stunted, he'd never understand. So instead I said, "It was almost twenty years ago. Are you telling me that people here are so lame, they're still talking about it?"

"People have long memories." He eyed me. "I will say, Alma practically dragged Dad to the hospital yesterday. I don't think there's any way she would've come back without you."

"Yeah, well, that's too little too late," I huffed, feeling another surge of righteous indignation.

"And when we got the news about the helicopter crash, she didn't come out of her apartment for days. I think she regrets it, Janie," John said quietly. "Your grandfather was seriously traditional. Having a daughter disobey him was probably too much for him to take."

"That's kind of racist, don't you think?" I snapped.

"No, it's the reality," he countered. "Your grandmother moved here when she was eighteen. It was an arranged marriage, and she was raised to obey her husband. I know that sounds kind of old-fashioned, but that's the way they were. If she'd gotten on a plane to Hawaii, he probably would've completely lost it."

"So she's a coward," I grumbled, wondering how he knew so much about Alma's life. She didn't seem like the type to share.

He shrugged. "I think it's more complicated than that. Alma loved him, and she didn't want to lose him. But that meant giving up your mom, and you. By the time he died, you were already ten years old. She probably thought it was too late."

He fell silent. I puzzled over what he'd said; it was nice to finally have some of the blanks filled in. That didn't mean I could forgive her, though.

"Why are you defending her?" I finally asked. "You're usually the first to say something awful about someone."

"Not Alma," he replied with a faint smile. "She's pretty much the only person who's ever been nice to me."

The way he said it pierced my heart; looking at him, I could see Nicholas in ten years. He'd also learn to bury the hurt so deep it would become nearly impossible to see, forming a cold shell around himself as protection. I hated the thought.

John gave me a funny look. "I was named after your father. Did you know that?"

I shook my head slowly.

"I met him once, when he came back for your grandfather's funeral. He slept on the couch in the study after dad got him drunk."

"When was that?" I asked, astonished.

"Let's see . . . I was fourteen, I think? So three years ago."

Of everything he'd told me, this was the most startling. I tried to wrap my mind around it. Dad had been back to San Francisco that recently? Why hadn't he taken us to the funeral, too? I'd been old enough to go, and even if I'd never met him, he was my grandfather.

Thinking back, I could remember my dad being unusually sad and introspective a few years ago. He'd sit on the porch staring out at the water for hours after dinner every night. Mom had been evasive when I'd asked what his deal was; she just said to give him space. At the time, I'd chalked it up to a midlife crisis.

I'd always thought the three of us were so close, much tighter than most families. And now that they were gone, I was discovering how much I didn't know about them. I sat back in the chair and blew out a breath, suddenly exhausted again. "Well, crap."

"Exactly," John said with a laugh. "See? I told you it was complicated."

I glared at him.

"So what else do you want to know?" he asked.

I wasn't sure I could process any more surprises, especially since my head felt like a melon on the verge of splitting in half. "Is there any aspirin around here?" I asked.

"Sure." John went to a cupboard on the other side of the room and sifted through a stockpile of bottles, coming back with aspirin and a glass of water. As I popped two in my mouth and washed them down, he asked, "So what are you thinking? Spa day? Or just a mani-pedi?"

"I'm going surfing," I announced. It had only just occurred to me, but that's exactly what I needed: a couple of hours in the water would help wash away the stress and anxiety.

John cocked an eyebrow and said, "Cool. I'll come with."

"Wait, what? But—"

He was already trotting away, leaving me scowling at his empty stool. I had no intention of taking him with me; the whole point was to spend some time alone. I gritted my teeth; what did he think, that I was going to give him a free surf lesson?

Minutes later, John reappeared in jeans, a long-sleeved shirt, and a fleece. It was pretty much the most dressed down I'd ever seen him.

"What?" he demanded, seeing my look of incredulity.

"Nothing," I said. "Listen, I'm really not up for babysitting right now."

"Neither am I," he said breezily. "I'm in the mood to catch some waves." He tossed me a pile of clothes. "There's a Speedo in there with the tags still on it; Georgie had a crush on a water polo guy for, like, a minute and bought a dozen of them. She won't even notice it's missing. The other stuff is from my personal closet."

I took the clothes and said, "Um, thanks. But listen . . . you need a wetsuit, and none of the surf shops are open yet."

His forehead wrinkled. "What makes you think I don't have a wetsuit?"

I shrugged, nonplussed. "You do?"

"Of course," he said. "In the back of the garage, next to my long board."

My jaw dropped. I hadn't seen any other surf gear in there, but then again, I hadn't really looked; Bob had allotted me a space by the front wall. And the garage was huge, large enough for five cars parked side-by-side.

John seemed to be enjoying my reaction. "So," he said. "Are you going to get changed, or what?"

I tugged at the pajamas self-consciously and grumbled, "Fine."

"Fantastic. Meet you at the car." He beamed at me, then headed for the door.

As I frowned after him, I realized he'd never finished explaining about Eliza.

TEN MINUTES LATER, I was wearing the Speedo under one of John's sweatsuits, and our boards were strapped to the top of John's black SUV.

"Gorgeous day," he commented cheerfully as we pulled away from the house. "Finally feels like spring. So, are you ready for the cotillion? It's next weekend, you know."

I stared at him as if he were insane. "You're kidding, right? I'm not going."

"Sure you are," he said evenly. "Dear old dad will insist. He did buy you that dress, after all. Well, technically you bought it for yourself, but still—"

By next weekend, I'll be back in Hawaii, I thought. *Even if I have to rent a canoe and paddle there.* But I wasn't about to let him know that. "We'll see."

"Now who's being secretive?" he asked, glancing at me. "Just so you know, if Fairfax isn't up for it, I'd be happy to wear the penguin suit."

I had to laugh. "Seriously? Are you asking me on a date?"

"Hardly. I'm offering to do charity work."

"Gee, thanks," I said, rolling my eyes.

"Your loss. But I can guarantee you'd have more fun with me, anyway."

I felt a pang, discussing Daniel with the person he considered to be his mortal enemy. I'd meant to call him after breakfast, but then John had distracted me, and before I knew it we were in the car. For a millisecond, I debated borrowing John's phone, but Daniel would totally freak out. I wouldn't exactly feel comfortable talking to him in front of John, anyway. I hated not having a cell phone; I kept unconsciously grabbing for it.

We'll only be surfing for a couple of hours, I told myself.

I'd ask John to swing by a drugstore on the way home so I could buy a disposable phone. There would be plenty of time to call when I got back to the house.

"NICE ONE!" I CALLED out, watching John cruise along a right break from my vantage point twenty feet offshore. I had to admit, I was impressed. He wouldn't be going pro anytime soon, but he was holding his own.

Definitely better than Daniel, I thought guiltily. As the wave mumbled away into gentle breakers, John hopped off the board, tucked it under his arm, and flicked hair out of his eyes. Giving me a thumbs-up, he strode back into the surf, then paddled back toward me.

We'd been at Ocean Beach for over three hours. It was a gorgeous day, with a perfect swell out of the northwest and just enough wind to kick the waves up. It was also unseasonably warm, in the low sixties. I drew a deep breath, loving the feel of salt air tickling my lungs. This was just what I'd needed; surfing had banished the nightmarish events of the past week to the back burner, at least temporarily.

"You going to catch another one, or just sit here checking out my ass?" John hollered as he shifted to sit on his board, forcing the tip of it out of the water.

"Just making sure you don't drown," I teased.

Since we'd arrived, I'd thrown myself into catching wave after wave; it felt good to spend a minute just taking it all in. Waiting for the perfect set was as much a part of the experience as riding: the feel of the board rising and falling beneath you, the constant crash of waves, steady as a heartbeat. It always gave me a sense of the vastness of the ocean and the pull of the moon. Sometimes that made me feel small and insignificant, but not today. Right now, it just felt good to be alive and free.

John's cheeks were red from the cold. He wasn't wearing a hoodie, but the frigid water didn't seem to bother him. "What?" he finally asked.

"Nothing," I said, tracing my hands through the water. "It's just . . . you actually look happy for a change."

He laughed out loud. "I can't believe it's been so long. Hell, I should be out here every day. It's not like I have anything better to do."

"Trust me," I said. "If I didn't have to go to school, and had a car, I'd be here all day, every day."

"I bet you would," he said, regarding me contemplatively. "I forgot how good it feels."

"Yeah," I agreed. The sun emerged from the clouds as a wave broke close to shore, sending a shower of rainbows cascading through the air. "I used to go at least once a day."

"Must've been nice."

"It's a lot easier when there's a break right in front of your house," I said ruefully.

"You miss it, huh?"

"So much," I confessed. "This is the only place I feel like I belong anymore."

"Funny. Seems to me you're starting to fit in fine."

I snorted in response. "Yeah, right. I'm practically the toast of the town."

"Play your cards right, you could be," he said smoothly.

I shook my head. "Not in a million years."

"Suit yourself. Hey, check it out." John tilted his chin, and I followed his eyes; a perfect wave was approaching, the swell visible against the horizon. "That beauty's all mine."

"Not if I catch it first!"

We both flipped onto our bellies and started paddling furiously, splashing each other and laughing. I edged him out and jumped up to ride the wave. My board coasted along the top, just below the crest. As I raced along, John yelled encouragement from behind me.

A solitary figure on the beach caught my eye. He was standing stock-still, staring at us. As I got closer, I realized who it was.

Daniel.

I cut out of the wave, hopped off the board, and raced toward shore, splashing as I went. "Oh my God, I'm so glad to see you!" I burst out, throwing my arms around him.

He didn't reply, and I realized he'd gone rigid in my arms. I pulled back and looked up at him. "What?"

Daniel jutted his chin toward John. "You're with *him.*" His voice was cold and flat.

I stepped back and pushed the hair out of my face. "Well, yeah," I said. "I really wanted to go surfing, and he offered me a ride. I was going to call as soon as I got back."

He barked a hard, short laugh. "Well, that's big of you."

I examined him. Daniel's eyes were bloodshot, and his scruff of beard was overgrown, like he hadn't shaved in a few days. "You know I lost my phone in the fire," I said slowly. "And then—"

"Then you attacked Georgie. I heard."

"I didn't attack her," I said with a flare of anger. "Well, I slapped her, but then she—"

"I had to hear about it from a kid in math class," Daniel snapped, cutting me off. "How do you think that made me feel?"

"Daniel, I was in a *mental hospital,*" I said, exasperated. "Drugged up and locked in a padded room, literally. I couldn't exactly send a text. And I didn't get out until late last night."

There was a flicker of hesitation in his eyes. I stepped closer and put a hand on his arm. "Seriously, the past few days have been . . . well, crazy," I said with a short laugh. "But I wanted to talk to you so badly."

He gazed at me for a long beat. When he finally spoke, his voice was strained. "I can't believe you came here with him. I mean, c'mon, Janie. This is *our* place."

I bit my lip, suddenly realizing he was right. The surf sessions were how we'd gotten to know each other, and we'd had our first kiss here. I'd been so eager to get on my board, it hadn't occurred to me that this would seem like a betrayal. "Listen, I'm really, really sorry. I wasn't thinking."

Daniel was still staring past me. I followed his eyes; John was standing in the breakers watching us. "He's not so bad," I said tentatively. "I think maybe he's changed—"

"Bullshit." Daniel snapped, turning on me. "So he's got you fooled, too. That's great, Janie. If you'd rather hang out with that asshole, I'll leave you to it."

There was an undercurrent of rage beneath his words. Throwing a final glare in John's direction, he turned and started walking up the beach, hands shoved in his pants pockets.

"Wait!" I called out. He didn't stop. Muttering to myself, I chased after him, catching up right before he reached the dunes. I grabbed his arm, forcing him to turn and face me. "Look," I said firmly. "I get that you don't like John, even though you've never told me why, which is insanely frustrating. But he's pretty much the only person in that house who's been even a little bit nice to me."

"Of course he has," Daniel scoffed.

"What's that supposed to mean?" I demanded.

"He's a user, Janie. John gets close enough to find out your weakness, then he takes advantage of it."

I glanced back at John; he'd gotten back on his board and was paddling past the break. I couldn't deny that he was as self-serving as the rest of the Rochesters. But I also couldn't see how helping me benefitted him. I hesitated, then asked, "So how did he take advantage of you?"

Daniel turned his head away, his jaw set. Tightly, he said, "We were best friends; or at least, I thought we were. He's the one who got me high the first time. And pretty much every time after that, too. Then he talked me into helping him get rid of some pills. 'Nothing major,' he said. 'Just helping out a friend.' Well, guess what. When the cops showed up, he shoved the baggie in my pocket. So I'm arrested and sent to rehab, while he waltzes off to boarding school. You want to know why I don't trust him? It's because he sold me out, Janie. And he'll do the same to you."

He turned and started walking again, head down.

I took a second to catch my breath, still processing everything he'd said. Then I hurried to catch up.

"Look," I said. "You're right, that sounds awful. I get why you hate him. But I'm kind of going through bigger things right now—"

Daniel spun around. "It's all about you, isn't it?" he shouted, stopping me in my tracks. "Poor Janie, who lost her parents. Who hears weird noises in the attic. Who thinks someone is out to get her. Well, you know what? I've been out of my head worrying about you. I heard about what happened at school, and I cut class and headed over there, but no one would tell me anything. Then you just vanished! I spent the past two nights lying awake, wondering if I should go to the cops—I was imagining all sorts of terrible things. And now I find out that you're fine, they let you out. But you didn't call—"

"I couldn't," I interrupted weakly. "I don't have a phone."

"Something wrong with the landline?" he asked.

I flushed red in response.

"I came here today, because—" His voice suddenly broke, and he looked away. After a few seconds, he said thickly, "Because this place reminds me of you, and I missed you. And when I show up, you're here with *him*, acting like nothing's wrong. Laughing and having a good time, and . . . and . . . surfing!" He threw his arms up. "It didn't even occur to you to let me know you were okay?"

"I was going to, as soon as I got home," I replied in a small voice. But it sounded lame to my own ears. He was right; my first thought hadn't been to run to him, it had been to come here.

Daniel drew a deep breath and looked down at his shoes. "I think this might've been a mistake."

"What might've been a mistake?" I asked tremulously. The steel in his tone scared me half to death.

He shook his head, and said, "My sponsor was right. This was too soon. I wasn't ready."

"Are you . . . are you breaking up with me?" I could barely form the words. My teeth were chattering from the cold. A new emotion, foreign and powerful, coursed through me. I felt sick again, and tasted my breakfast in the back of my throat.

"I'm sorry," he said curtly. "But I can't do this. Goodbye, Janie."

I stood rooted to the spot as he walked away. I kept hoping he'd turn back, but he marched purposefully to where his car was parked and slid behind the wheel. As he drove away, I blinked tears out of my eyes.

Could it really be over, just like that?

"Hey," John's voice said from behind me. "You okay?"

"Let's go," I mumbled, wiping my face with both hands. "I want to get out of here."

WE DROVE IN SILENCE back to the house; sensing my mood, John wisely (and uncharacteristically) refrained from commenting about Daniel. Honestly, the way I was feeling, I probably would've sucker punched him if he'd opened his mouth. Not that it was his fault; that was the worst part. This was all on me.

I felt gutted, like Daniel had reached inside and scooped out everything important. I was hurt, and really, really angry. Everything he'd said ran through my mind on an endless reel. *Poor Janie. Dead parents. Noises in the attic.* Like I was pathetic, wrapped up in myself and my own problems. And yeah, maybe I was. But I had damn good reason to be.

How could I *ever* have compared my feelings for him to what my parents had?

It was that, more than anything else, that made me feel like a fool.

I was so distracted, I forgot to ask John to stop so I could buy a new phone. It didn't seem to matter as much anymore, though. Who would I call, anyway? I wasn't even in the mood to talk to Kaila. I didn't want her comparing this to what had happened with Tommy; if she did, I'd probably snap at her, and that would only make things worse.

When we arrived at the house, I mechanically lugged my surfboard off the top of the car and hauled it to the garage. John watched silently for a minute, then offered, "I can handle that, if you want."

I shook my head. I needed to do something physical to distract myself. I rinsed the saltwater off everything, hung my wetsuit from a rafter to dry, and stacked my board along the wall. Then I stalked past John and into the house. I hesitated briefly on the threshold; the house was silent. Where should I go? Alma's apartment was off-limits. I needed to avoid Richard's wing of the house, too.

I took the stairs two at a time. When I reached the bend in the hall, I paused at the door to my old bedroom. A special cleaning crew had stripped it bare. All that remained were scorch marks on the red wallpaper and the lingering smell of smoke; huge machines hummed in every corner, probably to dry it out.

It was an apt metaphor for the barren wreckage of my life.

Turning away with a sigh, I walked down the hall and rounded the corner. Opening the door to Nicholas's room, I inhaled deeply. It smelled of baby soap and sweet sweat and tears. I crossed the room and collapsed onto his bed. Pulling the nautical-themed comforter over myself, I huddled there, shivering. It was always so cold in this house, just another thing I hated about it.

My shoulders shook with sobs. More than anything, I wanted my mother. Wanted to feel her hand on my forehead, brushing back my hair. The murmur of her voice in my ear, telling me it was all going to be okay. Her body curled up beside me, reassuring me with her presence. I cried as if my heart was breaking all over again; as hard as I had when the cops first showed up at our house.

"Mommy," I sobbed, burying my face in the pillow. "Oh, Mommy, I miss you so much."

Daylight shifted across the room. I clutched the comforter to my chin and used it to dry my tears, only to have more overtake me. I cried for everything I'd lost, all the things I'd never have in my life again. That, coupled with the hours of surfing, left me drained and exhausted. I closed my eyes and drifted off to sleep.

PERHAPS THE DREAM WAS provoked by lying in Nicholas's bed. It was strange, like watching a montage of old home movie reels: the Rochesters in black and white.

At first, I saw a younger version of Nicholas playing with a sickly-looking girl with pale hair. Eliza. Yet for once, the sight of her didn't terrify me. She and Nicholas were deeply absorbed in the castle game, galloping horses around the turrets. Marion came in and made a fuss over Nicholas, ignoring Eliza entirely.

An abrupt shift, and suddenly the little girl was standing in the front hallway. Her arms were wrapped around Richard's legs, her tear-stained face tilted up to him. There was no sound, but somehow I knew she was begging him to stay. Grimacing, he disentangled himself, patted Eliza's head, and walked out the door.

A shadow fell over her. Suddenly I *was* Eliza, turning with dread to face Marion, the tears still smarting on my cheeks. I felt raw terror as Marion dragged me upstairs by the arm. The door to the attic was thrown open and I was shoved inside, knocking my small knees painfully on the stairs. As the door latched behind me, I pounded my tiny fists against it, howling. The dream was so vivid I practically tasted the dust motes in the air and smelled the wood rot. I curled into a ball on the stairs, weeping. Nicholas was on the other side of the locked door, murmuring to me, but it didn't help. I felt forsaken.

Another jump: I was perched on Richard's lap, giggling blissfully as he bounced me up and down. Behind him, I could see Marion glowering, which made my smile fade, but for the moment, I was happy. *Daddy loves me,* I thought, over and over. *My daddy.*

More images, faster and faster. The banishments to the attic grew more and more frequent, until it seemed like I was up there permanently. There was a cot in a tiny room, and a thin rug that barely covered the floorboards. I sat in the corner, scrawling on the wall with a red crayon. No one came to see me. I was consumed by confusion; why was I so uncared for, so unloved? Why did Mommy hate me?

And then it was dark again. I was being shaken, so hard it felt like my head might come loose from my shoulders. Marion's face was inches from mine, her features twisted into an expression of pure loathing. *Bad girl,* she said, over and over. *You're a very naughty girl.*

In the background, a wisp of moonlight peeked through the skylight. Locking onto it, I made a wish, because that's what children did. I wished for my daddy to come save me. Wished for Mommy to stop hurting me. Wished that the pain would go away.

The shaking intensified, and I tried to scream, but no sound came . . . then suddenly I was airborne, flying.

A sharp jolt through my whole body as I crashed into something solid, then kept going, tumbling down the stairs. I felt myself shatter like a china doll.

As I lay there at the bottom of the staircase, panting, the sliver of moon vanished. I slipped into darkness, entering the place that deep down, I'd always known was waiting for me . . .

I AWOKE WITH A start. It was still light outside, probably late afternoon. The bedspread was damp from my tears. I rolled over on my side and stared at Nicholas's castle. A battalion of silent knights lined the ramparts, holding their swords at the ready.

The dream still held me in its grasp. It had felt so real. *Of course you're having nightmares about Marion,* I thought. *Not really surprising after what she did.*

This seemed like more than that, though. I tugged the comforter up around myself, shivering; the room seemed even colder than normal. Unnaturally cold. I drew in a deep breath, trying to quell my fear.

"Hello?" I said tentatively. "Eliza?"

I sat up in bed, shivering. As the minutes ticked by, I started to feel foolish. It was just a nightmare. As horrible and crazy as Marion was, she wouldn't have killed her own child. Right?

I shook it off. I had more pressing concerns right now; I had to get back to the people who cared about me. My hair felt stiff from salt water. I shuffled to the bathroom and took a shower. When I came back into the bedroom, towel-drying my hair, I saw that something had been left for me.

My cotillion dress hung on the door. It looked even redder against the white wood. I went over to it, feeling another pang of sadness. Daniel would never see me in it now; I wouldn't be walking in on his arm. Remembering all the hateful things he'd said that morning, my jaw clenched. Even if he apologized, I didn't think I could forgive him. Which meant there was nothing holding me here now.

After a moment's hesitation, I closed the door and carried the dress to the bed. I wrapped my hair in a loose bun to keep its dampness from damaging the silk, and slid it on.

Stepping in front of the full-length mirror in the corner, I actually caught my breath. The dress was even more beautiful than I remembered. I turned in a slow circle, flashing back to the flirty texts I'd sent Daniel from the fitting room. That was just a week and a half ago; it felt like a lifetime.

"Stunning," said a husky voice.

Startled, I whipped around. Richard was propped against the doorframe. His tie was loose, dangling below his open shirt collar. He held a nearly empty tumbler in one hand.

"Thanks," I said warily.

He stepped into the room, listing as if battling a strong breeze. "You know," he said, slurring slightly, "You look just like your mother."

I stepped back, trying to keep some distance between us. "That's weird. People usually say I look like my father."

Richard shook his head vigorously. "Nope. You've got Halina's face. It's funny, she wore a similar dress when I took her to the cotillion."

"My mom went to a cotillion?" I said dubiously.

Richard laughed sharply. "That's how she reacted when I asked her. Took me nearly a month to talk her into it, she kept saying she hated those things, everyone would be staring at us . . ." He lapsed into silence, glaring at the floor. "We had a great time until John swooped in. As always, he had some sort of drama going on with his date, and he begged Halina to help him out."

"Really? That doesn't sound like my dad," I said skeptically. Neither of my parents had ever even mentioned other relationships; it had never occurred to me that they might have dated other people.

"Trust me. John could be a real piece of work sometimes," Richard muttered. He took another slug of whiskey. I took a few steps back, trying to get the bed between us. The way he was looking at me over the rim of his glass sent a frisson of fear down my spine.

The ice cubes clattered as he dropped it back down by his side and continued, "He was just ticked off that Halina came with me. That was John all over. It wasn't enough that he already had everything, he had to take what was mine, too."

I bit back a retort; there was no doubt in my mind that my mother had *never* been his. She'd probably only agreed to be his date out of pity. But saying that might set him off.

Richard raised the glass back to his lips, then frowned when he discovered it was empty.

"I . . . I think they probably just fell in love, and didn't want to hurt your feelings," I finally stammered, surreptitiously taking another step toward the bed. I'd managed to put ten feet between us, but he could close that in three strides.

"Ha!" Richard snorted. His cheeks were bright red, and he was weaving. "Your mother didn't care which of us she got in the end."

"She wasn't like that!" I snapped, unable to contain myself anymore. "They got married even though it meant they'd be poor! They *never* cared about money. Not like you do."

Wrong thing to say. Richard's knuckles went white around the glass. He sneered, "You think you're better than me, too, don't you? Just like she did." His voice rose as he practically shouted, "I'm a goddamn Rochester!"

He'd marched forward as he said it, closing the distance between us until he loomed over me. Gone was every trace of the man who had offered to be my friend.

I wanted to defend my parents, to defend myself. But he was drunk. Volatile. Stronger than me. And we were basically alone in the house. John was probably out somewhere, and Alma was two floors down, too far away to hear me scream.

I took another step back, until the backs of my thighs hit the bed. Richard's gaze had turned inward, as if he'd gone to another place, swallowed up by the past. Fighting to keep my voice casual, I said, "I should go get changed."

Thickly, Richard said, "She was so beautiful. I would have done anything for her. Anything."

Run, the little voice in my head urged. I made a move to the right, trying to get around him.

His eyes narrowed, and he said gruffly, "What are you doing?"

"Nothing. I just . . . I want to get changed," I said, hating the pleading note in my voice.

But I'd never felt so afraid: not in the elevator, or during the fire, or even at the asylum. This was a different kind of terror.

Richard advanced another step and growled, "I'm not done with you."

I caught movement out of the corner of my eye; John had stepped into the room. He held his hands open by his sides, as if braced for a fight. In a measured voice, he said, "And here I thought the cotillion wasn't for another week."

Richard turned toward him, an ugly expression twisting his features. "Get out. We're talking."

"Nice to see you too, Dad," John said lightly. "If you don't hurry, Janie, we're going to be late."

"Late for what?" Richard asked suspiciously.

"Janie has an appointment," John said. Making a big show of checking his watch, he frowned and added, "If you still want a ride, we better get going."

"Right," I said gratefully, darting around Richard. On the way to the bathroom, I scooped up my clothes. "Be right out!"

I closed the door behind me and locked it. The dress nearly ripped as I yanked it off; not that it mattered, since I'd never put it on again. I could still feel Richard's eyes roving all over me. Trembling, I slipped on John's shapeless sweatsuit, leaving the dress in a pile on the floor. I splashed some water on my face, then leaned against the sink, bracing my hands against it. Richard's ugly words cycled through my brain. What would've happened if John hadn't shown up?

A knock at the door. Through it, John said, "Janie?"

"Yeah?" I called out, a quiver in my voice.

"He's gone."

I opened the door. John was standing there, his face etched with concern. "I was . . . I thought . . ."

"I know." Without warning, he wrapped his arms around me, holding me tight. "It's okay."

"Thank you," I said. Tears spiked my eyes again.

"Any time." He released me and stepped back, leaving an ache inside me; I hadn't been ready for him to let go yet. But now we were left standing there, staring awkwardly at each other. "I was thinking, it's probably a good idea for you to find another place to stay."

"Definitely," I agreed, cursing myself for falling asleep that afternoon. Instead, I should've been formulating a plan. "I need to buy a new phone, can you drive me?"

"Sure. And after that, I can help you find a hotel, if you want."

I considered for a moment. The thought of being alone in a sterile hotel room wasn't appealing. Plus, I'd have to charge the room to my card, and Richard might be able to track that.

"I have a better idea," I said. "Let's go."

Chapter XV

Do you think I am an automaton? — a machine without feelings? and can bear to have my morsel of bread snatched from my lips, and my drop of living water dashed from my cup? Do you think, because I am poor, obscure, plain, and little, I am soulless and heartless?

I rapped on the door again, willing it to open. *Please be home,* I thought. *Please, please, please. I can't handle any more weirdness tonight.* John's SUV was idling at the curb behind me. If Helen wasn't here, I'd have to find a hotel and hope for the best.

The thought was depressing, though. I really didn't want to be alone.

When the front door finally flew open, I did a double take. Helen looked like a tiny, futuristic Joan of Arc. She was wearing what appeared to be a full suit of armor, complete with enormous spikes that descended from each shoulder. Some sort of fur stole was draped across her shoulders, and her hair was spiked into a faux-hawk. There was a white handprint across her face, as if she'd been slapped.

If it weren't for the glasses still perched across the bridge of her nose, I honestly might not have recognized her.

She stared back at me, looking equally surprised. "Janie! You're okay!"

"Yeah, I am." I gestured toward her outfit. "Isn't it a little early for Halloween?"

"Oh, this?" Helen glanced down, as if she'd forgotten what she was wearing. "It's my cosplay costume for Comic-Con. What do you think?"

"It's really . . . impressive," I said, taking it in.

"Made these out of craft foam, but they look real, don't they?" she said proudly, jabbing at the spike on her right shoulder.

"Definitely," I agreed. "Who are you?"

"The Dragon Born," she said, sounding hurt. "From Skyrim?"

"Of course." I nodded, even though I didn't have a clue what she was talking about. *Maybe Daniel is right, and I'm not a very good friend,* I thought guiltily.

"Don't even bother pretending," Helen said with a grin. She squinted past me toward the street. "That's not Daniel's car."

"No, it's John's."

"Re-al-ly," she said, drawing the word out with all sorts of extra syllables.

I sighed. "It's an incredibly long story. Listen, can I spend the night? I'm kind of stuck for a place to stay."

She examined me warily. "It depends. You won't choke me in my sleep, will you?"

I flashed back to her horrified expression as they pulled me off Georgina at school. "This was probably a bad idea," I muttered, turning away. "Sorry to bother you."

"I'm kidding, silly," Helen said, rapping me on the shoulder. "Get in here." She waved toward the car. John lifted a hand in response; I could see his puzzled expression, and wondered what he thought of Helen's get up. "So that's evil Georgina's older brother? He's hot."

"He's a lot of things," I muttered, dragging my duffel inside. I still wasn't sure what to think about him. Daniel's warning lingered, but despite his snarky manner, John had always been kind to me. Earlier tonight, if he hadn't shown up when he did . . . the memory of Richard's hot, boozy breath chilled me again.

"You okay?" Helen asked as I took off my shoes in the front hall.

"I've been better."

"Yeah, I heard." She shook her head. "Jeez, Janie. You've set a whole new bar for gossip at Hamill. You're practically a legend now."

"Great," I mumbled.

"Actually," she said, leading me up the stairs, "You've got a cheering section. You're not the only person who felt like choking Georgina Rochester. But no one else was brave enough to try it."

"More like stupid enough," I mumbled, following her down the hall to her room.

"Of course I don't condone violence, unless it's virtual," Helen said loftily. "But I doubt she'll be spreading rumors for a while. Is it true that her mom checked you into a mental hospital? Or were they exaggerating about that, too?"

I dumped my duffel in the middle of her room, which looked like the aftermath of a foam factory explosion. "Yeah, she did." I sank down in her desk chair and added, "Plus, I have a grandmother that I didn't know about. Daniel dumped me. And oh, my new dad used to have a thing for my mom."

Helen's eyes went wide. "You're kidding."

I shook my head.

"Wow." Helen plunked down on the floor in front of me, sending smaller scraps of foam flying. "You want to talk about it?"

"Not really," I said. "Is that okay?"

"Sure," she said cheerfully. "You hungry? My folks went out, so I ordered a pizza. Hope you like sausage."

The mere fact that she wasn't pressing for details brought fresh tears to my eyes. I really didn't have the energy to explain everything that had happened over the past few days. I grabbed Helen's hand and squeezed it. "Thanks."

She squeezed back. "Sure. What're friends for, right? C'mon, let's get you some food."

JUDGING BY MR. BRIGGS'S response, I probably should have practiced what I was going to say before calling him. But finally getting my parents' attorney on the phone was such a relief that I'd basically just babbled for ten straight minutes, relaying everything that had happened since my arrival. I could understand how it all might sound nuts. Still, his attitude was irritating.

"I'm sorry, I'm afraid you've lost me here," Mr. Briggs said.

"At which part?" I asked impatiently.

A long pause, then he said, "Perhaps you'd better start over."

I sighed and flopped back down on Helen's bed. She was probably in the library right now eating lunch. I remained persona non grata at Hamill, which was fine by me. We'd gone shopping yesterday for some new clothes; it felt weird, whipping out that black card at the register. Even more disconcerting was how quickly I'd gotten used to it.

I drew a deep breath and forced myself to calm down. I needed him on my side. Which meant I should stick to the most important—and damning—parts.

"Okay," I said slowly. "So apparently my grandparents left me some sort of trust?"

"They did," Mr. Briggs acknowledged. "But as I explained in our initial meeting, there are very strict guidelines for how and when that money will be released to you. A third of it when you turn eighteen, another third at twenty-four, and the last when you're thirty."

"Okay," I said, not wanting to admit that the whole money thing hadn't even registered at the time. Those seemed like random ages to me, but whatever. Probably smart of them not to just hand it over in one lump sum; someone like Georgina could easily blow through a fortune in a few years. "And until then, my legal guardians are in charge of it?"

"Technically, no," he said guardedly. "The executor of the estate administrates it; in this case, that would be the Rochesters' family attorney. The Rochesters are allowed to draw on the account to cover any costs associated with caring for you."

"Okay," I said, thinking it through. "And we can check that balance, right? To see how much has been taken out?"

"Yes," he said. "But before we go any further, Janie, I should tell you that the Rochesters' attorney contacted me."

My pulse quickened. No wonder Mr. Briggs was acting so skeptical. "What did he say?"

He cleared his throat. "Apparently you've been acting erratically since your arrival, claiming that the house is haunted. And you're hearing voices."

"Bastards," I muttered. Daniel was right; I should've tried harder to get in touch with Briggs last week.

"Are you saying that's not true?"

"Well, not exactly true," I hedged. "But yeah, there's been some weird stuff going on."

"The Rochesters also maintain that you tried to set your bedroom on fire, though they're not pressing charges."

"That wasn't me!" I protested. "Someone else set that fire."

"And apparently you've been suspended from school for attacking Georgina Rochester?" he added, a note of disbelief in his voice.

"She went after me," I said, sitting bolt upright. "I was just defending myself!" I should've known that the Rochesters would mount a smear campaign to cover themselves. The worst part was that on the face of it, everything they'd told Briggs was true, and impossible for me to contradict. "Did they tell you that they tried to lock me up in an insane asylum? If Marion hadn't—"

"Listen, Janie," Mr. Briggs interrupted wearily. "I understand that this has been an extremely difficult adjustment for you—"

I snorted. "Have *you* ever been locked up in an insane asylum under a false name?"

"But in light of this letter," he went on, ignoring me, "I'm afraid that your options are limited."

My mind was spinning. I had to get him on my side somehow. Without his help, I was doomed. "Can you at least check and see how much money they've taken out of the trust?"

"I'll look into it," he said grudgingly. "But based on these claims, I wouldn't be surprised to see a fairly significant withdrawal."

"It would really make me feel better," I said. "Please?"

A heavy sigh; Briggs clearly thought he was dealing with teenage girl theatrics. I couldn't really blame him. We'd only met once, and that was right after my parents had died; I hadn't been at my best. I thought of that girl I'd overheard in the bathroom my first day at Hamill, snidely writing me off as "a hot mess." Briggs probably thought the same. He knew nothing about me. I pictured him sitting in the creaky leather chair in his small office, eager to get off the phone.

He let a low whistle. I frowned. "Um, Mr. Briggs?"

"Sorry, Janie," he said, sounding considerably less distracted. "Well, I have to say, this is more than I expected to see. Of course, cleaning up fire damage can be costly, and tuition at your new school is exorbitant. Still, there should be receipts attached to these withdrawals . . ."

"And there aren't any, right?" I said triumphantly. "See? I told you."

"It could be an oversight," he muttered. "Perhaps their bookkeeping isn't what it should be. I'll tell you what: I'll send a request for receipts, asking for a full inventory of where the money went. We should have a response in a few days."

"A few days?" I protested.

"That's the best I can do."

"Okay," I said, forcing gratitude into my voice. "Out of curiosity, how much did they take?"

He hesitated, then said, "Somewhere in the neighborhood of a quarter million dollars."

I nearly dropped the phone. Holy crap, the Rochesters *had* been robbing me blind. A quarter *million* dollars, over just a few months? I could hardly believe there had been that much money in the first place. I thought of yesterday's spending spree. Was I going to have to return all that stuff? Had those bastards already put me in debt? Anxiously, I asked, "So how much is left?"

"Oh, don't worry, Janie, there's plenty left," Mr. Briggs said with a laugh. "Haven't you been reading the statements?"

"What statements?" I demanded.

"They're sent quarterly," he said, sounding flustered. "You should have received one a few weeks ago."

"I haven't gotten any mail," I said. "None at all. Do you think that's just another 'oversight'?"

After another long silence, Mr. Briggs said, "Perhaps you should tell me again about your experience with the Rochesters."

I drew a deep breath. "Look. I know you barely know me, and their lawyer is making me sound nuts. But I'm not crazy. They're just trying to make it look that way, so they can get to my trust."

"That's a serious accusation, Janie," he said sternly.

"Listen, Mr. Briggs. I am not safe here," I said, firmly enunciating each word. "It's your job to protect me, right? That's why my parents hired you. So how do we do that?"

I held my breath; there had to be a solution, some way out.

"Well," Mr. Briggs said, speaking slowly, "We could petition to have you emancipated. It's a fairly long process, but based on their attempt to commit you to psychiatric care—"

"—Under someone else's name," I interjected. "Their dead daughter's."

"Right," he said, sounding discomfited. "I could file a petition on your behalf. In the short term, the court would suspend the Rochesters' access to your trust. I can have a forensic accountant start reviewing the records for evidence of misconduct. If we find any, that will strengthen your case."

"Great," I said, relieved. "So until then I can just stay with my friend, right?"

"Technically, I can't advise you to do that," Mr. Briggs said carefully. "The emergency court order will have to be filed by an associate who is registered with the California bar. And there needs to be a responsible adult willing to offer temporary custody. Are your friend's parents willing to do that?"

I hesitated. Helen's mom and dad hadn't blinked at having me stay over for a few nights; but would they be willing to become custodial parents? It seemed like a lot to ask, considering the fact that they'd just met me.

"I'll have to check," I admitted, deflated. "Um, what if they say no?"

Mr. Briggs sighed. "Well, unless you can find someone else, you'll have to stay with the Rochesters until the petition is approved. And I'm afraid that even an emergency petition will take a few weeks."

"Weeks?" I gasped, feeling my insides liquefy. "Mr. Briggs, no. I can't go back there."

"There's always foster care," he offered. "I know it's not the best option, but if you feel strongly that you're in danger, I can contact Children's Services. Of course, older children are usually kept in a foster shelter. And from what I understand, those can be . . . well, they're not the best."

My heart sank. It was hard to believe I had a fortune at my fingertips, but my choices were either to live with people who were actively out to get me, or to go to some sort of teen holding facility. "Please, Mr. Briggs. Can't I just check into a hotel or something?"

"I'm sorry, Janie. But legally speaking, a girl your age is not allowed to be on her own."

THE TALK WITH MR. Briggs disheartened me. I spent the rest of the afternoon listlessly waiting for Helen to come home. I tried to read a book, but couldn't focus. I flipped through every TV channel, but couldn't find anything worth watching. I even spent an hour trying to figure out Skyrim, but finally gave up. I couldn't seem to get more than ten feet into the game without having a giant kill me, which felt way too close to what I was going through in real life.

Sighing, I picked up my new phone and frowned at it. There was no one left to call. Kaila and Taka were in school. John Rochester? Forget it. And Daniel . . . well, I couldn't call him anymore, for obvious reasons.

Tossing the phone on the bed, I fell back against the pillows. I was staring up at the ceiling when Helen came in.

"That good, huh?" she asked.

I groaned. "I'd almost rather be in school."

"No, you wouldn't," Helen said, dumping her backpack onto the desk. "Trust me. Georgina's still on the warpath."

I sat up in bed, wary. "What's she saying?"

"Oh, you know. More of the same." Helen shrugged. "You're a nut job, your parents were crackheads. Nothing new." Her eyes shifted away at the end.

I scowled. "You're a terrible liar."

"So your lawyer had good news?" Helen asked brightly, changing the subject.

"Kind of," I hedged. Mr. Briggs had said that he couldn't "advise me" to stay with her family. Which I'd decided really meant that I could, as long as we kept it quiet. I moved to the edge of the bed and stared her down. "Enough stalling. Tell me what she's saying. I mean, it's not like it matters anymore. If things work out, I'll never see her again, anyway."

Helen's shoulders slumped. "It's probably as much of a lie as everything else she said, right?"

"Helen," I warned. "Tell me."

Focusing on a point past my shoulder, Helen said, "She's telling everyone that Daniel is taking her to the cotillion."

"What?" I blinked, trying to process the words.

"Seriously, Janie, she's got to be lying," Helen said, rolling her chair closer to me. "She's just trying to get under your skin."

I couldn't speak. I could hardly breathe. My eyes filled with the image of Georgina in that slinky white dress, twirling before the mirror. I swallowed hard, picturing her clinging to Daniel.

"Janie?" Helen asked uncertainly. "Are you okay?"

I shook my head. My voice sounded funny as I said, "It has to be a lie."

"Absolutely. I mean, he's not a bad guy, right? And that would be an absolutely awful thing for him to do."

I nodded, desperately wanting to believe her. Daniel *wouldn't* do that to me. He'd said that it was too soon for him to date, which was completely understandable. Being so close to all the drama in my life wouldn't be easy for anyone, especially not a recovering addict. Even if he was angry with me, he didn't seem like the vindictive type. And taking Georgina to the dance would be the height of cruelty.

Either way, though, I'd rather know for sure. "I'm calling him," I said, picking up my phone.

"Um, is that a good idea?" Helen asked worriedly. "Maybe you should take some time to cool off first—"

"I'm cool," I snapped.

"O-kay." She held up both hands. "I'll give you a little privacy, then." As Helen grabbed her laptop and left the room, I dialed with shaking fingers. I held my breath, half-hoping it would go to voicemail.

A click as the call connected. "What?"

"Daniel?" I asked hesitantly. "It's me. Janie," I added lamely.

"I figured," he said shortly. "No one else would be calling from an unknown number."

I bit my lip; he still sounded as angry as he'd been on Saturday. "Um, I just . . . I wanted to see how you were."

"Fine." There were mumbles in the background, like someone else was there. *Could it be Georgina?* Another wave of nausea swept over me. "Anything else?"

"Just . . . I'm really sorry." Before I could stop myself, I blurted, "I miss you."

He didn't answer. My chest ached, and tears pressed against my eyelids. "Daniel?" I finally said, desperate to break the silence. "Please, if we can just talk—"

"I have nothing to say to you." His voice was flat and cold.

"Nothing ever happened with John. I mean, seriously, I don't feel that way about him at all—"

"It doesn't matter." Another long pause, then he said, "The thing is, when you disappeared like that, I kind of lost it. I called everyone, trying to find out where you were. And when they told me what had happened . . ."

I held my breath, waiting for him to continue. His voice had changed; he sounded raw, emotional.

"I took some pills," he confessed.

"What?" I gasped.

"I messed up, Janie. When I saw you at the beach, I was still high. After I left, I drove straight to my sponsor's house, and he took me to a meeting. I'm cool now, but . . . it made me realize I'm not strong enough for this yet."

"But, Daniel . . ." My mind spun. I felt guilty; was it my fault that he'd succumbed to his addiction again? "I can help you."

"That's not how it works," he said wearily. "I have to help myself. And for now, at least, that means I have to be alone again."

After everything I'd been through, I didn't think there was a type of pain my heart hadn't experienced yet. I was wrong. Desperately, I said, "Please, can we just talk about this?"

"I'm sorry, Janie," he said, more gently this time. "But this is how it has to be."

"Daniel, wait!"

He'd already hung up. I tried to swallow past the lump in my throat. I hadn't found out about the cotillion, but it didn't seem to matter anymore.

Helen rapped lightly on the door and called out, "Hey, is it okay if I come back in?"

I wiped my cheeks and called out hoarsely, "Of course."

She entered, looking sheepish. "I just forgot to grab my phone."

"It's okay," I said with a sniffle. "I'm done."

"Oh." Helen plunked down on the bed and wrapped an arm around my shoulder. "So it didn't go great, huh?"

"He hates me," I said, my voice cracking at the end.

"I'm sure he doesn't hate you."

"I just can't believe it fell apart so fast!" I wailed.

"I know," Helen murmured as I leaned into her, soaking her shirt with my tears.

After a few minutes I sat up, feeling silly. With everything else that was going on, crying about boy trouble seemed like a self-indulgent waste of time. And maybe Daniel had the right idea; I should focus on what I had to do without any distractions, too. Because who knew what the Rochesters might try to pull next? I wiped my nose with the back of my hand and said, "Thanks."

"Don't mention it," Helen said. "I'm still living vicariously through you, after all."

I choked out a laugh. "Yeah? How's that going for you?"

"Meh," she said. "Honestly, it's kind of confirmed my suspicion that the virtual world beats the real one, hands down."

"Maybe I should try gaming," I tried to joke, but the quaver in my voice belied the words.

"Always happy to talk you through the first level," she offered. "So, um . . . there's another thing."

I met her eyes; Helen looked even more uncomfortable than she had before she'd spilled the cotillion rumor. "I'm guessing this isn't good news."

"It's just . . . my parents were wondering how long you needed to stay. Not that there's any rush," she added hurriedly, taking in my expression. "But Mom ran into Marion at a luncheon today."

"Oh, no," I groaned. Helen's parents were pretty cool, all things considered, but they still ran in the same circles as the Rochesters. "What did she say?"

"Nothing too bad," Helen said evasively. "But I guess they heard you might be staying with us. And Marion said something about getting her lawyer involved."

"Crap," I moaned. I should've known the Rochesters wouldn't let me go without a fight. "So your folks want me gone?"

"Not, like, right away," Helen said uncertainly. "But I think they're worried. They don't want to get into a legal battle with the Rochesters. Everyone knows how ruthless they can be."

"Right." I ran a hand through my hair. I could see that Helen felt terrible about it, but none of this was her fault. It wasn't fair of me to dump my problems on someone else's doorstep. And the last thing I wanted was to put her family in the Rochesters' crosshairs. "Listen, I totally get it. I'll leave tomorrow."

"But where will you go?" Helen asked with concern.

"Home," I said, reaching a decision.

"What, like . . . Hawaii?"

I nodded. If the Rochesters wanted to try something, they'd have to come to the Big Island. At least there, I had people who could be trusted to protect me. "I'll buy a ticket tonight."

Helen frowned. "I thought the lawyer said to stay put."

"I'll call him when I get there." I began grabbing my paltry belongings and stuffing them in my duffel bag. It actually felt good to take action. To be in control for once. "Kaila's mom can apply to be my emergency guardian, I'm sure she won't mind. And what are they going to do? Force me back on a plane?"

"Okay," Helen said doubtfully. "If you're sure."

"Positive." I could already imagine walking through Kona airport, with the thatched huts that made it look like a tiny village. Buying an ice while I waited for my bags. Maybe stopping at the kiosk where an elderly woman wove leis by hand. *Home.* The thought made my heart swell in my chest. Resolutely, I said, "I'll be safe there. They won't be able to come after me."

Chapter XVI

I am no bird; and no net ensnares me: I am a free human being with an independent will.

I checked Helen's room one last time to make sure I hadn't forgotten anything. Thanks to the fire, packing was easy; what little I owned barely filled the duffel bag.

That was okay; I didn't need much. Kaila was always happy to let me borrow things, and I could easily replace my island clothes when I got there. Just the thought of stepping into a new pair of flip-flops made me giddy. *Home,* I thought again with glee. The word had become a mantra, a prayer.

At dinner last night, Helen's parents had raised a few half-hearted protests about my leaving so abruptly, but I could tell they were relieved. Who wouldn't be? I was so scared of the Rochesters I was fleeing the city.

"You're sure you want to catch the red-eye?" Helen asked as we stood in her doorway.

"It's not really a red-eye. We'll land around midnight." It was going to be hard to sit still for an entire plane ride, I was so eager to get there. Tomorrow morning, I'd wake up to the sound of the surf outside Kaila's bedroom window. We could catch a few sets, then lounge around in pajamas and watch movies. San Francisco, the Rochesters, Daniel, and everything else would feel far, far away.

"I can't believe you're really going," Helen said with a catch in her voice. "I guess this means I'll never see you again."

"Hey!" I protested, wrapping an arm around her shoulders. "That's not true."

She tried to smile. "Well, you're not coming back *here*."

I bit my lip—Helen was right, I couldn't imagine anything dragging me back to San Francisco. "So you'll come visit me. Right?"

"In Hawaii? Have you seen my skin? I'd get a sunburn just thinking about it."

"We'll lather you up with SPF 50 and you'll be fine," I said. "Maybe I'll even get you on a surfboard."

Helen snorted. "Yeah, that's about as likely as you getting hooked on Skyrim."

"We'll see each other," I said firmly. "Promise."

She let out a deep breath. "There's an anime convention in Oahu, I looked it up. Maybe we could go together."

"I'm there," I assured her. "Just tell me where and when. Oh, and I'm guessing it's bring-your-own-armor?"

Helen whacked my arm. She was grinning, though. "Just for that, I'm making your costume myself. And you're wearing it, even if you hate it—"

The doorbell rang downstairs, cutting her off.

We stared at each other for a moment. "Guess it's that time." I slung my duffel bag over my shoulder.

Helen still looked worried. "You're sure it's safe to go back to their house?"

I nodded. "I've just got to grab my board and wetsuit, and say goodbye to Nicholas. John promised no one else will be there."

"Well, be careful."

I clasped her in a tight hug. "I'll miss you."

"Me, too," she said thickly. "Now get off, you're squishing me."

I released her and stepped back.

Noting my expression, Helen muttered, "Well, you don't have to be so cheerful about it." I tried to tamp down my excitement, but my heart felt like it was about to burst through my chest. I practically skipped downstairs, Helen plodding slowly behind me. John was standing on the stoop looking impatient. Motioning to his idling SUV, he said, "Your chariot awaits. We better get moving, there'll be traffic on the 101."

Throwing Helen a final wave, I hurried down the path.

JOHN WASN'T KIDDING. HELEN'S house was less than a mile from the Rochesters', but at this time of day traffic was heavy. As we inched along, I tried to quell a surge of panic in my chest.

"Maybe we should go straight to the airport," I said. "I don't want to miss the flight. You can ship my surfboard."

"Nah, we'll be fine." John waved a hand dismissively. "This will only take a minute. Besides, Nicholas will be crushed if you take off without saying goodbye. He's seriously attached to you."

Another pang. He was right, Nicholas would be devastated. I hadn't seen him since last week; and knowing him, he'd probably blame himself for my departure. I had to at least give him a hug and promise to stay in touch. "All right."

John shot me a sideways glance. "I gotta tell you, I'm pretty torn up about it, too."

"Really," I said dryly.

"Sure. I finally find a surf buddy, and she's abandoning me."

His words brought back that day at the beach, and the weird dreams I'd had afterward. I hesitated, debating; but what did I have to lose at this point? Drawing a deep breath, I asked, "John, how did Eliza die?"

He stiffened, and a cloud passed over his face. Cautiously, he said, "Wow, that kind of came out of nowhere. Why do you want to know?"

Shrugging, I said, "Just curious. I assumed she had leukemia or something like that."

Avoiding my eyes, John said, "There was an accident."

"What kind of accident?" I asked, flashing back to the sensation of slamming into something hard.

"I wasn't there. They called school to tell me afterward," he said curtly. "Eliza was found with a broken neck at the bottom of the attic stairs."

I stopped breathing for a few seconds. *That's exactly how it happened in my dream.* John was pretending to concentrate on the road, but we were barely moving. His face was twisted with an emotion I couldn't place. I pressed, "There's something you're not telling me."

He threw me an angry look. "Why are we talking about this?"

"Because," I said, grasping for a reason that would make sense. "I just . . . need to know."

The light at the intersection turned red. John shifted to face me. I met his gaze levelly. Finally, he sighed. "I guess there's no reason not to, since you're leaving anyway."

The light turned green, and we inched across the road. Three more blocks to the house; at this rate it would take a half hour. "So?" I pressed.

A pause, then he continued, "Eliza wasn't Nicholas's twin."

"What?" I asked, baffled.

John looked embarrassed. "My dad hasn't exactly been . . . well, he's not faithful. There were a lot of women over the years."

"I'm so sorry," I said. Of course, it wasn't exactly a huge surprise. And it went a long way toward explaining the constant tension between him and Marion.

"Yeah, well, one day he showed up with this little girl. He said she was his daughter, and she was going to live with us. Eliza was two at the time, the same age as Nicholas. Marion threw a fit, but Dad made it clear it wasn't up for discussion."

"Wow," I said, stunned. Even for Richard, that was beyond the pale. No wonder Marion had hated Eliza so much. "Who was her mother?"

John lifted his shoulders, finally picking up speed as the traffic cleared. "Dad never said. Nicholas was thrilled, of course, and he was so young . . . it didn't take much to make him think that Eliza had always been there."

Images from the dream returned; I could practically feel Marion's hand gripping my arm. Unconsciously, I rubbed it. "So that's why none of you talk about her."

John laughed sharply. "Yeah, Marion didn't exactly take to Eliza. She tolerated her, but—"

His mouth clamped shut.

"But what?" I asked softly.

"Nothing." He glared out the windshield. "Eliza just never got a lot of love in that house. I tried to help her, but then they sent me away. And the next thing I knew, she was dead."

He fell silent. I shifted in my seat, half-wishing that I hadn't asked. As awful and crazy as Marion was, did I really believe she could've killed a child?

Maybe, said a small voice in my head.

DREAD BLOOMED IN MY stomach as the iron gates in front of the house yawned wide before us. John pulled in and parked the SUV in front of the garage. I climbed out on wobbly legs.

"You okay?" he asked.

"Not really," I said with a short laugh. If anything, the house looked even scarier after a few days' absence. It huddled before me, like a great beast gathering itself to pounce. I bit my lip, trying to get control of my racing heart. All I had to do was duck inside, give Nicholas a quick hug, and leave. Five minutes, max.

"How about I go in with you?" John offered.

"Thanks," I said. "That would be great."

The house seemed abnormally silent and still. With a shaky hand, I reached out and turned the knob.

The hallway was empty. I flashed back to that first night,

when I'd followed Alma through this dark passage. It felt like a lifetime ago. But I was different now. Stronger. Squaring my shoulders, I stepped inside. "Let's go find Nicholas."

John closed the door behind us. When he turned around, I knew immediately by his expression that something was off. I felt a flicker of panic. "What's wrong?"

He held up both hands and said, "Listen, I swear he just wants to talk . . ."

My heart started to hammer in my chest. "Who wants to talk?"

Before he could answer, a familiar voice behind me said, "Welcome back, Janie."

JOHN WAS STANDING IN front of the door, an apologetic expression on his face. Blocking it, I suddenly realized. "You bastard," I hissed. "Daniel was right about you."

"It's not like that," he protested. "I promise, you'll end up thanking me for this."

"I seriously doubt that," I snorted. Crossing my arms over my chest, I turned to face Richard Rochester.

He was dressed immaculately in a pinstriped suit. For once, he didn't have a drink in his hand, and his eyes looked clear. Speaking in a conciliatory tone, he said, "Please, Janie. I just wanted to have a few words before you left."

"I have a plane to catch." The urge to turn and run was almost overpowering, but I didn't want to give him the pleasure. And I wasn't sure I could get past John anyway, if he was set on stopping me.

"I think you're going to want to hear what I have to say," Richard said. "I have a proposition for you. One that benefits all of us."

I shook my head angrily. "I don't care. I'm only here to say goodbye to Nicholas. If he's not around, I'll leave now."

Richard looked past my shoulder at John.

I snapped my head back and said, "I *can* leave, right?"

John had the nerve to look wounded. "Dad's telling the truth,

Janie. If you agree, he's willing to let you live with whoever you want, wherever you want. Legally. I've seen the papers."

"No more lawyers," Richard chimed in. "Hell, none of us wants to waste money on those leeches if we don't have to, right?"

I hesitated. It sounded too good to be true, which meant it probably was. "I'm guessing there's a catch. What do I have to do?"

Richard shrugged, looking embarrassed. "I'm afraid you've got me at a bit of a disadvantage. Perhaps we should go into the study to discuss—"

"We talk here," I interrupted. "Or I leave right now."

"Okay." Richard tucked his hands in his pockets and rocked on the balls of his feet. "Basically, I was forced to take a small loan from your trust to cover some stock transactions."

"Yeah, I heard," I said dryly. "Since when is a quarter million dollars considered 'small'?"

Richard's smile was forced. "Yes, well. Rest assured that if the market hadn't crashed, your trust would actually have received a substantial increase. But as it was—"

"You lost my money," I said. "And you weren't supposed to take it in the first place."

"Listen, Janie," John said, sounding alarmed. "Maybe—"

"No." I cut him off. "I'm not going to just fall in line like the rest of you." Taking a step forward, I spat, "You don't get to push me around, Richard. I'm not your wife, or one of your kids. My parents trusted you, and you stole from me. That's not okay."

The friendly mask fell away. Richard glowered at me, clenching his fists. In a low, menacing voice, he warned, "You should watch what you say."

But I held my ground. The rage made me feel strong, invincible. "Actually, you should watch what *you* say," I retorted. "You need me, remember? I don't need anything from you anymore. I have the money to drag this out in court. Hell, it might even be fun."

He reeled back as if I'd struck him. Behind me, John made a small noise that might have been a laugh.

Richard visibly composed himself, then said stiffly, "Will you at least look at the agreement?"

I made a show of checking my watch, then said, "You have three minutes."

Richard stared at me for a long moment. Then he turned and stalked out of the room, heading toward the study.

My entire body felt tense, like a cord drawn tight. John said, "Man. You have a set on you, I'll give you that."

I spun on him. "You lied to me."

"I know." His eyes fell. Kicking at an edge of the carpet, he continued, "But Janie, he said if I didn't get you to at least consider the offer . . . we're about to lose the house. Do you want Nicholas to end up living on the street?"

"It can't be as bad as that," I scoffed.

"Apparently, it is." John had a look I'd never seen in his eyes before: raw fear. "Dad mortgaged the house to the hilt. If we miss the next payment, we're out. Napa will be gone, too. They'll be sold at auction, and we'll literally have nothing but the clothes on our back."

"That doesn't make sense," I said, waving a hand at our lush surroundings. "Can't you just sell all this stuff? It has to be worth a fortune."

John barked a laugh. "Only if you consider a couple hundred grand to be a fortune. In San Francisco, that'll barely get us through a few months." He stepped closer, a pleading look in his eyes. "Please, Janie. I know how you feel about him—about all of us. But if you could just help out with the next payment, maybe Dad can fix this."

I stared at him, dumbfounded. "Wait. He wants more money?"

John looked uncomfortable. "Just enough to float us a little longer."

I shook my head, thinking *unbelievable.* Not only did they want to be absolved of stealing my money in the first place, now they wanted more of it? This seriously gave new meaning to a sense of entitlement. And I could tell that John didn't really believe that Richard could salvage the situation. They'd probably blow through the loan in a few months. Would that really solve anything?

Still, I couldn't help picturing Nicholas marching soldiers around his toy castle. I didn't want him to be forced out of the only home he'd ever known, not when he'd lost so much already. Not if I could do something to help.

"How much money?" I asked, resigned.

Richard's voice boomed behind me, filled with forced jollity again. "Not much at all!" He waved a sheath of papers as he approached. "And it says right here that you'll get it all back, with interest!"

Reluctantly, I took the papers. There had to be at least twenty-five pages total. Bright yellow tabs marked the spots where I was expected to sign or initial.

"You've been busy," I noted acerbically.

"Of course, if you want to look them over with your lawyer, that's fine," Richard said. "But I assure you, it's all legal."

Meaning that it's basically written in a foreign language, I thought with irritation.

Still, the basics were clear. Flipping through, I saw that Richard was asking for a loan of another two hundred fifty thousand dollars from my trust, at a twelve percent interest rate; I had no idea if that was fair or not, but then, chances were I'd never get a dime back regardless.

The last section, though, piqued my interest.

It stated that Richard Rochester was ceding custodial guardianship of Janie Mason to the adult of her choosing, effective immediately.

A lump rose in my throat. *What if we settled this right here and now?*

I could still get on a plane tonight. Kaila's mom could take over as my guardian. The Rochesters would be able to hold on to their house, for at least a little while longer. And this whole ordeal would be behind me, once and for all. I skimmed the papers again. Richard and John watched silently, the air practically humming with tension. I couldn't find anything overtly wrong with the document, nothing that gave the Rochesters continued access to my trust, or about any other money changing hands. "Anything in here about signing away my soul?" I finally asked.

Richard laughed sharply. "We are going to miss your sense of humor, Janie."

I snorted. "Right. Listen, this looks fine, but I want my lawyer to go through it before I sign."

Richard's eyes flashed to John. A worried look crossed his face, and his brow furrowed again. "Of course, I completely understand. But we're on a bit of a deadline here."

I sighed. "How much of a deadline?"

"Well, there's a payment due tomorrow. I would have asked sooner, but we weren't entirely certain where you'd gone . . ."

"Whatever," I said curtly. "I'll sign it." After all, if there *was* something illegal, I could always claim I'd been forced to comply. And it wouldn't be a lie—they were effectively blocking the front door.

"Thank you, Janie." Richard's shoulders sagged. "This means so much. I can't tell you—"

"What is *she* doing here?"

I froze.

Marion was standing at the base of the stairs. Her Chanel suit was rumpled, her hair mussed, and she was barefoot. I hadn't seen her look this dispossessed since that night in the hallway.

"Marion," Richard said sternly, "Go back to your room."

"Not in my house," Marion hissed, stalking toward me with her fingers spread wide, as if preparing to claw out my eyes. "Did you think I wouldn't find out you were sneaking in your whores again, Richard?"

"Mom," John said, quickly stepping in front of me. "This is Janie. Remember? Janie."

"A whore, just like her mother." Marion's lips twisted into a sneer as she turned on Richard. "I heard the whispers about how she rejected you. Everyone knew. We all thought it was *pathetic.*" She tossed her head and continued, "I told you what would happen if you ever brought another one into my home, Richard. I warned you."

"Shut up, Marion, and go upstairs!" Richard said, desperately jabbing a finger toward the landing.

"I'll kill her, just like—"

"That's enough!" he snarled, grabbing hold of her arms. She snarled like an animal, her eyes flashing. Richard shook her hard, once, and she suddenly fell still.

Almost without realizing it, I'd backed up against the door. My heart hammered in my chest; Marion had brought a dark, manic energy into the hall with her. The hysteria in her voice struck a chord deep inside me. I felt like a child again; I felt what Eliza must have felt, all the time.

"John," Richard said tightly, without releasing his grip on Marion. She looked like a trapped bird, flailing helplessly against him. "Please take your mother upstairs and make sure she takes her pills."

John didn't move. "Um, I'm not sure—"

"Do it!" Richard yelled. "Now!"

John turned to me. I wasn't eager to be left alone with Richard, not after the way he'd behaved the other night. But the front door was right there; all I had to do was turn the knob and run if I sensed any danger. And I'd feel a lot better if crazy Marion was gone. "I'll be fine," I said, trying to reassure myself as much as him.

"Okay. I'll be right back down, then we can go," he said.

Marion muttered as he led her away. She threw me a final, filthy look.

Richard stood stock-still, listening to their retreating footsteps. After a moment, he cleared his throat and said, "I apologize for that, Janie. My wife is not well."

"Clearly," I said, but my voice was shaky.

"So." He held out a pen. "Can we finish this?"

I hesitated. He sounded helpless and frantic. The same way I had in the mental hospital. He hadn't been willing to help me then, so why should I bail him out now? When it came down to it, I didn't owe these people anything. Every night under their roof had been hell. Besides, I still wasn't convinced that things were really that dire. They probably just wanted to maintain their lavish lifestyle. Downsizing might be painful, but they wouldn't starve. I pictured Marion behind the wheel of a battered Honda. That clinched it. "Sorry, no."

He blinked. "What? But you said—"

"I know what I said." My hand was wrapped around the doorknob; it felt cool against my skin. *Just walk away. Let them clean up their own mess for a change.* "It just doesn't feel right. I'm sorry."

"Sorry? You're sorry?" He sounded disbelieving. "Janie, listen to reason. Can't you see I'm just trying to help you?"

I had to fight the urge to laugh. Since my arrival I'd been terrorized, insulted, nearly burned alive, and committed to a psych ward. Richard certainly had a funny definition of "help." "Yeah, right. Like you helped Eliza?"

He reared back. "What?"

The look on his face should have stopped me, but I was too angry to back down. Instead, I spat, "It's your fault she's dead. You knew what Marion was like, and you brought her into this house anyway."

"I loved Eliza," he said in a strained voice. "She was my daughter."

"If you loved her, you should have protected her."

"I tried!" he snarled, lunging toward me. I recoiled, pressing back against the door. Richard drew up short a foot away; I could see him fighting to regain control. Heavily, he repeated, "I tried. What happened to Eliza was an unfortunate accident."

"It was no accident," I hissed. "Marion murdered her."

His eyes narrowed. "Who told you that?"

I shook my head; telling him about the dream would be a mistake. There was no way I'd give him ammunition to commit me again. Turning the knob, I said, "Tell John I'll be waiting in the car."

"Stop!" With a look of panic, he grabbed my arm.

I tried to pull away, but his grip was iron. "Let me go, Richard. Right now."

"You don't understand." His eyes were wild, the vein in his temple pulsed. "I can't be the Rochester who loses the house. Do you have any idea what people would say?"

"I don't care," I snapped. "You made bad decisions, and now you're going to have to pay for them."

He choked out a laugh. "Pay for them? Like you'd know anything about that. Why do you even care? It's not like you earned that money."

"Neither did you!" I retorted. "You blew through everything you inherited, and from what I hear, that was a hell of a lot. So deal with it."

I fumbled for the knob. As I pulled the door open, he slapped a palm against it, slamming it closed again. I let out a small yelp of surprise.

Richard loomed over me, his face inches away as he spat, "You're nothing but a little piece of trash, just like your mother."

That did it; I was tired of these monsters badmouthing my parents. "Your own family hates you," I said, seething. "And soon *everyone* will know what a loser you really are. My mother was a hundred times better than you."

Richard's face went florid with rage. As if in slow motion, he drew his hand back.

And suddenly I was on the floor, my head ringing. Sharp stabs in my chest as he kicked me, the crack of ribs breaking . . .

And then, darkness.

Chapter XVII

I have an inward treasure born with me, which can keep me alive if all extraneous delights should be withheld, or offered only at a price I cannot afford to give.

I woke up sneezing. Blearily, I opened my eyes. I was lying on my side, bare wooden floorboards beneath me. The room was dim, the only illumination a thin rectangle of light seeping under the door . . .

With a jolt, I realized where I was.

The attic.

I was in the tiny room where they'd kept Eliza—I could just make out the crayon figures scrawled on the wall.

Suddenly frantic, I tried to sit up, only to discover that my hands were bound behind my back with what felt like rope. My feet were tied, too. Every breath sent pain ricocheting through my rib cage, and there was a constant pulsing throb over my left ear. I lay on my side panting, trying not to panic as it all came back: he'd *hit* me. Richard had beaten me, right in the front hallway. I'd thought he was going to kill me . . .

But instead he'd tied me up and locked me in the attic.

I started hyperventilating, and my vision blurred. Had he completely lost his mind?

I heard voices outside the door: Marion's first, then Richard's. I held my breath, listening intently.

"She'll tell everyone," Marion said.

"Shut up and let me think," Richard growled.

"That lawyer of hers called again. Richard, what are we going to do? The house—"

"I said shut up!"

Marion whimpered, making me wonder if he'd hit her, too. Then he muttered, "I can handle this. It'll all work out . . ."

It sounded like he was trying to convince himself. My heart thudded hard.

"We'll lose our membership in the club," Marion fretted. "And Napa, where will we stay for—"

"Jesus, you really are insane," Richard said heavily. "Don't you get it? She's going to shoot her mouth off about Eliza, and you'll go to jail. And I'll be right behind you for hitting her. The house will be gone, who knows where the hell the kids will end up . . ."

"No one will believe her," Marion said dismissively. "Not against our word."

"She looks like hell," Richard growled. "What do we tell them? That another one of our kids just happened to fall down the stairs?"

"Richard—"

"Just go to bed," he barked. "I told you I'll handle it, just like last time."

My panic kicked up another notch as I wondered how he planned to "handle" it. *I should have just signed the damn papers. Then I'd already be on the plane home.* At the thought, the tears started to flow.

A long silence, then the door creaked open. I squinted in the sudden brightness. Richard stared down at me, his face cast in shadow.

I licked my cracked lips and croaked, "Please untie me."

He shook his head. "Not until we've had a little chat." He leaned against the doorjamb.

Lying at his feet made me painfully aware of my helplessness. "I'll give you the money," I offered. "All of it. I don't care about it anyway."

Richard snorted. "Please. Everyone cares about money. They might pretend they don't, but they're lying to themselves. Without it, everything is meaningless."

The words spilled from my mouth before I could stop them. "My mother didn't care. Neither did my dad. They gave it all up, just so they could be together."

"And you think that's romantic?" he jeered. "Your father was an idiot. He could've owned this town, and he threw it all away."

"Because none of it mattered to him," I said disdainfully. "The stupid parties, the cotillions. Nobody aside from people like you cares about that sort of thing."

"Of course they care. You're just as naïve as he was." Richard shook his head.

"You need to let me go," I urged. Talking about the past wasn't going to solve anything; it was the future I was worried about. "I'm supposed to be sleeping at my friend's house tonight. If I don't show up, she'll call the cops." At least, I fervently hoped Kaila would; she and her mom might just assume my flight had been delayed, or my plans had changed.

"By the time anyone starts looking, it'll be too late," Richard said ominously.

"What's that supposed to mean?" The finality in his tone terrified me. Panic overrode my physical discomfort; my whole body started trembling.

"You shouldn't have asked so many questions," Richard said over his shoulder as he stepped back into the hall.

I called after him, "Where are you going? You can't just leave me here!"

The door groaned as it closed behind him. A click as the bolt engaged.

I was trapped.

I lay there, hyperventilating, listening to his heavy tread descending the staircase. There was a soft thud as the door at the bottom closed; no doubt he'd locked that one, too.

I'd been frightened when I woke up; now I was scared witless. Should I scream for help? Who would even hear me? The Rochesters had probably sent the staff home.

Helen and her family weren't expecting to hear from me for a few days. Kaila would wonder why I hadn't shown, but in actuality it might be a day or two before she got suspicious.

No one was looking for me. And by the time they started to, whatever Richard had planned would be over and done with. The room went dim around me. Bright stars spiraled through my vision, and my ears roared. It was like getting sucked under the waves, the surf consuming me . . .

No, a voice in my head insisted. *You're stronger than this.*

Gradually, the tide receded.

With great effort, I drew my legs close to examine my bindings. The rope was thin and black, wrapped numerous times around my calves. I tried to shift my feet, rubbing my ankles together. After a few minutes, I'd only managed to painfully chafe my skin.

Panic flared again. I took a few seconds to relax my breathing the way I would after a wipeout, then told myself, *Okay. Hands next.* My wrists were bound so tightly, I'd lost all feeling in my fingers. Still, I struggled with the cords. Richard knew his knots, that was for sure; they didn't give at all.

I finally gave up, defeated.

You've got options, I tried to reassure myself. *You just need to figure out what they are.*

Maybe I could roll to the door, edge up it, and try the knob. I'd heard the bolt turn, though. And even with my hands free, I couldn't pick a lock like Daniel could.

Daniel. Thinking of him, my shoulders slumped. How would he feel if I just vanished? Sad? Relieved? Maybe he wouldn't feel anything at all.

I started to tremble again, which sent jolts of pain through my damaged ribs. God, how could my parents have been so wrong about these people? It sounded as if Richard had always resented them. Had they just not realized it?

What was going to happen to me?

"Please," I said out loud. "Someone, please help me . . ."

There was a sudden chill.

I tried to peer into the shadows, but the room was just as bare as it had been when Daniel and I explored it. The temperature kept plummeting. A breeze wafted past my cheek, even though the doors and windows remained closed.

I caught movement out of the corner of my eye. I shifted to see what it was—then froze.

The ball of light was back.

It was the size of a basketball now, hovering a few feet away. I sucked in air, staring at it.

Fighting to quell my fear, I said softly, "Eliza? Is that you?"

The ball started to bulge at the edges, stretching while simultaneously fading. As I watched, mesmerized, it slowly morphed into the faint image of a young girl: the same one I'd seen in my dream. She shimmered, as if trapped underwater. She was wearing a pale white nightgown, the edges frayed. Her eyes were big and bottomless, her hair so pale it shone. She stared at me, looking unnervingly like Nicholas.

"Eliza?" I whispered.

She nodded slowly.

In a trembling voice I said, "You tried to warn me, didn't you? You tried to scare me away from here."

Eliza nodded again. The motion made her image shift, as if she was having a hard time holding herself here.

"Well, you could've been a little clearer," I muttered.

A faint smile curled at her lips. In her bottomless black eyes I saw tiny glimpses of what looked like clothes flying through the air . . . I squinted hard. My room: getting trashed and rearranged. I understood. Nicholas hadn't been lying; it was never him. Eliza was just a kid. Scare tactics were probably the best she could come up with.

"I'm so sorry about what Marion did to you," I said.

Eliza just stared as the images faded, not responding. I wondered if she could talk; it didn't seem like it.

"Eliza," I said. "Is there any way you can untie me?"

She hesitated, then nodded again.

"Great," I said, relieved. "I think we have to hurry, though."

Suddenly she vanished. I whipped my head around, trying to catch a faint glimmer—but she was gone. Just as I was about to call for her again, I felt cold, icy fingers on my wrists. The knots started to give.

I held my breath, hardly daring to believe this was happening, and trying not to be creeped out by it. The ropes loosened. A few tugs, and my hands were free.

Relief flooded through me. "Thank you," I gasped, shaking out my fingers to get sensation back in them. "Thank you so much, Eliza." I reached down and struggled to untie my ankles, wincing at the pain in my ribs. It felt like an eternity, but probably only a few minutes passed before I was completely free.

I stood slowly, unsteady on my feet. My head pounded, my wrists and ankles ached, and the stabbing pain in my ribs was even worse when I was upright. I touched a hand to my temple: it came away sticky with blood. That steeled me: I was getting out of here. And then I'd make sure Richard and Marion ended up in jail for what they'd done to both of us.

I turned in a slow circle; there was no ball of light, no shadowy presence, but somehow I sensed that she was still with me. "Eliza, I owe you my life. Thanks again."

A click as the door to the room unlocked. Hurrying forward,

I pressed my ear against it. Nothing but silence on the other side. I eased it open. The attic hallway was dark; there was no one there.

Holding my breath, I carefully stepped out and hurried down the corridor. I flinched every time a board creaked, my heart pounding unnaturally loudly. It was quiet below. Marion was probably in her bedroom, per Richard's orders. He could be anywhere—though I suspected he was holed up in his study, downing a few drinks while working on his plan. If my luck held, it could be hours before they realized I was gone.

I charted a course in my mind: first, down the attic stairs, where hopefully Eliza had unlocked the door at the bottom. Then I'd take the back stairwell down two flights to the pantry off the kitchen. From there, I could sneak out the back door and make my way around the house to the front gate. Once I reached the street, I'd run down the block. And if they chased me, I'd scream bloody murder until one of their rich neighbors called the cops.

You can do this.

The door at the base of the attic stairs slowly creaked open. I held my breath as I went through it, grateful that I was still wearing my sneakers. As quietly as possible I made my way down the hall, past the ruins of my old bedroom. Quickening my pace, I practically jogged toward the servants' staircase that divided the two wings of the house. It was narrow and dark; rarely used by anyone except Alma.

I drew a deep breath and turned the knob.

The stairwell door didn't budge.

Frowning, I tried again. Nothing. I strained with all my might, throwing my back into it, but the door refused to move.

Something brushed against my feet, making me jump. I suppressed a scream, stifling it in my throat. Looking down, I discovered a mangled stuffed rabbit staring up at me from the floor.

What was Bertha doing here?

I nudged the toy aside with my toe and tried the door again.

Another nudge. I cursed when I saw that Bertha had shifted and was now resting against my right ankle, as if pleading to come with me.

"Eliza!" I hissed in a low voice. "Let me out!"

The bunny slowly shook from side to side.

"C'mon!" I begged. It didn't seem fair. I was so close, and up until now, she'd been helping me. So what had changed?

One of Bertha's paws lifted, pointing down the hall. My brow furrowed. "I can't go that way, they'll catch me!"

The rabbit's arms waved insistently.

I let my head drop against the door. I'd been so close. What the hell did Eliza want from me?

Suddenly, I got it. *Nicholas.* Eliza wanted me to take Nicholas. "I can't!" I whispered.

In response, Bertha started hopping down the hall. I groaned. Was I really supposed to wake a sleepy six-year-old and drag him from his home? Wouldn't that make me a kidnapper? I tried the door again, struggling with the handle. But it was as if a giant was pushing it closed from the other side.

"He'll be okay!" I insisted. "They're not going to hurt him."

Bertha didn't seem to agree. Obstinately, that damn rabbit kept heading for his room.

I swore under my breath. There was no point in trying to reason with a five-year-old, dead or alive. "Fine. But this is a lot more dangerous for both of us."

My ribs throbbed as I bent down to snatch up the rabbit. I raced down the hall, thankful for the thick rugs that muffled my footsteps. Passing my room again, I took the corner at a near run and skidded to a stop outside Nicholas's bedroom door. Drawing a deep and painful breath, I pushed it open.

Nicholas was awake.

He sat up in bed, blinking at me. "Janie? Why did you take Bertha?"

"I didn't, exactly," I said quickly, keeping my voice low. "Listen, Nicholas, we have to leave. Right now. I'll explain later."

"Oh. Okay." He shifted his legs out from under the covers and got to his feet. I stared at him: he was fully dressed. As I watched, he started to pull on a pair of shoes.

"Why are you dressed?" I asked in a whisper.

"Eliza told me to be ready," he explained. "Can you tie the laces for me?"

My fingers trembled as I tied his sneakers; there were so many ways this could go wrong. "Okay," I said, helping him into his coat. "We're going to be really, really quiet, all right? Stay close to me."

"Sure, Janie!" He sounded excited, as if this were all a big adventure. Tucking Bertha under his arm, he whispered, "Let's go!"

I paused on the threshold, thinking I'd heard something. Holding my breath, I listened; whatever it was had stopped. Nicholas was peering up at me, a question in his eyes. Trying to look like I knew what I was doing, I flashed him a reassuring smile—or the best version I could manage under the circumstances—and motioned for him to follow.

We tiptoed down the hall as quickly as possible. Nicholas struggled to keep up, but his short legs made it difficult and I was forced to slow down. As we passed my old bedroom he suddenly stopped, tugging urgently on my arm.

"What?" I hissed.

"Eliza says to wait," he explained, staring up at me with enormous blue eyes. "It's not safe."

"Well, it's not safe here," I answered. "We have to keep moving." I dragged him around the corner. The door to the servant's stairwell was ajar; Eliza must still be marking a path for us. I approached it cautiously: all clear. Still, the hairs on the back of my neck were standing up. I said a silent prayer and opened the stairwell door all the way.

A dark shape lunged at me. Nicholas let out a high-pitched yelp, and his hand slipped from mine. I landed hard, the wind knocked out of me. Shocks of pain radiated from my ribs, making me gasp. Reflexively, I fought back. Using every ounce of my strength, I threw off my attacker and scrambled away, breathing hard.

Marion.

She slowly rose to her feet. Her face tilted toward me, pale skin glowing. She'd changed into a long, black silk nightgown; her hair was wild, her eyes full of hate.

"You're a naughty child," she snarled.

Nicholas was huddled against the far wall, clutching Bertha to his chest.

Marion turned toward him. "And you," she hissed. "You're a very bad boy."

He whimpered and started crying. That galvanized me. I could handle one batty society lady, right? Paddling through the surf had given me strong arms and shoulders. Despite my injuries, I still had a size and strength advantage on her.

"Get out of our way," I said firmly. She was between us now, blocking the stairwell door. I just had to get Nicholas, then get past her. I gestured for him to take my hand.

Marion extended her arms to the sides, blocking us. "You're not going anywhere, Eliza."

"You know what?" I said in a low voice. "I'm really sick of your nonsense. C'mon, Nicholas."

Hesitantly, he stepped toward my outstretched hand.

Marion's eyes blazed. "Evil children!" she hissed. Her hand whipped out, python-like, grabbing him by the throat. Nicholas made a strangled sound as she dragged him toward her.

Marion clutched him to her chest. His eyes were wide with terror, his tiny hands batted at the arm wrapped around his neck. As I watched, horrified, his face started to turn purple. *She's going to kill him.*

I lunged toward her, but she yanked Nicholas out of reach, hissing at me. She was holding him off the ground, and his legs kicked futilely at thin air. With one movement, she could snap his neck. I couldn't risk it.

"Marion, stop," I begged. "You're hurting him! For God's sake, he's your son!"

"You're all bad children," she muttered. "So bad. You simply won't behave."

Nicholas's eyes were bulging out, and he was starting to turn blue. "Eliza!" I cried in desperation, not caring if Richard heard us. "Help! Please!"

Footsteps behind me. I whipped around, expecting to see a bobbing ball, or the echo of a little girl. Instead, Alma was barreling down the hall, looking determined. Without breaking stride, she opened her hand and blew some sort of smoky powder directly into Marion's face.

Marion cried out. Her hands went to her eyes. Nicholas dropped to the ground, coughing and gasping. Wheezing, Marion collapsed back against the wall, knocking paintings askew. Her hands groped at her face.

I grabbed Nicholas and hauled him toward the staircase.

Before I could get there, my ears popped. The temperature dropped; it was suddenly Arctic in the hallway. I could see my breath; it was so frigid my teeth started chattering.

Marion fumbled toward us, her eyes swollen shut, her arms outstretched and grasping. I backed up, keeping Nicholas behind me. Alma was babbling in Filipino, waving for us to follow her. But Marion was still in the way.

Suddenly, it was as if she'd been sucked into her own private tornado, buffeted by winds. She rocked back and forth, swiping at the air, moving like a person possessed. Her hair flew out from her scalp, and her nightgown whipped around her legs. She slammed into the opposite wall, then careened away from us down the hall.

I heard Alma calling for me, but it sounded like her voice was crossing a great distance. The gale lashed my hair and drove tears from my eyes. Marion opened her mouth to scream, but nothing came out. She howled silently as an invisible force dragged her backward.

The attic door swung wide on its hinges.

Marion scrabbled at the frame frantically. Her hands clutched at air, her feet kicked as she was lifted off the ground. There was a loud sucking noise . . . then she vanished through the doorway.

The attic door slammed shut, and the bolt turned.

The wind dissipated. I stared at the door, stunned. "Come!" Alma ordered, holding open the door to the staircase.

Her voice brought me back to my senses. I grabbed Nicholas by the hand and urged him along. Richard was probably charging toward us already, alerted by all the noise. We had to move fast.

Alma wasn't wearing her wig, and her scalp shone like a beacon, leading us down the stairs. Each step sent another jolt through my ribs. I gritted my teeth and tried to take shallow breaths. We reached the first landing; nearly there, just one more flight of stairs. Nicholas was completely silent, probably in shock. I didn't have time to reassure him, though; the most important thing was to get him out of the house.

At the bottom of the stairs, Alma pressed her ear to the door, then waved us forward.

The pantry was dark and still.

We hurried into the dimly lit kitchen. The outside door was at the far end of the room, just twenty feet away. I picked up the pace, and Alma scuttled after me, towing Nicholas in her wake. I reached the door and turned the deadbolt, then threw it open.

"Hurry!" I hissed, holding it for them. They stepped into the yard. I was about to follow when suddenly the kitchen flooded with light.

I stopped dead in my tracks, my heart plummeting.

Behind me, Richard thundered, "How the hell did you get out?"

At the sound of his voice, Alma and Nicholas froze. They were only ten feet from the door. Slowly, I turned around. Richard was standing on the other side of the kitchen island. He had a handgun pointed directly at my chest.

But he hadn't spotted Alma and Nicholas yet. I could bolt after them, but then he'd see all of us; even drunk, he'd move faster than an old woman and a six-year-old boy. I couldn't risk him doing something crazy with the gun. There was only one way to save them.

Drawing a deep breath, I slowly closed the door. Out of the corner of my eye I saw Alma open her mouth as if to protest. I made a small motion with my head, hoping she'd get the message: *Run. Get help. Come back for me.*

I just had to stall Richard until then.

Slowly, I raised both hands in the hair and said, "The ropes came loose."

Richard was swaying and sweating, drunker than I'd ever seen him. His hand wavered, which made the gun shift alarmingly. "Bullshit. I tied those myself. Besides, the doors were locked."

I shrugged slowly, careful not to make any sudden movements that might startle him into pulling the trigger. "I dated someone who taught me how to pick locks." Which was at least partly true.

A small noise from the yard, followed by the sound of the gate on the side of the house creaking open. Richard's eyes narrowed. "Who's out there?"

"No one," I said quickly. "Listen, I'll go back upstairs. You can even tie me up again if you want."

Richard ran his free hand through his disheveled hair. His cheeks were bright red, his eyes bloodshot. "This isn't how this was supposed to go," he slurred.

"We can figure this out," I offered. "I meant what I said upstairs, I'll give you all the money you need."

"They're going to take the house," he said, acting as if I hadn't spoken. "This house! I can't be the Rochester who loses it."

"You don't have to be," I said, trying to sound soothing. "Whatever you need, I swear."

He shook his head. "I don't believe you. You'll turn on me, just like everyone else. Like your father, and your mother. You'll betray me, too."

I swallowed hard, wondering how long it would take Alma to find help. "I'll sign the papers."

"So what? You'll tell them what I did," he said morosely, as if the beating had somehow been my fault. "You'll say I forced you to sign the contract, and they'll arrest me."

"I won't. I'll sign it and go straight to the airport. No one has to know. You'll have the money, and none of you will have to deal with me, ever again."

"You're lying. You'll tell them about Eliza, too."

"What proof do I have?" I said, desperate to convince him. "You're right, everyone will just think I'm crazy. You've already made sure of that."

The gun slowly lowered, until it was pointing at my waist. I held my breath: this was working. "Please, Richard. Get the papers. Let's end this."

Before he could answer, footsteps approached. I gripped the edge of the counter, braced to dive behind it for cover. Were the cops here already? But they'd have to ring the bell or announce themselves or something, wouldn't they?

John appeared in the doorway, hair tousled, jacket undone. Taking in the scene, he asked, "What the hell is going on? I thought you took a cab to the airport."

He couldn't see the gun from where he stood. I wanted to scream at him to run for help, but Richard was too unpredictable. "Um, I decided to stay," I lied.

John stepped closer and frowned. "What happened to you?" My eyes darted to Richard, and John's face clouded over. "Jesus, what did you do, Dad?"

Richard spun on him. John's eyes widened when he saw the gun. Richard waved it in a circle as he said, "This is none of your damn business. Go to your room."

"The hell I will," John retorted. "Come on, Janie," he added, beckoning to me. "I'll get you out of here—"

"She's not going anywhere," Richard snarled. "Not until she signs the damn papers."

"Christ, you are crazy." John snorted. Inwardly, I cursed; he'd showed up at precisely the wrong moment.

"It's fine, John," I said, trying to keep the quaver from my voice. Richard was swinging the gun back and forth between us, like he couldn't decide where to aim. "Really. I'll sign the papers, then we can go."

"We're going *now*," John said, glaring at his dad. "I messed up, bringing you here tonight. I shouldn't have trusted him." He stepped forward, getting in Richard's face. "If I'd been here that night, Eliza would still be alive. I'm not letting you do that again."

Richard's face darkened. Before I could call out a warning, he lashed out with the gun, knocking John across the temple. John staggered backward, looking startled. His right hand went to his head. Then he growled and sprang forward, shoving his father against the kitchen island.

For a second I stared at them, mesmerized; then I came to my senses and raced toward the kitchen door. My heart pounded in my chest, all I could think was *go, go, go . . .*

The loud crack of a gunshot stopped me.

I spun around. John was clutching the edge of the kitchen island. He gazed in disbelief at the blood saturating his white T-shirt. I watched, horrified, as he sagged and fell to the floor.

Richard stared down at the gun dangling from his hand, as if wondering how it got there. He looked dazed, too.

"Oh my God," I gasped.

Richard's head snapped up. His features twisted into an expression of pure hatred as he spat, "Look what you made me do!"

"We have to call 911," I said, rushing toward the phone.

"Stop!"

I paused, my hand on the receiver. Richard had the gun pointed at me again. His hand shook as he said, "Put the phone down. You're not calling anyone."

"But he could die!" I protested.

John was clutching the wound in his side. His mouth opened and closed as if he were trying to form words, but couldn't. A pool of red slowly spread across the floor, lapping at the toes of Richard's loafers.

There was a battle raging across Richard's sweat-drenched face. Finally, he said, "He was always a disappointment."

"You're a bastard," John gasped through clenched teeth.

Richard laughed sharply. "See? He hates me. They all hate me."

Where the hell were the police? I stared down at John. His chest rose and fell in accelerating pants, and his eyes were glazing over. He was dying right in front of me. "I'll tell them it was an accident," I said, grasping at straws. "You were cleaning your gun, and it went off."

"John will never go along with that," Richard said darkly. "He'll make them lock me up."

"He won't," I protested, although he was probably right.

Richard shook his head hard, as if to clear it. When his eyes locked on mine, they were blazing. "Maybe you shot John, then killed yourself out of guilt."

There were sirens in the distance. *They were coming!* Hopefully they'd bring an ambulance, too. Emboldened, I said, "That won't work. Alma went to the cops."

"Alma *what*?" Richard said incredulously. "She wouldn't dare."

"She's *my* grandmother," I retorted. "She'll tell the truth. So just put down the gun. It's over."

"Everyone betrays me," he said forlornly, as if to himself. "After all I've done for this family. No one gives a shit."

John had fallen still. Was it already too late? "Please, Richard. Help him."

"No." Crossing the distance between us in two steps, he snarled, "Let's go."

"Go where?"

Keeping an eye on me, he bent over and grabbed John's keys from the floor where they lay by his outstretched legs; as he palmed them, his fingers left a bloody smear behind. My heart thumped against my battered rib cage: *Should I try to run? Could I make it to the door before he shot me?* And where the hell was Eliza? If there ever was a time for ghostly intervention, this was it. I'd done what she wanted and retrieved Nicholas; had she just abandoned me in favor of tormenting Marion in the attic?

Probably. This was her chance for payback.

Richard motioned toward the door with the gun. "Move. Now!"

On shaky legs, I walked out of the kitchen. He propelled me through the house, prodding me in the back with the barrel of the gun whenever I slowed. The sirens were getting closer. Hustling me out the front door, he pushed me toward John's SUV and growled, "You're driving."

I hesitated—the police were so close.

"I will shoot you right here," he hissed, leaning in. "In the head. You think they can save you then?"

On leaden feet, I approached the SUV. Richard kept the gun trained on me as he rounded the car, aiming through the windshield until he slid in the passenger side. He tossed the keys in my lap and barked, "Drive!"

The lump in my throat was making it hard to swallow. "Where are we going?" I asked hoarsely. My eyes scanned the surrounding streets, but there was no sign of a patrol car. Had they even been coming for me?

Richard's free hand was shaking. He ran it through his hair over and over, making it stand up in tufts. "Take a right."

Obediently, I turned down Jackson Street. The hill descended steeply toward the water. According to the clock on the dash it was nearly 1 A.M., which explained why the streets were so deserted.

We drove in silence. At the bottom of the hill, Richard ordered, "Left."

I drove slowly, constantly checking the rearview mirror for help. With every mile, my panic grew. I was being held hostage by a madman. I toyed with the idea of doing something I'd seen in a movie once, crashing the car into a telephone pole; but with my luck, I'd be the only one injured.

Richard shook his head. "I can't believe I've been reduced to this. I let my wife kill my youngest daughter. The rest of my children hate me. I've lost everything." He glared at me. "I shot my son. Do you think I'd hesitate to kill a piece of trash like you?"

"Please," I said shakily. "There's still a way—"

"Just shut up and drive."

"I still don't know where we're going."

"The beach."

That was the last place I would've expected. "Why?"

"You'll see," he said moodily, settling into his seat. "Keep your mouth shut until we get there. I need to think."

It was eerie, retracing the route that I'd driven so many times before with Daniel. At this hour, most of the streetlights were set to blinking red or yellow; it took half as long as normal to traverse the seven-mile stretch of road. As we drew inexorably closer to Ocean Beach, I fumbled through one potential escape plan after another. All of them seemed likely to end with me getting shot.

"Park there," Richard ordered. I turned off the Great Highway and into a parking lot bordering the beach. It was completely empty, no bonfires this late on a weeknight.

"Stop the car." Richard's voice was steadier. That scared me more than anything else.

"Richard, please," I pleaded. "You were my father's best friend. Are you really going to kill his daughter?"

"Your father," he spat venomously, "stole everything I had. Your mother was mine. Mine! And he took her away from me."

"That was years ago! Besides, my mother is dead." Thinking of her, I almost started crying again. It would break her heart to know that this was the life they'd abandoned me to. How could they ever have thought that sending me here was a good idea?

"Halina wouldn't be dead," Richard growled, "if she'd just done the smart thing and chosen me. That's what started all this." He stared out the windshield toward the waves, white smudges against the horizon. Pointing with the gun, he continued, "You know, I proposed to her right down there. She always loved the beach."

My mother had never mentioned anyone else proposing to her; yet another thing she'd declined to share with me. "I'm sorry," I said, just to keep him calm.

"I am too." Richard shook his head. "Marion never really loved me, she just wanted to be a Rochester. Your mother, though; she was something. I think that if I could have gotten her to understand how I felt, then maybe . . ." His voice trailed off.

I sat there barely breathing, gripping the steering wheel with sweaty palms.

Finally, he said, "Well, it's too late. John took her away from me, and I never got her back. I was supposed to get her back."

Leaning in so close I could smell the whiskey on his breath, he said, "You know how close I came to killing your father, the night he showed up for the funeral?"

I couldn't respond. The blood in my veins had turned to ice. I pictured my sweet, oblivious father asleep on a couch, and Richard standing over him with a gun.

"I was too weak to go through with it." He smiled ruefully. "This time, I don't have a choice."

"You do!" I said desperately. "I'll tell the cops whatever you want!"

"It's too late," he muttered. "You've ruined everything. Now get out of the car."

I hesitated. Impatiently, he nudged me with the barrel of the gun. My hands were almost shaking too hard to open the door. When it swung wide, my legs were so wobbly I nearly fell to my knees.

He motioned me around to his side, directing with the barrel of the gun. Then he opened the door with his free hand and clumsily climbed out. A strong offshore wind blew my hair back from my face. Frantically, I scanned our surroundings: there were no lights on the beach, and all the houses across the highway were dark. How could a city this size be so deserted, even at this hour?

"Go on," Richard said, nodding toward the water.

Biting my lip, I walked on unsteady legs toward the surf. It was high tide, and the waves were silent giants rearing out of the water. They were nearly twice the size of the ones John and I had ridden just a few days earlier.

Breakers washed over my feet, making me shiver. "What now?" I demanded.

"Now, I disappear." Richard straightened his arm and spread his legs in the sand, centering himself. The moon lit his face with an eerie blue glow.

"What?"

“I’ll clear out as much of the cash as I can tonight,” he said. “Drive to Mexico. It’ll be enough for a fresh start.”

“But then you don’t have to kill me!” I said frantically. “You can just drive away, I won’t tell anyone!”

Richard shook his head. “Sorry, Janie. I truly am. But it has to be like this. They’ll think you shot John and ran away with the money.”

I gaped at him. “But Alma will tell them it was you!”

“Maybe.” He cocked his head to the side and added, “But by the time they find you and figure it out, I’ll be across the border.”

I reeled. Richard had actually come up with a plan while we were driving. And crazy as it sounded, it might actually work. Or at the very least, it would end with me dead.

“Please!” I begged. “Just let me—”

As if in slow motion, I watched his finger tighten on the trigger. Behind me I heard a rumble, like a freight train approaching. The sound of a wave about to crash against the shore . . .

I dove straight backwards.

It was like plunging into a bucket of ice. The shock of the cold water almost made me release my held breath. I struggled against the weight of my sodden clothes, my sneakers suddenly dragging me down. With an awkward backstroke, I swam away from shore. I held my breath as long as I could, my lungs searing, until I was forced to come up for air.

I blinked the salt water from my eyes, treading feverishly. The wave ahead of me broke, and I saw a livid Richard standing onshore. I was still only twenty feet away from him.

His head jerked toward me. I heard the gun go off as I dove back down, determined to get farther this time. My fingers and ears were already numb, and I had to clench my teeth to keep them from chattering. *How long before hypothermia set in?* Fighting toward the horizon, I battled the current that was trying to force me back toward shore.

The next time I broke the surface of the waves, I couldn’t see

Richard anywhere. I twisted my head from side to side, scanning the shoreline: he was gone.

Had he given up? Maybe he thought I'd already drowned. I had to get out of the water soon, or the cold would kill me.

I started paddling in, aiming for a spot a half-mile down the beach. I kept checking anxiously over my shoulder, looking for Richard.

I was ten feet from shore, about to ride a wave in, when I felt an iron grip on my shoulder.

RICHARD ROSE FROM THE waves like a leviathan, his face a grotesque mask of rage. I tried to kick away from him, but he grabbed my other shoulder and bore down with his full weight, driving me underwater.

I'd been too startled to draw a full breath. I kicked and punched at him, trying to get free. But he was too strong, and I was too tired. My lungs strained for air, it felt like they were going to burst through my chest.

Just let go, I thought. *What do you have to live for anyway?*

At least I'd die in the water. It would be quick, and relatively painless. Maybe there was an afterlife, and I'd see my parents again. An image of them filled my eyes, from the photo I'd kept on my nightstand. It was taken at their secret place, the anniversary spot they'd been returning from the day they'd died. The camera must have been propped on a log, because the image was slightly off-kilter, but that only made it more charming. My father had his arms wrapped around my mother in a bear hug, and she was laughing, chin tilted slightly upward to catch the blades of sunlight sifting through the tree cover.

Opening my eyes, I stared into the darkness. Small swirls danced before me: my air bubbles, gradually diminishing. All I had to do was inhale a mouthful of water. The rest would be easy.

I went limp and stopped fighting, letting my hands drift

upward. Richard was still pressing down on me. My head started to pound, and the roar in my ears grew louder. Still, I waited.

His hands released.

With a final burst of strength, I tucked in my knees and drove my heels into his stomach as hard as I could. The motion propelled me backward. I surfaced, gasping for breath. I inhaled deeply and then dove back down, swimming away. This time, I wasn't stopping until I was sure he was gone.

A hand grasped my ankle; I kicked it away and kept swimming. I broke for air three more times, then finally checked back over my shoulder. To my surprise, I discovered that we were a few hundred feet offshore. We must have gotten caught in one of Ocean Beach's infamous riptides. This far out, the waves were just starting to gather strength, the swell creating dark bumps against the horizon. Richard was fifteen feet away. Seeing me, he started to swim closer.

"Stay there!" I screamed. "Get away from me!"

"Janie!" he gasped. "I'm drowning!"

He was paddling clumsily toward shore, probably having as much trouble with his heavy clothing as I was.

I treaded water, watching him. My arms and legs were so tired; I tried to minimize my movements, not using any extra energy.

"Help me!" he cried, reaching an arm toward me imploringly.

The trick to beating a riptide was to let it suck you out to sea, then swim parallel to shore until it eased. Then, and only then, could you make your way back in. Fighting it only fatigued you, and the current would always win.

My father had taught me that.

I kept moving away from Richard. He tried to follow, but his strokes were progressively slower and feebler. I heard him choking on seawater, sputtering.

As he sank below the waves, the current released.

My whole body felt like it was encased in ice, and my teeth were chattering hard enough to make my head shake. I was four hundred feet offshore. Slowly, I turned toward the beach. I pretended I had my board beneath me, and that it was a beautiful, warm day. The water wasn't cold, that was just my imagination; it was actually nearly the same temperature as the air.

I could see the small stand of palm trees in front of our house. My mother was on the back porch reading a novel, her bare feet propped on the rail. My father was waxing his board on the patch of grass right below her.

I paddled toward them. My board carried me over the waves, slicing through the water like a shark. I wondered what we would be having for dinner. Maybe we'd all play a board game afterward. That would be nice.

My feet brushed against something: sand. I could practically feel the particles separate beneath my toes, the gentle ripples carved along the bottom. I dragged my board out with me and left it there.

I was close to home, but suddenly felt very, very tired. I should probably rest before going up to the house. Catch my breath. I'd just lay here for a minute. It was such a nice day. I closed my eyes and tilted my chin up, soaking in the sun.

"Janie! It's time for dinner!"

My mother was calling me. But it was so lovely and quiet here, so still. I just needed a little nap, then I'd go to them.

"Hang on!" I called back. "I'm coming!"

Chapter XVIII

. . . and, best of all, to open my inward ear to a tale that was never ended—a tale my imagination created, and narrated continuously; quickened with all of incident, life, fire, feeling, that I desired.

I'm told that the truck driver who encountered me on the Great Highway at two in the morning nearly had a heart attack, convinced I was a ghost that had crawled from the sea. Once he'd determined that I was a living, breathing person—though very nearly not, by that point—he rushed me to a hospital where I enjoyed a solid week of terrible food and way too many pokes and proddings.

A ghost. I honestly had to laugh at that.

The police had arrived at the house shortly after Richard dragged me away; once they'd discovered John bleeding to death in the kitchen, they sprang into action. Apparently a dragnet descended on the city; half the cops in San Francisco had been looking for us.

They found Marion Rochester locked in a tiny room in the attic. She'd pulled out most of her hair, and was ranting and babbling incoherently. Last I heard, she was confined to the psychiatric ward at SF General. Sometimes I wonder how she and Dr. Lloyd are getting along.

Weeks later, what was left of Richard Rochester's body was

recovered by a crab fishing boat a few miles up the coast. Which was a relief—up until then, I'd awakened every night with terrible nightmares of him standing over my bed dripping wet, clamping giant hands around my throat and slowly suffocating me.

The nightmares haven't stopped, not completely. But I'm not afraid of ghosts anymore.

The Rochester house was foreclosed upon a month later. It sold in a short sale, but inexplicably burned to the ground before the new owners moved in.

There were rumors that neighbors had seen a small girl standing at a window in the attic, hands pressed against the glass as flames rose up around her.

I hoped that the fire had released Eliza, that she wasn't still trapped there among the ashes. Nicholas claimed that she didn't talk to him anymore; he'd lost that haunted look, and with every passing day was becoming more of a normal, happy little boy. He'd made a lot of friends at summer camp, and would be starting at the island school in the fall. If he missed his parents, he never said so. In fact, he never mentioned them at all.

"Ready to catch a set?"

I held a hand up to shield my eyes.

John was grinning down at me, a longboard tucked under his arm. He was wearing board shorts and a rash guard shirt that showed off his deep tan. It also concealed the angry-looking scar on his side. I was still amazed at how fully he'd recovered. Granted, he'd been in the hospital for weeks; it was touch-and-go at first. But he turned out to be stronger than his father gave him credit for.

"I thought you were working today," I said.

"Nope. The beach shack messed up and overstaffed, so I graciously offered to let someone else take my shift."

"Big of you," I smirked. John was working full-time at a resort a few miles from my new place; he and Nicholas were renting the house next door.

I still didn't trust him completely. But he'd been amazing with Nicholas in the aftermath of everything that had happened. In light of that, despite his betrayal, I'd decided to give him a second chance.

I just wished he'd stop flirting with Kaila. She was spending almost as much time at their house as she was at ours.

"Have you heard from Georgina?"

"She's in Dubai with some sketchy guy." John shrugged, but there was concern in his eyes.

"Maybe he'll turn out to be okay," I offered.

"Doubtful. But it's her life, right?" John gave me a thin smile. "I can't exactly picture her taking a job as a maid."

I had to laugh at the thought. "No, I guess not."

"Georgie will be fine, she's a survivor."

"Aren't we all," I muttered. By the time I checked out of the hospital, my constant nausea had vanished. Had the Rochesters been poisoning me, in addition to everything else? I'd never know for sure.

"So what do you say?" he asked, gesturing behind him. "There are some great sets rolling in."

I lifted my head off the hammock and peered past him toward the surf: he was right, the conditions were perfect. I'd already spent the morning catching waves, though, and my arms were burning. "Maybe later. I promised Nicholas I'd take him out for a lesson after camp."

"Suit yourself." He winked at me, then trotted toward the break.

I lay back and sighed.

Our new house was only a mile away from where I'd grown up. It was nicer, actually, with an extra bedroom for guests. Not that Alma and me had many of those. Although just last night I'd gotten an email from Daniel, asking if he could come visit.

I hadn't responded yet. I was still sorting out how I felt about everything that had happened between us. He'd apologized for the way he'd treated me, and said that his recovery was going well.

I just wasn't sure I was ready for anything.

San Francisco seemed very far away, even though we'd only been gone a few months. It felt like I'd finally gotten firm ground beneath my feet again. I had a family, albeit an ad hoc one. I had a home. Alma and I were slowly getting to know each other; she was even teaching me Filipino. The one thing I'd learned from all of this was forgiveness: For her, for John, for my parents. And for Daniel.

But I had a lifetime to see if there was anything there. For the moment, it was enough to enjoy everything I had. When I thought of my parents now, I tried to focus on the happy memories, leaving the anger and bitterness behind me. None of us is perfect, after all.

We struggle mightily against the challenges life throws at us: the unexpected tragedies, the cruelties we inflict on each other, the pain and suffering. Some of us rise above it; others are swept away by the tide. And the only way to learn how strong we are is by facing those hardships.

I closed my eyes, feeling the sun on my face, the whisper of a breeze teasing my hair. Sometimes, when I listened carefully, I swore I could hear a faint voice riding the wind, humming a nursery rhyme . . .

Ladybird, ladybird, fly away home
Your house is on fire and your children are gone . . .

<<<<>>>>